The Devil's Bargain Series

THE DEVIL'S CANVAS

SARA MCCLAFLIN

First Edition

ASIN: B0DYB8XNJ3

ISBN (trade): 979-8-9914135-6-5

Book Cover by Pia

Editing: Brandy Gibson

Social Media: Tawny Gratto

PA: Ashley Sullivan

Marketing & PR: Wildfire Marketing Solutions

Author Note

T his book wrecked me before it ever healed me.

It started with a question I couldn't answer. Then a feeling I couldn't ignore. And somewhere along the way, it turned into a story I couldn't stop writing, no matter how hard it hit or how much it asked of me.

It's a story about choices—the ones we make when we think we're right, and the ones we make when we're desperate. About power and love and the cost of both. But more than anything, it's about expression. About the ache of having something to say and not knowing how to say it. About what happens when the one thing you thought defined you is taken away—and what's left behind.

If you've ever felt like you were too much or not enough—if you've ever been silenced, underestimated, or made to feel small—I hope you see yourself here. Not just in the brokenness, but in the strength it takes to keep going anyway.

There's nothing easy about finding your voice again. But you're allowed to. You're allowed to speak, to feel, to take up space. Loudly. Messily. Unapologetically.

Thank you for reading this. For trusting me. For stepping into the fire with me.

Sara

Content Warning

This book contains themes that may be triggering or distressing to some readers. Reader discretion is strongly advised.

Content Warning:

This book contains depictions and references to emotional abuse, psychological manipulation, self-harm (graphic), suicidal ideation, depression, parental neglect, sibling betrayal, obsessive behavior, stalking, possessive and controlling dynamics in romantic relationships, power imbalances (both supernatural and emotional), gaslighting, verbal degradation, emotional isolation, trauma responses, toxic family structures, substance use as a coping mechanism, supernatural coercion, identity suppression, non-consensual magical binding, and morally gray acts of vengeance. Themes of death, damnation, immortality, and loss of autonomy are present throughout, including intense emotional and physical consequences tied to supernatural contracts and soul-bonding.

Please take care of yourself while reading. Your wellbeing matters. If you need help, reach out.

Support Resources

International:
   findahelpline.com
   United States:
988 Suicide & Crisis Lifeline | 988lifeline.org
Crisis Text Line: Text HELLO to 741741
   thehotline.org | loveisrespect.org
   United Kingdom:
Samaritans: 116 123 | samaritans.org
   Canada:
Talk Suicide Canada: 1-833-456-4566 | talksuicide.ca
   Australia:
Lifeline: 13 11 14 | lifeline.org.au

Contents

A Sacred Vow of Binding and Judgment

By the Depths of the Abyss, by the Shadows That Watch, by the Chains of Fate that no force may sever—

Let it be written. Let it be known. Let it be sealed.

I, **Julian Duvain**, of my own will and without coercion, do stand before the Unseen Council and swear this Oath, binding my existence to the Eternal Laws of Bargains, Punishments, and the Seven Sins.

I take upon myself the mantle of **Deal Maker and Deliverer of Judgment.**

I wield not the sword, but the contract, for a promise is sharper than any blade.

I wield not chains, but consequence, for a choice freely made is a fate unchangeable.

I wield not force, but inevitability, for what is agreed shall come to pass, no matter the pleading.

I walk among mortals not as a savior, but as a test—**to tempt, to offer, and to take.**

Thus, before the **Shrouded Thrones and the Abyssal Hosts**, I inscribe my vow into the **Book of Binding**, knowing that once my name is burned into these pages, my path is set.

THE LAWS OF THE OATH

I. The Deal is the Beginning.

To speak is to shape. To offer is to bind. Once my words seal a deal, there shall be no undoing, no regret, no escape.

II. The Bargain Holds Weight.

What is given shall not be returned. What is promised shall not be denied. No mortal, angel, or demon shall unravel the contract once it is set.

III. The Cost Shall Match the Desire.

Each soul shall be measured, and its burden weighed. The greater the sin, the greater the consequence. No deal shall be granted without its proper price.

IV. The Collector Does Not Pity.

I shall not sway, nor shall I falter. I shall take what is owed in its due time. No tears, no pleas, no prayers shall alter fate.

V. The Soulmate is Fate, But Duty is Eternal.

If I should find the one who bears my mark, the soul bound to mine by fate, I shall not deny them, for fate cannot be rewritten. To love is not a sin, but to forsake my duty for love is unforgivable.

Though my soul may recognize its other half, my purpose remains unshaken. I shall not waver, nor shall I allow this bond to weaken the will I have sworn to uphold.

If I place my soulmate above my duty, if I let them turn me from my path, then let my name be burned from the Abyss, my power stripped, and my soul cast into the void, lost to both fate and eternity.

VI. The Unseen Council Holds the Final Word.

Though their presence is unknown, their law is absolute. No punishment shall be given beyond what is agreed, and no deal shall be struck that defies the Balance.

VII. The Reckoning Shall Always Come.

No bargain shall go uncollected. No debtor shall go unpunished. In pain or in ruin, in torment or in nothingness—the price shall be paid.

SO IT IS WRITTEN.

SO IT IS SEALED.

SO IT SHALL BE.

SIGNED IN BLOOD AND HELLFIRE BEFORE THE UNSEEN COUNCIL

Julian Duvain

Signed in Blood, Marked by the Shadows, Sealed in Fire

Prologue

JULIAN

There is no word for what I do. No simple pleasure, no fleeting satisfaction. It is a craft. Every deal, every signature, every carefully placed word is a deliberate act, a test of control, a game where I have already won before the other side realizes they have begun to play. It's an art—one most will never understand.

A simple exchange. A promise sealed. And when the time comes... I collect.

Not just souls. That would be too easy.

They always fixate on what they are gaining, desperate and blind, never stopping to consider what they are losing. They believe they are making a choice. That is the greatest illusion of all.

The price must be paid. And I ensure they feel every moment of it.

Pain is part of the process, the suffering is inevitable. Some shatter the moment they realize what they have done, while others hold on, convinced they can fight fate itself. *Those are the ones that amuse me the most.*

Everyone breaks eventually. The trick is knowing when to push... and when to wait.

Control is everything. And I have never lost it.

I decide the terms, the timing, the moment of collapse. I decide when the scales tip, when the realization dawns in their eyes.

After all, why should I take what is owed quietly... when I can make them beg for it first?

It's not just the moment of the deal. That's the easy part. The signatures, the final words, the inevitable realization that they've made a mistake. No, the real work comes after—the documentation, the records, the endless paperwork that no one warned me about.

It could be worse, I suppose.

I lean back, setting aside the final contract of the day. The library is quiet, just as it should be. The scent of aged parchment and enchanted ink lingers in the air, woven into the very foundation of this place.

My library. My space.

Endless bookshelves stretch along the walls, towering and full. Some volumes are harmless—fairy tales, old myths, records of human foolishness. Others are sealed, bound with protection wards so intricate that no one but me can touch them without consequence. They are private. Personal. Mine.

And the last thing I want is one of my brothers or cousins anywhere near them.

My desk sits at the heart of the room, massive and unmoving. Obsidian-black wood, older than most life on Earth, its surface worn only by time and my own hands. A relic, an anchor, a thing of permanence in a world that constantly shifts.

The library belongs to me. And in it, I am in control.

Or at least... I should be.

I hear it. A voice, distant at first, slipping through the cracks of my focus.

I put my pen down and lean back, closing my eyes. I need to concentrate. The voice is too soft, too weak.

It sharpens—a thread of power curling through the silence, laced with something fragile, desperate. Someone is calling.

I call to the ones who walk between shadow and flame. Let one who would bargain step forth.

It hits, clear and undeniable.

I'm being summoned.

No wonder I didn't hear it at first. The blood used to summon me must be weak. Too diluted, too fragile, barely enough to get my attention.

I exhale, already irritated. *Why am I the one getting this call?*

I don't want it.

So, I reach out—casting my mind through the tether that binds me to my brothers and cousins, testing if any of them will take it. One of them should. Anyone but me.

Julian: *Guys. Anyone hear that call?*

Silence.

I sigh, rubbing my temple. Of course. They all hear it. And instead of responding, they're pinging it back to me.

Julian: *I can't believe none of you assholes are answering me.*

Owen: *What do you expect?*

Julian: *Oh, so you can respond to this, but not when I actually call?*

Seth: *Kinda busy. Is this important?*

Caleb: *Seth, put the mortal down and tell Julian why you're not answering.*

Adrian: *We all know why Seth isn't answering.*

Julian: *Shut the fuck up. Did anyone hear the call?*

Lucas: *No.*

Damian: *No. Could have. Didn't feel like it.*

Caleb: *No. Had better things to do.*

Adrian: *No. And if I had, I would've ignored it just to watch you react like this.*

Owen: *No. Would've let it ring just to piss you off.*

Julian: *Are you all fucking kidding me?*

Owen: *Seems unanimous.*

Seth: *Wait, we were supposed to answer that?*

Julian: *I fucking hate all of you.*

I force out a slow breath, reigning in my irritation. Fine.

Julian: *Just—stop what you're doing and focus. Listen.*

Thirty seconds of absolute silence.

The summoning won't leave my mind. It's relentless, coiling around me, persistent despite its fragility.

Lucas: *Yeah... still nothing.*

Damian: *Same.*

Caleb: *Nothing.*

Adrian: *Absolutely nothing.*

Owen: *Total silence. Peaceful, actually.*

Seth: *Thought I heard something—never mind, just the mortal screaming.*

Julian: *I am going to kill all of you.*

Caleb: *It sounds like they're calling you specifically.*

Julian: *No.*

Adrian: *You're the only one hearing it.*

Julian: *I hear: "I call to the ones who walk between shadow and flame. Let one who would bargain step forth." That's not my name.*

Owen: *Sounds like it belongs to you.*

Julian: *I am not answering that.*

Seth: *But you kinda already did.*

Julian: *I am—*

Owen: *—Going to kill all of us. We know. Go see what they want first.*

I grit my teeth, fingers flexing at my side. I could ignore it. Let the call fade into nothing, let the summoner grow desperate. But I don't.

Instead, I stand, grab my black wool coat, and follow the pull.

Closing my eyes, I focus. The voice is weak, flickering like a dying flame, barely enough to get my attention. Blood must have been used sparingly. Amateur work.

When I open my eyes, I'm standing in the middle of a room. An office, it seems.

Candlelight flickers against the walls, casting shadows that stretch unnaturally. A man stands near the center, tense but composed, his eyes sharp with something that amuses me. Desperation. It's always desperation.

I glance at the table in front of him, lined with the expected ingredients—salt, sigils, melted wax, and the faint scent of iron. And surrounding me, carefully drawn on the floor, is the thing that makes me want to laugh.

A demon trap.

Really?

I exhale slowly, shaking my head. Humans and their ridiculous ideas. They watch a few television shows by people who claim to know us, and suddenly they think magic is as simple as drawing a few symbols on the floor.

Just to show him that I am the one in power here, I step forward.

The man flinches, his confidence slipping as I move freely.

"You are?" I ask, though I already know.

"Cassius Arden," he says.

I lean back, studying him, unimpressed. "Cassius." I let his name settle between us like an afterthought. "What a surprise. And what, exactly, do I owe the pleasure of this intrusion?"

"I want to make a bargain."

"Do you?" My amusement is effortless, bordering on boredom. "And what makes you think I would make a deal with you?"

He doesn't hesitate. "I have something to offer."

I exhale slowly, watching him. Humans love to think they hold power when they call to us, but Cassius Arden doesn't understand the first rule of negotiation.

"You seem mistaken, Cassius." My voice is measured, even. "I make the rules. Not you." I pause, letting that settle before I continue. "You came to me. That means I decide the terms. I decide the price. And you, well—" I tilt my head slightly. "You decide whether or not you're willing to pay it."

Cassius adjusts his cuffs, exuding the confidence of a man who believes himself to be in control. "Tell me the price."

I almost laugh. Humans always assume they can buy what they want, that power is nothing more than a transaction waiting to be completed. I tilt my head, watching him carefully. "Let's start with the basics, shall we? Power is not created. It is transferred. Stolen, taken, bartered away. You don't simply wish for something and have it appear—you take it from another. And the greater the gift, the greater the loss."

Cassius doesn't flinch. "I understand," he says smoothly. "I know where the gift should come from."

"Do you?"

"My daughter," he says without hesitation. "Ophelia."

The name lingers in the air, and though I don't react, something inside me sharpens.

"She was born with something she never should have had," he continues, voice measured. "A gift wasted on someone who refuses to use it. She isolates herself, locks herself away from the world, creating nothing of value. And worse—she's spiteful. Vindictive. Her entire existence is designed to bring others down."

Ah. So this is his angle.

"And you believe Melanie is the one who deserves it," I say, though it isn't a question.

Cassius stiffens, his polished exterior cracking for just a second. It's quick—just a flicker of tension in his jaw, the briefest hesitation—but I see it.

He knows. He knows that I didn't need him to tell me who she is.

And I watch as the realization settles in, as his carefully crafted confidence wavers.

I smirk, slow and deliberate, letting the silence stretch between us.

Cassius doesn't speak.

I don't rush him.

I like watching people squirm.

"She was meant for greatness," Cassius insists. "She commands attention, captivates with her presence. She was always the one meant to shine, yet Ophelia—" His lips press together as if the very thought of her disgusts him. "She stands in the way. She manipulates, she poisons, she drags everything down with her. She is selfish, cruel. The world would be better if she were nothing at all."

I tap my fingers against the desk.

Humans love to rewrite their own narratives. Villains must be villains. Heroes must be heroes. There is no room for nuance in their minds.

I exhale slowly, considering his conviction. "Fair," I say, weighing the word. It never means what they think it does.

Cassius waits, still convinced this is a clean exchange—a gift taken, a gift given, a transaction that benefits him and his favored daughter. He expects power without consequence.

Humans always make that mistake.

I don't answer immediately. I watch him instead, letting the silence stretch, letting it press down on him. It unsettles the humans, makes them question things they were once so sure of.

Not Cassius.

He stands tall, his expression unreadable, his confidence unwavering. But confidence means nothing here. Not in my domain.

"You want her gift transferred," I say finally. "A simple request on the surface. But again, power is not created, Cassius. It is taken, bound, and reshaped. And you—" my gaze sharpens slightly, "must carry the weight of that exchange."

He squares his shoulders, unwavering. "Explain the terms."

"From the moment this bargain is sealed, Melanie's rise or fall will be tied to you. Her victories will be yours. Her failures, yours as well. If she succeeds, you succeed. If she falters—" I tilt my head slightly, "so do you."

A flicker of calculation flashes in his eyes. He expected a price, but he did not expect it to be this personal.

"And Ophelia?" he asks, his tone void of hesitation.

"She will still feel," I say, smooth and deliberate. "But she will never be able to express it. Not in words, not in action, not in art. Every emotion she experiences will be locked inside of her, unheard and unseen. She will carry joy, sorrow, rage, and love—" I pause, letting it settle, "but she will never be able to release them."

Cassius doesn't react.

"And more than that," I continue, "she will lose the ability to feel the emotions of others. No connection, no understanding of what lies beneath the surface. She will be an island, alone in a world of people she can no longer reach."

Still, nothing.

"And in exchange," Cassius says, "Melanie will have what she deserves."

"Melanie will have what was not meant for her," I correct. "And it will change her."

"She was meant for this," he says, with the certainty of a man who has already convinced himself of his own righteousness.

I nod, letting a flicker of something—amusement, curiosity, calculation—pass through me. "We have an agreement."

But before I seal it, I add one final thought.

"One last thing, Cassius."

He straightens, waiting.

"Melanie's success—" I pause, "it will not come easily. You will push her, shape her, mold her into something greater. And she will resent you for it. She may never know why, but she will feel it. The pressure. The unseen hand guiding her every move."

"She will understand in time," Cassius says dismissively.

I smile slightly. "Perhaps."

He doesn't ask what happens if she fails.

Because he doesn't believe she will.

And that is his first mistake.

Cassius believes he understands the terms. He thinks he has out-maneuvered fate, that he is correcting an error rather than condemning a daughter. He does not hesitate. He does not question.

He should.

Because there is one last price—the part he has not considered, the part he will not realize until it is far too late.

His bond to Melanie is not just one of success and failure.

It is one of soul and consequence.

Because the brightest star before the trade—the one who carried the gifts, the one who was meant to succeed—is always the cost.

The parchment appears the moment I will it into existence, the paper thick and edged in black ink that does not bleed, does not fade, does not forgive. Cassius doesn't hesitate. He reaches for the quill—one crafted from a feather long since turned to shadow, its tip razor-sharp.

I do not offer ink. Deals like these are sealed in something far more permanent.

He presses the tip to his finger, just enough to break the skin. A bead of crimson wells before he signs—smooth, practiced strokes, like it's nothing more than another business contract.

The moment his name settles onto the parchment, the ink shifts, darkens, burns. The letters twist into something older, something binding and final. The air tightens around us, the room pressing in as the bargain takes hold.

I lift the parchment, inspecting it. The seal has formed. The terms are set. The contract is complete.

At the height of Melanie's success, when her gift has flourished, when the exchange is absolute, the price will come due. And the soul that must be collected—the daughter with the most success—will be Ophelia Arden.

I look at Cassius, and he looks at me, and in this moment—he does not know what he has truly done.

But he will.

Soon.

One
Ophelia

Painting used to be everything. Now, it's just a habit. A necessity. A lifeless motion of brush to canvas that means nothing.

I paint because I have to. Because I need to make a living somehow. Because moving back in with my father is not an option.

He's an asshole.

I stare at the canvas in front of me—technically perfect, completely meaningless. It should be beautiful, but it isn't.

It wasn't always like this.

I glance toward the paintings stacked in the corner, the ones from when I was sixteen. They're nothing like what I paint now. They're alive. The colors clash and meld, raw and unfiltered, as if something inside of me had been spilling out onto the canvas.

They make me feel.

They make others feel.

I never thought I would lose that. But I did. Slowly, bit by bit, it slipped away. The world didn't change all at once—it tipped, tilted, unraveled one piece at a time.

At first, it was small. A dullness in my chest where excitement used to be. A hesitation where inspiration should have struck. I could still paint. I could still feel. Just... less.

Less turned into nothing at all.

I'm twenty-six now. And what little expression I had is gone. Completely.

I can't even fucking see color anymore. Everything is just shades of gray.

I drop my brush onto the table beside me and sit on my bed, rubbing my hands over my face. The apartment is small, but it's mine. It's open space, nothing excessive, just a bed against the wall, a desk covered in paint-stained rags, and canvases leaning near the window.

It's quiet. Safe. Controlled.

And yet, right now, I just want to throw myself on the floor and scream.

The misery, the frustration, the absolute agony of being unable to get any of it out—it's crushing me.

Painting was my escape. My release. The way I used to make sense of things.

Now, it's nothing.

And crying? That won't fix anything either.

I could talk to someone. Hang out with friends. Try to be normal.

But I don't like that.

Instead, I get to be the sister of Melanie Arden, the princess of the entertainment industry. The media's golden girl. The one who gets everything, the one the world adores. The one who is perfect.

Melanie, who is getting married to Dominic fucking Forsythe, award-winning actor, tabloid darling, every media outlet's obsession.

Melanie, who plays the role of a golden girl so flawlessly that people believe it.

And me? I'm just her frumpy older sister.

Not by much. Just four months.

My father had an affair. My mother had me. My stepmother had Melanie.

Two years later, she had Arabella.

Melanie and I? We aren't close. We never were. But Bella? She's my person. Two peas in a pod. She just moved out, and she's out there doing something good, being a social worker, changing lives.

And Melanie?

Melanie was mediocre at best. She started acting when she was ten, and it was obvious from the start. No emotions. No depth. No connection to anything. She could memorize lines, but there was nothing behind them.

Until she was sixteen.

That's when it changed. That's when she suddenly found her way—when she gained emotional intelligence, empathy, depth.

Right around the time I started losing mine.

If karma exists, I got the shit end of the stick.

And maybe it's nothing. Maybe it's just a coincidence.

But something about it bothers me.

Still, it's impossible. She couldn't have taken my emotions, my ability to express them. That's not how the world works.

My phone rings, startling me.

No one ever really calls me. Not like I'd answer anyway. I don't have a whole lot to talk about.

I push aside a half-dried canvas and feel something cold beneath my fingertips.

"Found it," I exclaim, lifting my phone into the air.

I glance at the screen and my stomach twists.

Cassius Arden.

I groan, thumb hovering over the decline button. I don't want to answer. But ignoring him never makes anything better.

I exhale sharply and swipe to accept.

"Hello, Father," I say, voice even. Detached.

"Ophelia," he replies, his voice smooth, impassive.

I don't say anything else.

There's no point. I know how this goes. It doesn't matter what I say—he'll talk over it, dismiss it, ignore it entirely.

So I wait.

"You need to call your sister," he says. "She needs you and Arabella to help her. We can't trust anyone else."

Of course. *We*. Not 'Melanie needs you.' Not 'This is important to your sister.' *We*.

Because none of this has never been about Melanie. It's about him.

I exhale slowly. Controlled.

"Bella would love to assist," I say, pushing it onto someone who actually cares.

"Arabella and you, Ophelia," he corrects, his tone sharpening.

Here we go. Full names. No shortening. No warmth. Cassius Arden speaks like every word is a signed contract, like everything is already decided before I have a chance to react.

I press the phone tighter to my ear, already regretting answering.

"Melanie built something of herself. A career, a future, a life. You, on the other hand? Wasting away in that apartment, painting things no one cares about. She knows how to uphold this family's name. I wish I could say the same about you."

The words hit like cold steel. Blunt. Precise. Cutting.

I swallow, but I don't react, don't bite, don't snap back. I just stare at my own reflection in the window.

"I don't expect you to contribute much, but at the very least, you will be there. Looking presentable. Acting appropriately."

"So that's why you called," I mutter. "To make sure I show up and behave?"

"This wedding is not about you, Ophelia," he says, unimpressed. "Try not to make it difficult."

I clench my jaw. I'm well aware that nothing has been about me, nothing that involves him, anyway.

"You are an Arden. That means something. It is about time you started acting like it." The final blow comes effortlessly, like it means nothing."Melanie is everything this family needs. You are just a reminder of past mistakes."

The line clicks dead.

No goodbye. No room for response.

Just silence.

I lower the phone, staring at the screen, his name still glowing, his words pressing into my skull like an imprint I can't erase.

I don't throw it. I don't scream. I don't cry.

But my hand is shaking.

I squeeze the phone tighter, pressing it into my palm until the edges bite into my skin, sharp and unyielding. Something solid to anchor myself to.

A mistake. That's all I am to him. A lingering reminder of something he should have erased.

And yet—I'm still going. Because he told me to.

I don't waste any time in calling Bella. If I have to deal with Melanie, so does she.

The phone barely rings once before she answers. "Hey, Lia!" Bella's voice is bright, easy, like she was expecting my call.

I lean back against the wall, exhaling. For the first time since Cassius called, I don't feel like I'm bracing for impact.

"Hi, Bella. Has Dad called you yet?" I ask, already knowing the answer.

"Not yet, but I'm assuming he called you," she says.

"Yup. To talk about Melanie's wedding."

Bella groans dramatically. "Ah. Yes. The event of the year for the media's prince and princess." Her voice turns mockingly haughty, like some over-the-top reporter announcing breaking news.

I laugh. Not because it's funny. But because she's right.

"Dom isn't a bad guy though," Bella adds, more thoughtful now.

"No, he's not," I admit. "But he doesn't know the real Melanie."

Bella hums in agreement. We both know what that means.

Silence stretches for a second, but not the uncomfortable kind. The kind where I know Bella's about to say something I don't want to hear.

"So, let me guess," she says, tone lighter but laced with understanding. "Dad made it sound like you have no choice?"

I scoff. "What else is new?"

"And you're going, aren't you?"

"I don't know yet," I lie.

"You do," she corrects, amused. "You always do."

I rub my temple, sighing. "Yeah, well. It's not like I have a real excuse."

"Not one he'd accept, anyway."

"You okay?" Bella asks. She gets it. She always has.

I hesitate. Just long enough for her to notice. Just long enough for me to almost say something real.

But I don't. "Yeah. Just tired."

She lets it slide.

"If Melanie's already planned every second of this, why does Cassius want us to call her?" I ask, changing the subject. Because that's the last thing I need—to think about any of this longer than necessary.

"Probably some power move," Bella says. "You know how he is—he needs to make sure we acknowledge how important she is. Like we haven't spent our whole lives being reminded."

"Or maybe he just enjoys making us suffer," I mutter.

"That too," Bella says. "But you know what's weird? He made it sound like it was urgent, like we were supposed to check in with her. As if Melanie doesn't already have everything planned down to the last second."

I sigh. "She probably planned this too. Maybe we're supposed to beg her for instructions so she can feel even more important."

"Obviously," Bella scoffs. "She probably has an itinerary, including the precise angle the cameras should catch her from at all times."

"And a breakdown of what emotions to display," I add.

"Right," Bella says. "Shock and delight at the ring. Graceful amusement at Dominic's jokes. Deep, contemplative love during the vows. All carefully rehearsed."

"Nothing about this is real," I mutter.

"Of course not," Bella says. "It's a production. And we're the extras in her perfect, award-winning love story."

"Maybe if we lay low, we can avoid being in too many scenes," I suggest, though I don't believe it.

Bella snorts. "Yeah, good luck with that. You know how she is," she pauses, voice hitching slightly. "You sure you're okay?"

I exhale slowly. "Why wouldn't I be?"

"Because this should've been you," she says softly.

My stomach clenches.

"Bella—"

"You and Dominic were together for years," she continues. "You were going to get married. And suddenly, he's with Melanie. Engaged after, what? A few months?"

I grip the phone tighter. "It wasn't sudden."

"Yes, it was," she says. "One day, you and Dominic were planning your life together, and the next, he was with her. And now they're about to get married."

I press my lips together, refusing to respond. Because I know she's right.

One day, Dominic told me he loved me. That he saw a future with me. That I was it for him. And after that... I wasn't.

I wanted to love him the way he needed me to. I did love him. But I couldn't *show* him. I couldn't express it, not the way normal people did. Not the way Melanie could.

I remember the way he looked at me the night it ended. How exhausted he seemed. How hurt.

"You don't love me."

"That's not true."

"Show me."

I couldn't.

Melanie could.

"You never talk about it," Bella says after a beat. "Not once. Not even when it happened."

"Because there's nothing to talk about."

"Lia—"

"It wasn't some big betrayal," I cut in. "We broke up because it wasn't working. He and Melanie just... made sense."

Bella scoffs. "Melanie doesn't 'make sense' with anyone but herself."

I don't argue.

"Did you love him?" Bella asks.

The words land like a weight in my chest.

I force myself to respond. "It doesn't matter."

She's quiet for a moment. "You did."

I don't confirm it. I don't have to.

"Do you still?" she asks softly.

I close my eyes. "Bella, let it go."

She sighs. "Fine."

A beat of silence. "Do you want to just call her now?"

"Might as well get it over with," I mutter.

The phone goes silent for a second before clicking.

"Finally," Melanie says, smooth, controlled, like she's been waiting for this call. Not a greeting, just acknowledgement.

"Hey, Mellie," Bella says, voice dripping with fake sweetness.

"Don't call me that," Melanie snaps immediately.

I smirk, shifting my phone to my other hand. At least I'm not the only one suffering.

"Right, right," Bella says innocently. "Forgot how much you hate stupid nicknames."

Melanie ignores her.

"Father has spoken to you both, I assume."

"He called me," I say.

"And now you're calling me," she muses, like she's pleased we're following some unspoken order. "I suppose it's better than being ignored."

Bella sighs loudly. "So, what's the plan here? You just want us to show up, sit through the ceremony, and pretend this whole thing isn't one big PR event?"

"It is not just an event, Bella," Melanie corrects, voice clipped. "It's my wedding. My career. My future. Everything has to be flawless."

There it is.

"The press will be watching. The entire industry will be watching. This isn't just about me—" she pauses, correcting herself, "well, it is, but it's also about the image of this family. This is a moment to solidify everything I've built. I cannot afford distractions."

I roll my eyes. Of course, she means us.

"And not about Dom?" I ask, leaning back against the couch.

Silence.

Her voice sharpens like a blade. "It's Dominic. Not Dom." She doesn't stop there. Her tone shifts, controlled but pointed. "And we both know he was meant to be mine, Ophelia."

I grip my phone tighter. The casualness of it, the certainty, makes something twist deep in my chest.

"Right. Of course," I say, keeping my voice even. I should let it go. I should move on.

I met him first. I loved him first. But that doesn't matter. Not to Melanie. And now he's marrying her.

I swallow the thought down like it doesn't matter. Like it doesn't make my stomach twist. Like it's not another piece of something I had stolen from me.

"So, what exactly are you expecting from us?" I ask, forcing the words out.

Melanie, of course, doesn't hesitate. "There's a schedule. You're both expected at the rehearsal dinner, the press brunch, the charity gala, and, obviously, the wedding itself. I'll send over the itinerary, and I expect you to follow it exactly."

She doesn't wait for acknowledgment. Doesn't ask if we're available. It's already decided.

As if this entire conversation hasn't been nothing but orders, she tacks on a sickly sweet, "Gotta go. Smooches."

And just like that, the line clicks.

She's already hung up.

I pull the phone away from my ear, staring at the screen. Of course, she didn't wait for a response. She never does.

"Bye, Melanie," Bella says, voice flat and unamused. "So great catching up."

"Yeah. Can't wait for all of it," I add dryly.

Bella groans. "We are going to need so much alcohol to get through this."

"So much," I agree, finally exhaling as I let my head fall back against the wall.

She sighs. "Anyway, I have to get back to work. I just took a late lunch, and I swear if I hear one more person tell me I have a 'heroic profession,' I might scream."

"You're doing good things, Bells," I say, even though I know she hates when people say it.

"Yeah, yeah," she replies, but I can hear the smile in her voice. "Text me later?"

"Of course. Bye, Bella."

"Bye, Lia."

The line clicks off, leaving me alone with my thoughts. A soft chime breaks the silence.

I glance at my phone, expecting a message from Melanie, but it's not a text. It's an email. From Melanie's assistant.

Still, I tap the screen. The email opens, and there it is—a meticulously curated timeline of my impending suffering.

From: Kimberly Cho, Assistant to Melanie Arden

To: Ophelia Arden, Arabella Arden

Subject: Dominic Forsythe & Melanie Arden Wedding Itinerary – Finalized Schedule

Cover Story Photoshoot – Required. Full family participation. No opt-outs.

Engagement Documentary Interview – Pre-scripted testimonials. Be prepared.

Bridal Press Conference – Live-streamed. Designer sponsors featured. No mistakes.

Exclusive Bachelorette Celebration – Industry event. Cameras everywhere. Smile.

Charity Gala – High-profile attendance mandatory. No plus-ones.

Wedding Feature Special – Documentary-style footage. Minimal speaking.

Rehearsal Week – Daily prep, media staging, and curated family moments.

Rehearsal Dinner – Filmed. Dress code enforced. Individual statements expected.

Pre-Wedding Brunch – Final press event. No opt-outs.

Wedding Day — International coverage. Press interviews guaranteed.

Post-Wedding Magazine Feature — Additional press appearances may be scheduled.

I scroll to the bottom, where a final note from Melanie glares back at me in bold text.

This is a carefully curated event. Any deviations will reflect poorly. Please don't make this difficult.

I stare at the words, gripping my phone tighter. Translation: Don't embarrass me. Don't complain. Show up and play your part.

I press my lips together and exit the email, as if ignoring it will make it go away.

But it won't.

It never does.

# Two
JULIAN

I don't attend mortal celebrations. They're boring and a waste of time. But at least this one has alcohol.

I knew it the moment I stepped through the doors—wealth pressed against every surface, suffocating in its extravagance. Gold-trimmed tables stretch beneath chandeliers, their crystal facets refracting artificial warmth. The scent of expensive perfume and freshly cut flowers clings to the air, mixing with the undertone of champagne and desperation.

Another human spectacle. Another display of power disguised as romance. I should leave.

And yet, I stay.

Something feels off.

I straighten my tie as I step inside, the fabric smooth beneath my fingers. My suit is dark, crisp, tailored to fit a presence that was never invited yet never questioned. A shade too sharp for a place meant to feel warm. A hint of midnight against the forced glow of celebration.

Something pulled me to this moment. I trust my intuition, it's never led me astray before.

I sigh and grab a flute of champagne, taking an idle sip as I scan the room. This is the wedding of Melanie Arden, the pinnacle of a deal sealed ten years ago. Her father bargained for success, and he received it. She is at her peak, thriving, untouchable. She is not a failure.

Which means it isn't time to collect.

I may never collect Cassius Arden's soul at all. Who knows? Melanie may always be successful. That's what they wanted, isn't it? They don't care about the price.

Pride is something. Ego is more.

I walk further into the venue.

The ceremony is over. The applause has died, the vows already dissolving into memory, meaningless words wrapped in spectacle. Now, the real show begins—the reception, the stage where the perfect couple plays their part for the world.

Even the guests are accessories. Selected for status, influence, and their ability to elevate the illusion.

Not a single thing about this wedding is real.

My gaze drifts to the newlyweds.

Dominic Forsythe, Hollywood's golden prince, a man who has played so many roles, I wonder if he remembers which one is truly his. His smiles, effortless and charming, are perfectly attuned to the cameras that linger.

Melanie Arden, standing at his side, holds his hand like she's holding a trophy. She does not look at him. Not really. Her gaze flickers over the guests, the press, the performance unfolding around her.

This is what Cassius Arden wanted. A daughter who could captivate,r one who could shine.

I take another sip of champagne. The taste is fine, but it's human, forgettable.

This is not why I'm here.

These people know I don't belong here. The way they glance at me. Uncertain. Drawn in without understanding why.

The women are the most obvious. Staring. Wanting.

One in particular.

She watches me like she already knows how this ends. Sex eyes. A silent offer. An invitation.

I don't care who she is. Her name, her voice, none of it matters.

But her body?

The way she shifts, tilts her head just enough to expose the curve of her neck, the way her dress clings to every place that matters—that is something worth noticing.

And of course, that's when I hear it. A voice I'd rather ignore. Sharp. Entitled. Cassius. It cuts through the space, low and furious, laced with that same arrogance he always carries. But this time? There's something else beneath it. Something fraying.

"What the hell is wrong with you?" His voice snaps through the air, barely muffled by the closed door. "Look at you—pathetic. You can't even handle yourself for one night?"

A pause. Silence. No response.

That's when the woman decides to strut over like she always gets what she wants. Like the room was made for her, and I'm just another trophy to collect. Her hips sway with practiced precision, confidence bleeding from every step. She stops in front of me, too close, eyes sharp with expectation.

"You look like you need a break from all this," she says, fingers brushing my jacket like she's done this a hundred times. "Come with me. Just for a minute."

I don't answer. The voice I'm listening for isn't hers.

She leans in, pressing against me like her body's an invitation I should be grateful for. "Please," she whispers, breath warm against my neck. "I can make it good. I swear."

Still nothing. My attention is elsewhere.

She grabs my lapels, tighter this time, her tone breaking. "Don't walk away. Just one more minute. Please."

I take her wrists and pull her off me—calmly, precisely. Not a struggle. Just removal.

"No."

She laughs. Cold. Cutting.

"You act like a god, but I see what you are. All that power—still begging for scraps like the rest of us."

I let it happen. My eyes shift—the color bleeding into something deeper, richer, consuming. Blood-red.

Her breath catches. Her body goes stiff. The room disappears. She sees. Her deepest fear. Her worst future. Her own death.

A strangled, broken sound slips from her lips. She stumbles back, nearly tripping over her own feet as she claws at her chest like she can rip the terror out of herself.

I step forward, slow, unbothered. I let her drown in it for one second longer than she can bear.

My eyes shift back to normal in a blink.

She crumples against the wall, shaking, panting, clutching at her chest as if she can still feel the shadow of what I showed her.

I straighten my tie, adjust my jacket, and step forward.

I stumble walking around the corner. It's slight, barely noticeable, but I feel it. A shift. A crack. Something inside me is catching on an edge it shouldn't have.

My breath tightens. The world blurs at the edges, everything fading into meaningless shapes, meaningless noise.

Until I see her. And the world stops, nothing else exists.

She isn't just beautiful. She's something otherworldly, something that doesn't belong in a place like this. She shouldn't be here.

But she is.

Her hair is dark blonde, messy even now, strands slipping free from whatever careless attempt had been made to tame it. Crystal blue eyes, striking against the dim lighting, sharp but unreadable, guarded in a way that makes me want to break past the walls and see what's inside.

She's dressed for the occasion, but it doesn't suit her.

The dress is skimpy, tacky—a thing meant to demand attention rather than deserve it. It clings to her in a way that cheapens her beauty, a costume forced onto someone who doesn't belong in the role. Like she didn't choose it. Like someone else did.

Sunkissed skin, dusted with freckles that don't belong in a world of polished vanity. I wonder if she had to scrub herself raw to fit in tonight. If she stood in front of a mirror and erased the paint smudges from her hands, her arms, her face, stripping away every piece of herself that didn't match the setting.

Slender but strong. The kind of strength that doesn't come from power but from survival. Delicate in appearance, but something about her feels unbreakable.

She's stiff beneath Cassius' grip, her face blank, expression carefully set, but I see it. The tension in her shoulders. The slight tremble in her fingers. The way her body screams against being handled.

And her eyes. Crystal blue, but hollow.

That's what stops me, not her beauty, her presence. Not even the way she looks in a dress she clearly hates. It's her emptiness.

Something inside me pulls tight. Painfully tight.

I don't know what it is. But I know it's never happened before.

I inhale sharply, pulse steady but pounding too loud in my ears. And before I can think, before I can even try to understand why this feels like fate snapping into place— A force rips through me, through the room, through everything.

It isn't a shift. It isn't a warning. It's a reckoning. Something I was told would come for me one day. Something I never truly believed. My parents, my aunt, my uncle. They all warned me.

I never listened, never thought it was possible. But now, it's happening. And there's no stopping it.

The air thickens, pressing down like an invisible hand closing around my throat, suffocating the moment into existence. Pressure builds—not just around me, but inside me, in my ribs, my veins, something ancient and undeniable forcing itself into reality.

The first spark hits—a flicker of gold beneath her skin. It slithers through her veins like fire, curling, twisting—spreading.

Her body seizes, jerking violently as heat erupts from within, searing through her, deeper than bone, into her soul.

She screams. Not a sound. A rupture.

Raw, agonized, primal—not just pain, but something being ripped from her very core. It crashes through the room, through me, the force of it sinking into my ribs, my lungs, my very being.

And I feel it.

A sharp, visceral sting lances through my chest, piercing muscle, threading through marrow, a burning that isn't mine but still binds itself to me.

Cassius moves before anyone else.

He doesn't hesitate.

He doesn't check if she's breathing, doesn't kneel beside her, doesn't even acknowledge the way she writhes on the floor, gasping for air.

Instead, his jaw tightens, his eyes burning with something sharp, not fear—but rage.

"Get up," he snaps.

She doesn't move. She can't.

Her body is still wracked with pain, her breath ragged and uneven. She presses her forehead against the floor, fingers digging into the marble as if she can anchor herself, as if she can make it stop.

Cassius doesn't care.

His fingers clamp around her arm, yanking her up like she's nothing.

She stumbles, legs barely holding her, knees buckling under the weight of whatever just tore through her. Another broken cry slips past her lips as she tries to wrench away, but his grip only tightens.

"You are an embarrassment," he hisses. "Do you hear me? An embarrassment to this family."

Her chest heaves, her body still trembling, but she doesn't speak.

She doesn't have to.

I see the way she bites down hard, pressing her lips together, her shoulders locking into place. She won't fight back.

Not because she agrees with him. Because she knows it's useless.

Cassius shoves open a door—a small, dimly lit room, *somewhere to discard her, to keep her out of sight, out of mind*—and throws her inside.

She hits the floor, gasping, curling into herself.

And before Cassius can step away—I move. My hand grips the back of his collar, and with a sharp yank, I throw him out.

His back slams against the opposite wall, the impact shaking the framed art behind him. He blinks, stunned for a fraction of a second, his breath hitching as he looks up, confusion twisting into fury.

I adjust my cuff, exhaling slowly, my pulse still thrumming from something I don't want to name.

"You've done enough."

Cassius' jaw tightens, his fists clenching at his sides, but he doesn't step forward, doesn't try to re-enter the room.

Good.

I step toward the woman, now cowering on the floor. I should be annoyed by this. But something about her—something about this moment—sinks its teeth into me before I can shake it off.

"Just breathe," I murmur, more out of instinct than intent. "Where does it hurt?"

She moves her dress away, trembling fingers peeling back the fabric to expose the skin just above her heart. My gaze drops, and I see it.

My mark.

My soulmate mark.

The Mark of Duvain.

It is not a simple brand, not ink, not magic in the way mortals understand. It is something deeper, something alive. The shape is ancient, the design unmistakable—a twisted sigil of darkened gold and deep crimson, curling like fire that has been frozen in time. The edges pulse faintly, like embers waiting to be reignited, sinking into her skin like it was carved there by something older than existence itself.

Over her heart. It's flawless, absolute. And it shouldn't be on her.

I inhale sharply, pulse steady but pounding too loud in my ears. I don't need to touch it to know it's still burning, still settling into her body like a claim that can never be undone.

She's still gasping for breath, her hand hovering just above it, like she's too afraid to touch it, too afraid to acknowledge what's now a part of her.

"What is happening to me?" she asks, her voice barely more than a whisper.

"I'm sorry," I sigh. "I'm so sorry, but it means—"

A pounding on the door cuts me off.

"Ophelia! Get out here now!"

The name slams into me like a fist to the ribs.

Ophelia.

She exhales sharply, still shaken but forcing herself up. "I'm coming!" she yells. "I'm sorry. My father's calling me."

She rushes out of the room.

I don't move.

I can't.

All of a sudden, it hits me.

Ophelia Arden.

The painter. The girl I stripped of emotion, gifting her talent to a sister who never deserved it. The woman whose suffering is tied to my own.

My fucking soulmate.

Deals are unbreakable. Final. Absolute. I should forget about her, let fate take its course.

But I don't.

I start to pace, pulse thrumming with something sharp, something I don't want to name. I don't find loopholes. I don't break the rules.

But for the first time, I want to. I don't care what the contract says.

Cassius will never fucking touch her again. No one will.

She belongs to me. Not because of a deal.

Because fate decided it.

Three
Ophelia

I run out of the room as fast as my legs can carry me.

"What the hell happened, Ophelia?" my father says.

"Nothing. Do you know him?" I ask.

"You need to stay away from him. Got it?" he says, without any additional information. Of course, he doesn't answer my question.

"Fine," I say, crossing my arms, refusing to budge. I won't give him the satisfaction of walking away first.

My father grabs my arm again, leading me out to the ballroom. I shift this stupid dress around and trip a little over these heels.

The champagne-colored satin clings too tightly, smooth and flawless. The sheer panels at the sides feel like an afterthought—delicate, designed to hint at skin without revealing too much. The neckline plunges lower than I would have chosen, the slit creeping high up my thigh.

I feel like a stripper.

Melanie obviously picked this. It's elegant, expensive, the kind of dress that should make me look like I belong in this world. But on me, it feels wrong—too polished, too curated, like I'm wrapped in something artificial. Like an accessory to the perfect image she wants to maintain.

The ballroom is a display of wealth more than a celebration. Gilded accents, towering floral arrangements, and polished marble floors that reflect everything back in pristine perfection. The air smells of expensive perfume and champagne, a careful elegance that feels more like a showroom than a wedding.

Paparazzi are everywhere. What a joke.

My father drifts off into the room, probably greeting guests and making his rounds.

I rub the spot on my chest. The mark is there, still burning, still peeking out just enough that I have to adjust my dress to hide it.

I don't know what this is or if it means anything, but I want it off. Now. It still fucking burns like hell.

"Hey, Lia," I hear. I turn and see Bella walking up to me. In the same bridesmaid dress, it looks just as forced on her as it does on me, at least we match perfectly.

Her dark brown hair is swept up, a few loose waves already escaping, she doesn't bother to fix them. Her deep hazel eyes dart around, filled with the same discomfort I feel. She tugs at the fabric like it's suffocating her.

"I hate this," she mutters under her breath. "You look just as miserable as I feel."

She just huffs and takes another drink. The music begins, and I look over to see Melanie and Dominic walking onto the dance floor.

She's trailing behind him, her hand in his, holding her dress. It's massive, layers of ivory tulle billowing around her like a cloud, shimmering embroidery catching the light with every step. A true fairytale ballgown. The kind of dress meant to take up space, to demand attention, to make sure no one forgets who the bride is. I don't care about the dress.

I care about the man holding her hand. It hits harder than I want it to.

I press my palm over my chest. The mark tingles, not painful but present—like it knows something I don't. Like it recognizes something before I do.

Seeing him hurts.

The tenderness beneath my ribs lingers from whatever happened before, a reminder I don't want but can't shake. I don't know what it is, but I'll figure it out later.

Melanie and Dom are dancing. She moves like she's floating, graceful, effortless, every step rehearsed to perfection. He holds her close, his hand at her waist, guiding her like she's the only person in the room.

He's looking at her like he used to look at me.

And honestly, it's heartbreaking. Not that I can show it.

The music swells, their movements slow, intimate—something that should feel private, but isn't. The cameras flash, the guests watch in admiration, and Melanie smiles like she knows exactly what she's doing.

They finish their dance and break apart.

"The dance floor is now open for couples," the announcer booms through the microphone.

"Great. Now we have to dance," Bella says.

"Speak for yourself. No one is going to ask me," I say.

The music shifts, a slower beat threading through the air. I barely register it before a guy steps up beside Bella, confidence rolling off him like it's second nature.

"Can I have this dance?" Bella blinks, caught off guard.

He tilts his head, a smirk playing at his lips. "Or are you going to leave me standing here looking ridiculous?"

"See, I told you," I tell her. I can tell she's about to say no. "Go," I say.

Bella hesitates, glancing at me like she's waiting for an excuse to decline the offer. I meet her gaze and nod—a silent go ahead.

Her shoulders relax slightly, and after a beat, she takes the guy's outstretched hand, letting him lead her onto the dance floor, disappearing into the crowd.

I rub my chest again, fingers brushing against the mark. The tingling doesn't stop.

There's a presence next to me that sends a shiver rocking through me. Not from the chill in the air, but from something else. I look to my right and see him. The guy from earlier. What is he doing here?

He shifts beside me, gaze flicking toward the dance floor. "The couples are heading out for a dance," he says.

I follow his line of sight. "I guess so," I reply.

"And you're not," he adds.

It's not a question. It's a statement.

I glance at him, but he's already looking at me. Steady. Knowing. Like he sees something I don't want him to. It feels like he knows me.

"Dance with me," he says. It's more demand than request.

I look at him, stunned. "Okay," is all I can muster.

We walk out with all the other couples. The moment his hands find my waist, something shifts. He pulls me into his arms like I was always meant to be there.

All of a sudden, something clicks.

We fit. Perfectly.

Like his body already knows mine, like I was molded to fit against him, like this was always supposed to happen.

His hand presses firm against the small of my back, keeping me steady. He's warm, solid, I'm not sure how I know it, but I know for a fact that he's unshakable. My fingers curl against his shoulder, my body reacting before my mind catches up.

His scent drifts between us—dark, expensive, something rich and unfamiliar. I breathe it in without meaning to, and it settles somewhere deep, curling into my lungs.

The warmth beneath my skin spreads, sending tingles through me. The mark.

I swallow hard, not understanding this, not understanding *him*.

It shouldn't feel like this. It shouldn't feel effortless, like breathing.

"You don't belong here," he says suddenly.

My eyes snap up to him. "Neither do you," I fire back.

He chuckles at me. Actually chuckles. And I hate that it curls low in my stomach, like I'm the punchline of an inside joke only he knows.

"I suppose not," he says, his grip tightening just slightly. "But I'm glad I came."

I scowl before I can stop myself. Yeah, this guy pisses me off. Not that I can express that—God forbid I show anything real.

I clear my throat instead. "I never caught your name," I say, watching him carefully.

For a second, he doesn't answer. His smirk flickers, barely, but it's enough to make me think I've surprised him.

"I never gave it," he says smoothly.

I narrow my eyes. Of course he didn't. Of course he's that kind of man—smirking, mysterious, and too pleased with himself to give anything away unless it benefits him.

His gaze lingers on my face, studying me like he's reading a particularly complicated sentence.

"You look upset," he muses, like my irritation is entertaining. "So, I'll tell you. My name is Julian Duvain."

He noticed. *Wait.* Noticed?

I haven't been able to show anything in years. No one sees through me. No one even tries anymore. So how the hell did he?

"My name is Ophelia Arden," I decide to go with.

"I know," he says, his voice steady, unbothered.

Something about the way he says it sends a strange prickle down my spine. It's too certain, too effortless. I narrow my eyes slightly, testing him. "You do?"

"I heard Cassius calling your name earlier," he says.

Of course he did. That should be explanation enough, something logical, something I can accept. But it doesn't quite sit right. There's something in his tone, in the way he's looking at me, like he's just been waiting for me to confirm it myself.

I try to focus, but my thoughts slip sideways. I want to kiss him.

The realization hits so fast it knocks the air from my lungs. Where the hell did that come from? I press my lips together, forcing my attention back to the dance, back to the steady movement between us, back to the warmth of his grip tightening ever so slightly as he pulls me closer.

Neither of us speaks. The silence stretches, but it isn't uncomfortable. It lingers, charged and heavy, the kind that doesn't need to be filled.

A throat clears behind me.

I turn, pulse still uneven, to find Dominic standing there. His expression is unreadable, but there's something deliberate about the way he watches me.

Melanie is nowhere in sight—yet. But I know better than to let my guard down. She'll make her appearance any minute.

Dominic's gaze flickers between me and Julian, his expression unreadable, but there's something sharp beneath the surface. Something he's holding back.

"You're really dancing with him?" Dominic asks, his voice low.

I blink, forcing my expression to remain neutral. There's no right answer to that question.

Julian doesn't move. Just watches, taking in every detail.

"Why wouldn't I?" My voice comes out flat, distant. Just like always.

Dominic exhales sharply, jaw tightening. "Because I don't know who he is."

Julian chuckles, quiet, dark. "Then ask."

Dominic ignores him. His focus is on me. "Are you okay?"

That question. The one he always used to ask me. The one I could never answer the way he wanted me to. I swallow. "I'm fine."

Julian's fingers press slightly against my back, his hold still firm, still steady. He hasn't let me go.

"You're not." Julian's voice is smooth, certain.

Dominic stiffens. His gaze flickers between us, something unsettled in his expression. "How would you know?"

Julian doesn't hesitate. "Because she doesn't have to lie to me."

Dominic's jaw clenches. His hands curl into fists at his sides, but he doesn't speak. Before the tension can break, a sharp, too-familiar voice cuts through the moment. "Well. Isn't this interesting?"

Melanie. She walks up, chin high, her perfect mask slipping just enough to show the irritation underneath. Her gaze flicks between me and Julian, sharp, calculating.

"You looked like you were enjoying yourself," she says, but it's not directed at me. She's talking to Julian.

Julian smiles—slow, amused, like he's already two steps ahead of whatever game she's trying to play.

"Your sister's a good dancer," he says casually. "She doesn't need to be the center of attention to make an impression."

Melanie's lips press together, the first crack in her performance. "How sweet. Though I didn't realize she needed a date tonight. Funny, she didn't bring one."

Julian hums, his hand still resting lightly on my back it's not possessive. Just enough to remind her that I'm not alone.

"I go where I'm needed," he says easily. "And right now, she seems to need someone who sees her."

Melanie's nostrils flare. For a second, she doesn't know what to say. I wait for her to recover, to turn the moment around, to make me feel small like she always does.

But Julian doesn't give her the chance.

"You should be more concerned about your husband," he continues, his smirk widening. "Considering he's been standing here watching her dance longer than you have."

Melanie stiffens, just slightly, but I see it. She turns to Dominic, her expression smoothing into what is supposed to be natural, but there's unease there. "Are you coming?"

Dominic hesitates for only a second. But that second is long enough for me to see it. Melanie sees it too.

Her fingers curl into the fabric of her gown before she forces them to relax. "I'm sure you've had enough fun for one night, Ophelia," she says, voice airy but her face is laced with ice.

She turns before I can respond, slipping her hand into Dominic's and pulling him back toward the crowd. I should feel victorious, but I don't.

Julian's thumb brushes lightly against my spine, a subtle reminder that he's still here. "That was fun," he muses.

I exhale, staring after Melanie and Dominic. "For you, maybe."

I'm ready to leave. I'm tired—physically and mentally, in a way I can't quite name.

I'm over all of this. The crowd, the noise, the empty conversations that don't mean anything. The way people glance at me like they're trying to figure something out, like I'm supposed to be someone I'm not.

I need to get out. Away from the expectations, away from the unspoken tension that lingers in every corner. I don't want to think about why. I just want to be anywhere but here.

"Picture time!" Melanie yells. "Come on, Arabella, Ophelia!"

Great. I sigh, stepping back from Julian. I miss his touch immediately. Like I never wanted to leave his side, or even his arms for that matter.

"Thank you for the dance. Maybe I'll see you around." My voice is even, but I don't quite meet his eyes.

"I'll wait to make sure you're okay," he says, his tone calm, certain.

I shift, glancing toward the crowd. "You don't have to," I say. "You don't even know me."

"But I want to," he says.

Something flickers in my chest. I ignore it. Before I can even comprehend that statement, Melanie yells again. "Ophelia! Let's go!"

I hesitate, my pulse still too fast, my skin still too warm. I look at Julian one last time.

He's staring at me, and he doesn't look away, unashamed. Not when I step back, not when I turn, not even when I move toward the flashing cameras. I feel his gaze on me the entire time.

The photographer directs us into position, arranging us like perfectly placed dolls in a family portrait. Melanie at the center, Dominic at her side, my father standing tall with his pristine, handpicked family.

I take my place, but I don't belong in the frame.

I don't belong here at all.

"Smile," the photographer calls out.

My lips don't turn up, the camera flashes, and I have to hold back a flinch. My focus doesn't stay on the camera, I can't do what they're asking me to do, instead my eyes drift to the side of the room, toward him. Slowly, an electric pulse starts at the mark and spreads throughout my body.

The mark.

The sensation isn't painful, but it's there—burning softly, an echo of something I don't understand.

The camera flashes again. My pulse jumps, my body is still aware of Julian's touch, the ghost of his hand on my back, the imprint of his fingers against my skin.

I shouldn't be looking at him, but I can't tear my eyes from him.

Another flash. Another second of pretending.

He holds my stare unflinchingly, and suddenly, this entire performance doesn't feel so heavy. I can hear Melanie say something, but I don't know what she says because Julian lifts his chin slightly and smirks as his gaze rakes over my body.

The mark ignites again, heat licking beneath my ribs like it's reacting to him, like it recognizes him.

Heat coils deep in my stomach, but I tear my eyes away before I do something reckless.

"Ophelia," Melanie snaps under her breath, voice sharp. "At least *try* to look like you want to be here."

My fingers curl slightly into the fabric of my dress, but I don't answer. The mark is still thrumming with energy, pulling my focus.

Because all I can think about is the way Julian is still watching me.

And the way my body wants him.

Four
Ophelia

The first thing I feel is the heat.

It's not the blankets, not a dream fading into reality. This heat is real, it's inside me, and it feels like it's alive.

I inhale sharply, my body stiffening, heart kicking up like I've just startled awake from a nightmare—except there is no nightmare. Just silence and my bedroom, dim and still. Too still.

My fingers curl against the sheets, but my skin feels wrong—tight, electric, too aware. I feel it. A pulse, a hum beneath my ribs, a presence.

I don't want to look, don't want to confirm what I already know. But I have to.

My fingers shake as I peel the sheets back, tugging the collar of my shirt down—and there it is. The Mark. It's bright against my heart, beating in sync with it. The color is different today, it's a dark gold, twisting, *moving*.

My stomach drops and my breath locks in my throat.

No. No, no, no. It wasn't a dream.

I throw the blankets back and get out of bed. Maybe a shower will get rid of it. *Yeah, let's go shower.*

I walk past my dress from last night, crumpled on the floor where I left it. It doesn't matter, it's not like I'm ever going to wear it again.

The water is too hot when I step in, but I don't turn it down. I scrub hard—hair, skin, everywhere, like I can wash off whatever is clawing under my ribs.

Soap and bronze glitter swirl down the drain. Jesus. I feel five pounds lighter.

The makeup is gone, scrubbed from my skin, but the mark remains. Not glowing this time, just there—dark, strange, like an ink stain that won't wash away. A reminder.

What now?

I stare at the blank canvas in the corner of my studio. *Might as well paint.*

Painting is everything to me, or it used to be. Now, it's different. I stare at my half-finished canvas. Gray. Again.

I loved color once, it meant *feeling*. My emotions used to cling to the paint—deep, visceral, and uncontainable.

Now everything is muted, caged, like I can't quite reach it.

I can't let them out. Hell, I can't even say them. Every time I try, the words won't come. It's so fucking frustrating. It's why Dominic broke up with me.

I sigh and start painting. With gray, of course.

I think about Ophelia of the past. The one who loved a man. And the man who loved her. But that was back when I could show it.

The first stroke is red.

Color floods the canvas, spilling from my brush without thought. It moves the way it always has—effortless, reckless, and alive.

Like I don't have to think, don't have to try.

My fingers are already smudged with paint, streaks of crimson and burnt orange smeared against my wrist, my forearm, the hem of my tank top.

I don't care. I never do. The mess is part of it.

Arms slip around my waist from behind, broad hands settling low against my hips.

Dominic. I don't have to turn to know it's him. His body molds against mine, the warmth of him sinking through my clothes, his chest pressing firm between my shoulder blades.

"You're making a mess," he murmurs, voice low and teasing as his lips graze the shell of my ear.

"So?" I drag a streak of deep blue through the red, watching them bleed together, shifting into a rich purple, something wild.

"So," he echoes, fingers skimming beneath the hem of my shirt, slow, searching, like he's mapping out every inch of bare skin.

"You're a distraction."

"You say that like it's a bad thing."

I roll my eyes, but my pulse stutters when his mouth brushes my shoulder. My grip on the brush falters, the next stroke coming out uneven.

"I'm working." The words are thin, weak, barely holding weight.

"You're always working." His lips curve against my skin, then press lower, open-mouthed, warm. His hands tighten against my hips, pulling me back into him, fingers flexing against my waist.

The brush slips from my fingers, clattering to the floor.

His chuckle is soft, smug, and vibrating against my neck.

"That's what I thought."

I twist in his grip before he can say anything else, turning to face him. He's already looking at me like he knows he's won, like he's already felt my body melt against his, already heard the breathless sigh I don't want to give him.

Smug bastard.

I drag my fingers through the red paint and swipe it across his jaw.

He startles, eyes widening slightly before amusement flickers across his face. "You little—"

I laugh, stepping back, but he catches me before I get far, gripping my wrist, pulling me back in, pressing me against the edge of the table.

His mouth crashes against mine, all heat and teeth and hunger. I gasp against him, fingers tangling in his shirt, smearing red between us.

His hands find my waist again, firm, grounding, and he's pulling me closer like he needs me there. Like he can't stand the space between us.

I kiss him back, letting the heat take me, letting the world shrink down to just this, just him, just color and warmth and the way he tastes like coffee and something sweeter.

His teeth graze my bottom lip, and I shiver. His hands slide beneath my shirt, fingers pressing into my skin, spreading heat low in my stomach, between my thighs, making me ache.

"Dominic—"

"Shhh," he murmurs, lips brushing mine between words. "Keep painting."

I laugh against his mouth, shaking my head. He knows damn well I'm not picking up that brush again.

Not when his hands are on me. Not when I can feel the heat of him pressing closer, stealing my breath, making me forget what I was even working on in the first place.

I miss that, not just the way he touched me, but way we were. The laughter, the ease, and the way he made everything fun.

He may be a celebrity, but with me, he was just Dom. I never walked a red carpet with him. Never sat beside him at an award show, smiling for cameras.

He knew I hated that. He knew the spotlight was everything I tried to avoid. And he loved me anyway.

"You're such a liar."

"Excuse me?"

"I said," I repeat, crossing my arms, smug, sure of myself, "you're a liar, Dominic Forsythe. You cheated."

He gasps dramatically, hand clutching his chest. "I would never."

I scoff, pointing at the Scrabble board between us. "You absolutely did. Quotidian? Who the hell just has quotidian sitting in their brain like that?"

"Intellectuals." He smirks, leaning back on the couch like he isn't the most insufferable person I've ever met.

"You're an actor."

"Actors can be intellectuals."

"Uh-huh." I narrow my eyes, reaching for my phone. "I'm checking the dictionary for that one."

Before I can unlock it, he lunges, grabbing it from my hand and scrambling backward across the couch like a child trying to escape a time-out.

"Cheater!" I yell, laughing as I dive after him.

"Strategic genius," he corrects, ducking just in time to avoid my swipe.

"Strategic my ass!"

"Your ass is very strategic," he mutters, and I punch him in the shoulder, hard enough that he almost loses his grip on my phone.

"You're ridiculous," I say between laughter, climbing over him, wrestling my phone from his hands, half-trapped in his lap now.

"I'm adorable."

"You're insufferable."

"And yet, you're still sitting here, all tangled up in me."

I freeze just long enough for him to take advantage, flipping me onto my back against the couch, hovering over me with that same smug, knowing grin. "You play dirty," I murmur.

"You love it," he says, kissing me before I can argue.

I don't fight him. I never do.

Those moments, those times. I want that again, I miss that. I hate that he started to notice me change.

The slow shift in my personality happened in a way that I was able to convince myself that it wasn't happening. I still laughed at his jokes, still kissed him in the morning, still cuddled at night.

Still painted in color.

But there were cracks—tiny, hairline fractures that I ignored. Until I couldn't anymore.

"Are you okay?"

I blink up at him, pulled from my thoughts. We're in bed, Dominic lying on his side, propped up on an elbow, watching me.

"Yeah," I say automatically.

His brow creases, a flicker of something uncertain in his eyes.

"You sure?"

"I'm fine, Dom." I reach for him, trying to make it true.

He lets me pull him in, lets our mouths meet in a slow, familiar kiss. But when I open my eyes, he's already staring.

Like he's trying to see something beneath my skin. Like he's searching for proof that I'm still here.

"You don't look at me the same anymore."

It's not an accusation, it's something much worse. A realization.

My stomach twists.

"That's ridiculous," I murmur, rolling onto my side, pressing closer to him, trying to drown in the warmth of his skin so I don't have to feel the way his words sink into my ribs.

"Yeah," he says, but he doesn't sound convinced.

His fingers skim over my back, slow and thoughtful, like he's trying to memorize me before I slip away completely.

I close my eyes and pretend I don't feel it.

Well, after that, things got a thousand times worse. We argued constantly, but I never had anything to say.

Actually, I had a lot to say. But it wouldn't come out, no matter what I tried. I couldn't even change my facial expression.

And that wasn't even the worst part. The first thing to go was my happiness.

And what was left in its absence? Anger.

That was the all I had left. So, I used it, clung to it, let it consume whatever broken parts were still inside me.

Eventually, there wasn't even anger.I became nothing. A statue.

"Why don't you love me anymore?"

Dominic's voice sounds raw, desperate, but I don't flinch. I just stare at him, arms crossed, body stiff, waiting. Waiting for what? For him to stop asking questions I can't answer? For him to finally see that I don't have anything to give?

"You don't touch me the same," he continues, his voice edged with frustration. "You don't smile at me. You don't laugh with me. You don't—fuck, Ophelia, you don't even look at me like I matter anymore."

"So?" The word scrapes out of me, sharp and reckless, before I can stop it.

His brows pull together, hurt flickering in his eyes before something heavier settles in. Anger, resentment.

"So?" he repeats, voice tight. "That's all you have to say?"

I exhale through my nose, my jaw locking. I don't want to fight. I don't want to talk. I don't want to feel. "What else do you want from me?" I ask, my voice colder than I mean it to be.

"I want you to care!"

"I do!"

"No, you don't."

The words are a punch to my ribs. I know he's right, I know he's seeing it now, really seeing it. That the happiness, the love, the warmth—it's all gone. It drained out of me, and I don't know when or how it happened.

But anger is still there.

Anger is the only thing left.

At least I had anger.

But what's worse than that? Not being able to show anything at all. That's what really broke us. It wasn't the fights or the distance, it was the nothingness, that was what ended us.

And now he's married to Melanie. Maybe he wanted her all along, she could give him what I lost. He could have the smiles, laughter, and softness that left me.

A woman who could stand beside him in front of the cameras. Walk the red carpet at his side. Someone he could be proud of.

Someone who wasn't me.

"I need to tell you something." Dominic's voice is quiet. Careful.

I look up from the table, blinking at him. He's been shifting in his seat for the past ten minutes, fingers tapping against his glass, shoulders tense. Something is wrong, I feel it in the air between us, in the way his jaw tightens before he exhales.

"Okay," I say.

"I've been talking to Melanie." The words don't register at first. "Not like that," he adds quickly, shaking his head. "Not at first."

"At first," I echo, my voice sounding far away.

His throat bobs as he swallows. He looks down, twisting the ring on his finger—the one he used to turn absentmindedly when he was nervous.

"I didn't mean for it to happen."

"For what to happen?"

Dominic exhales, but I already know. I already fucking know. "For me to fall for her," he finally says.

Something inside me splinters. The words don't just hit me. They tear through me, sharp and deep and horrifyingly real. My stomach twists, my pulse spikes, and pain floods through me like a tidal wave.

And I can't show a single fucking ounce of it. I'm stuck sitting here, my fingers locked together in my lap. "Oh," I say. That's it. That's all that comes out.

Dominic exhales sharply, his chair scraping as he leans forward, elbows on his knees. His hands thread through his hair, his body folding in on itself like he's bracing for impact.

"I tried, Ophelia," he says, his voice lower now, more wrecked, more desperate. "I really, really fucking tried."

I want to tell him I know. I want to tell him I'm sorry. I want to scream, cry, shake him, beg him to stay. But, I do none of it.

"Say something else," he pleads.

"Like what?"

"Like you care."

I do. God, I do. But my mouth won't open, my fingers won't unclench, my body won't move, won't shake, won't react. I feel everything. And he sees nothing.

"I don't think I do," I say instead.

His eyes snap shut, and when he exhales again, it sounds like something inside him breaks.

"Fuck," he mutters under his breath, rubbing a hand down his face. He looks wrecked. Like he wanted me to fight for this. For us. For him.

"I think I've known for a while," he says after a long pause, his voice quieter, sadder than I'd ever heard it.

I want to tell him he's wrong. I want to scream that I still love him, that I never stopped. But I can't, even if I could it would fall flat. Love means nothing when you can't express it.

Dominic watches me for a moment longer, like he's memorizing me, like he's saying goodbye before he actually says it. "Goodbye, Ophelia."

He doesn't shout, or slam the door, he doesn't storm out in a rage like I want to. He just quietly leaves. And I do nothing to stop him.Because even as I shatter, even as I bleed out inside—he will never, ever know.

I can't help it. The frustration, the grief, the rage—they snap all at once. I throw my paintbrush across the room and scream.Because I lost the ability to express my emotions everywhere.

Except here, where I'm alone. And what the fuck is the use of that? I'm going to be alone forever.

The thought should sit heavy in my chest. It should weigh me down, sink me into the emptiness where I belong.

I think about Julian Duvain, and suddenly, for the first time in a very long time, I don't feel empty at all. He saw me, it was like he could see the emotions trying to burst free. He looked at me and knew—knew everything I was feeling before I could even name it.

And I'm starting to realize that what I thought was forever with Dominic might not have been right. He was too perfect, too clean, too safe.

But Julian? Julian is none of those things. And as I stand there, breathless, paint on my hands, my chest still heaving from the scream, I know one thing.

He's dangerous. But I'm not afraid of him. I want him.

And that thought scares me more than anything.

Five

JULIAN

I watch Ophelia leave for the night. She kept looking at me, but she never approached.

I close my eyes and picture home. When I open them, I'm in my living room.

The space is vast, but not cold. Black marble floors stretch beneath my feet, polished obsidian veins flickering with molten gold. Shadows coil at the edges of the room, shifting with the low hum of power that lingers in the air.

A fireplace, wide and ancient, burns with fire that isn't entirely normal—it's deeper, alive. The walls are lined with towering bookshelves, dark wood, filled with tomes older than time itself. A decanter of whiskey sits on the sleek, onyx table in the center of the room, next to an untouched glass.

It's all the same. Everything exactly where I left it. But it feels different now, because for the first time, I'm not thinking about Hell. I'm thinking about her.

I need a walk.

The space bends subtly as I step outside my house. The air shifts constantly, its never still, never settled. Hell doesn't sleep. It adapts.

Hell isn't fire and brimstone—not entirely. It's deeper than that. Older. It breathes. Moves. Changes.

The Infernal Palace rises around me, a fortress of obsidian and shadow, shifting with every step. It never looks the same twice, bending to the will of the demons who rule it. Hallways stretch or collapse, doors appear where they shouldn't, and entire wings vanish and reassemble as if Hell itself is deciding who deserves to walk them.

I've never gotten lost, but tonight, something feels off. Power saturates the air, humming beneath my skin, in the walls, in the sigils etched into the floor. The Throne of the First Demon stands at the heart of it all, empty, untouched. No one dares claim it. The last demon who tried was never seen again. The air around it is thick, expectant, waiting for the fool who will test it next.

I keep walking.

The halls of the palace twist as I move, paths folding over themselves, redirecting me toward the Binding Vaults.

I don't have to see them to know they're there. The strongest contracts in existence are housed here, burned into the foundation itself. The sigils glow, carved deep into the stone, pulsing like living things. Some are too old for a human mind to comprehend, they're ancien. And one of them belongs to Ophelia's father.

I exhale sharply, rolling my shoulders, trying to shake the thought of her. But the Mark on my forearm pulses, faint but insistent, and I grit my teeth.

The streets pulse beneath my boots, veins of molten gold threading through the cracked onyx ground. The Market of the Damned sprawls ahead, chaotic and ever-changing just like the rest of Hell. Stalls flicker in and out of existence, their wares equally unnatural—human memories bottled in vials, stolen voices trapped in enchanted glass, broken promises wrapped in parchment.

A merchant eyes me from a shadowed corner, hesitating before he speaks. Some demons give me a wide berth, while others weigh their odds.

I cross the River of Forgotten Oaths, black as ink, whispering as it winds through the city. The voices rise from below, twisting through the air, thick with regret. Those who betray their contracts feel its pull. The ones who step too close, never come back.

The Mark flares again. Instinctively, my fingers brush over it—slightly sensitive, not painful, but there. I roll my sleeve down, ignoring it.

I turn down a side street and enter the Shadow District. I can sense the demons lingering in the alleys, They know the Duvain name. And that's enough to keep them back.

We don't control this place, no one does. But we control enough of everything else to give them pause.

I don't stop moving, there's no need to. The moment my power bleeds into the space around me, the tension snaps. Shadows retreat and the demons lower their heads. It's a small amount, just enough to remind those that may have forgotten just who was walking in their midst.

My path leads me to the Eternal Flame Pits. The fire burns endlessly, a place of torment and rebirth. Some demons are sent here as punishment, their bodies burned away and reforged in agony. Others enter willingly, sacrificing themselves to regain lost power.

This place is for the desperate—the fallen, the broken, the ones who lost too much and will sacrifice more just to feel whole again.

I don't belong here. I don't need it. And yet, as I watch the fire consume another demon, something in me itches—like a part of me is already burning.

The Mark pulses again, threading fire through my veins. I exhale, turning away.

I need answers, maybe even guidance. I need to know what happens next. What I'm supposed to do.

My parents know this feeling. My father went through the same thing, he had always been immortal, my mother had not. I don't know much, they've only ever told me the basics.

It was a different time, a different world. His Mark appeared first, glowing in that same dull way mine does now. It didn't matter right away—not to him. Soulmate bonds are rare but not unheard of, and he had lived long enough to know that fate has a cruel sense of humor.

She was mortal. A warrior, they say, one who defied fate itself. My father doesn't talk about it much, and my mother only smiles wistfully when asked, as if the truth is a secret too precious to share.

But I know one thing as fact—she chose him.

She chose him, and the bond changed everything. She was supposed to die. But the Mark doesn't care for rules, it doesn't allow for endings.

She is immortal now. Their souls entwined, their fates sealed.

Julian: *Dad. Are you home?*

Evander: *Yes. I'm with your mother. Your aunt and uncle are here too.*

That may actually be a good thing.

I've never asked about Aunt Selene and Uncle Theron. Their bond is older than most things, and whatever happened between them isn't something they offer explanations for.

My father never speaks of it. If he acknowledges it at all, it's only with a simple *"It was always meant to be."*

Theron never speaks of it either. But sometimes, when he looks at her, there's something unshakable in his expression. Like she is the only thing in existence that has ever made sense.

Aunt Selene only meets his gaze in response, steady and certain. Not unreadable or indifferent. Just... sure.

Julian: *Okay. I'll be right over.*

I pictured my parents' living room, took a deep breath—and I was there, standing in front of them.

Liora, my mother, sat closest to the fire, poised and untouchable, her dark eyes sharp, assessing. Power sat on her effortlessly, a quiet, unshakable presence.

Evander, my father, stood behind her, arms crossed, silent but absolute. He had always been a fixed point, a force that never yielded, never broke.

Theron, his brother, my uncle, leaned against the far wall, his expression stoic. He had the same control as my father, the same presence, but where Evander was sheer, immovable force, Theron was a strategist, a blade hidden beneath layers of patience. The kind of power that stayed quiet until it needed to be seen.

Selene sat beside my mother, pale and sharp, her silver eyes unreadable. She was never careless, never rattled. Selene was a blade honed too sharp to dull, one that never struck unless the kill was certain.

Theron's gaze flickered toward her. She met it without hesitation. A silent conversation. A thread between them that had long been woven, impossible to sever.

They all looked at me now, waiting.

"Son," my father says, his voice calm, certain. "What can we do for you?"

"I—" I am cut off when I hear people entering. Of course, this couldn't be a conversation alone. They're all here.

Owen is the first to speak. "You didn't block your call." His voice is even, controlled, but his expression is sharp, searching. He's broad-shouldered and built like a warrior. There's no accusation in his voice, but he's waiting for an explanation.

Lucas exhales, arms crossed with a smirk tugging at his mouth. "Since when do you screw up?" He's the tallest of us, lean and deceptively relaxed. He has the kind of face that's always on the verge of amusement—until it isn't. He sounds entertained, but his eyes flicker with curiosity.

Damian leans against the wall, arms folded, gaze locked onto me. "Didn't think that was possible." Dark-haired and quieter than the rest, he fades into the background—watching everything. He isn't waiting for an answer; he's already piecing it together.

Seth drags a chair out and drops into it lazily, stretching out like he has all the time in the world. "Maybe he's finally losing his edge." There's always something reckless in his posture, something unpredictable in his golden eyes.

Caleb exhales sharply, arms tight across his chest. "We were all pulled into a call because you made a mistake. You never make mistakes." Built solid, with a gaze that sees straight through people, he's always the one who cuts through the noise. He doesn't care about the teasing—he wants an answer.

Adrian stands near the back, he hasn't spoken, but his presence is heavier than all of theirs combined. Dark-eyed, always composed, he watches first, waits second, speaks last. I exhale, rolling my shoulders. "And yet, here we are."

They don't look convinced. Because Julian Duvain doesn't make mistakes. And they want to know why this time is different. I don't say anything. I just roll up my sleeve and show them my forearm.

Owen's posture shifts—just barely. His arms, once loosely crossed, stiffen for half a second before he schools himself back into stillness. His gaze locks onto the Mark, and I see the flicker of recognition behind his eyes.

The others stay quiet, but I can feel the shift in the room, the way the air seems to thin.

My father steps closer. "So, it has begun."

"What is that supposed to mean?" Seth says, his eyes flicking between me and my Mark.

"Looks like one of you found your soulmate," my uncle says, one brow raised and the corners of his mouth pulling up just slightly.

"And faster than expected," my mother says.

"A soulmate..." Owen trails off, his gaze fixed on my forearm.

My father exhales, rubbing a hand over his jaw before speaking. "For the demon, the bond is a tether. It starts as a hum beneath the skin, an awareness that builds until it's impossible to ignore." His gaze flicks to me, steady, knowing. "It doesn't fade or break, it only gets stronger."

My uncle leans forward, arms crossed. "And it changes everything. Whether you want it to or not."

My mother tilts her head slightly, her dark eyes assessing. "For the mortal, it's different." Her voice is even, but there's something else beneath it—something maternal. "The Mark doesn't appear on their skin the way it does for the demon. It lives inside them, in ways they can't see but will always feel."

My aunt, quiet until now, finally speaks. "At first, they don't realize it's happening. They resist it, fight it. They'll try to rationalize it, to push it away." A pause. "But they can't."

My mother's gaze flickers to me, sharp. "Because for them, it burns." She lets the words settle, lets them sink into the air between us. "The Mark doesn't settle on their skin. It carves straight into their soul. It burns, slow and merciless, searing into every part of them until it's undeniable."

My uncle's expression hardens. "And it is agony."

Selene's voice is smooth, matter-of-fact, but there's something cold beneath it. "They wake up fevered, with their skin burning like an open wound. Some scream for hours. Some don't stop for days."

A slow, creeping dread coils in my gut. It's not shock—I knew it would be bad. But hearing it like this, laid out so plainly, makes it worse, makes it real.

Owen shifts beside me, exhaling through his nose, his posture tightening.

"And for the demon?" Lucas asks.

My father's jaw tightens. "It's nothing compared to what they go through. The bond doesn't carve into us the same way. It starts as a pull, an awareness, a force we can't fight. But..." He trails off for a moment before finishing, "watching them suffer is worse than any pain we could feel ourselves."

I roll my sleeve back down, my jaw locking. "And when does it stop?"

My mother watches me. "Normally, it takes decades. The body learns to survive, the soul learns to endure. But this bond... it's already rewriting the rules."

My uncle nods. "But it doesn't settle. Not until it's accepted." I already know the answer before they say it. "When the mortal chooses. Freely."

My aunt's silver eyes flick to me. "The demon has no control over it. He can't take what isn't given."

Owen exhales. Lucas mutters something under his breath.

"And if they don't?" I ask.

My father holds my gaze. "The bond never completes. It remains... unfinished. They live, but they are never whole."

"And if they're forced?" My voice is quieter this time.

My mother's expression darkens slightly. "It isn't a bond. It's a wound. A wound that never heals."

My aunt's voice is steady, final. "And a wound like that... festers."

"It gets worse. I made a deal with her father. I took her emotions. Empathy. The ability to express them. And I gave them to her sister," I say.

My aunt tilts her head slightly, her silver eyes sharp. "Well, that's a problem."

"But I can see them," I say.

My mother watches me closely, unreadable. "You can see her emotions despite the bargain you made with her father? Well, that's good, that means your bond is strong."

My uncle exhales. "It's progressing faster than it should."

My father nods, his gaze unwavering. "A bond this strong, this early—it means you're already sinking into each other. Soulmates can sense each other in ways no one else can."

I don't move. "Explain."

My mother folds her hands in her lap. "When a bond starts, the connection is weak, like a thread barely tied together. At first, it's the unshakable knowledge that they exist and that they are yours."

"It will grow," my father continues. "The bond strengthens over time, weaving the souls together, letting them sense each other. And once it's strong enough, soulmates can do more than just feel each other."

"They can hear each other," my uncle says, his voice measured, deliberate.

"Read each other," my aunt adds. Her gaze lingers, steady but distant, like she's remembering something she can't forget. "Not just surface thoughts. The deepest parts of them. The pieces no one else can touch."

My mother's voice is steady, absolute. "And once the bond fully solidifies, distance doesn't matter. You will always know where she is. If she's in pain, you'll feel it. If she speaks to you, you'll hear her—no matter where she is."

The room feels smaller. I already feel her. Already see her emotions when no one else can. And if this is moving faster than it should... "So what does that mean for me?"

My father's expression darkens slightly. "It means whether you wanted this or not... you're already tied to her in a way you can't undo."

I roll my shoulders, inhaling slowly. "This is complicated."

My aunt exhales softly. "Soulmates are never supposed to be easy."

The room stays silent. No one disagrees.

Because we all know—this will break something before it fixes anything.

Six
Ophelia

I t's opening night at my friend, Emilien Marchand's, gallery. I've never missed one of his openings, and although he's been begging me for years to let him put my art on display, I just can't. It's not good enough.

I straighten my earrings and adjust the high collar of my jumpsuit. I've been trying to cover the 'Mark' as I'm calling it, but nothing is working other than clothes. When I tried to put makeup over it, it literally *melted* off, as though there's some sort of heat source inside it. I've tried scrubbing, wiping, scar serums, the only thing I haven't tried was burning it off and scar removal surgery.

His name is burned into my very being.

The pressure in the room plummets, the air growing dense, suffocating, pressing down on my skin like something unseen is closing in. My lungs tighten, my pulse skitters, a slow, creeping awareness settling deep in my bones. The mirror trembles, a ripple moving across the glass—slow, deliberate—like a breath exhaled onto frozen air, like something stirring beneath the surface.

It shifts again. The reflection warps, bending inward, stretching like liquid metal, its edges pulling in on themselves. It should stop there, should snap back to normal, but it doesn't. Shadows coil at the edges, thick and shifting, blurring the line between real and fantasy, smearing the glass like ink bleeding into water. My chest tightens, my fingers curling against my sides as my stomach twists, and for a second, I think it's a trick of the light, some distortion from my own movement—until I blink and realize that my reflection is gone.

A slow dread creeps over me, settling deep, a weight in my chest that refuses to let go. The mirror moves, the glass swirling like a storm caught beneath the surface, silver and black churning together. The frame vibrates, a faint hum rising from it, not from the walls or the floor but from the mirror itself, a pulse, an exhale, something waiting on the other side. The center darkens, stretching open, swallowing the light in the room. My heart pounds against my ribs as I step back, my legs locking in place, because this isn't normal, this isn't possible. But it is happening, whether I understand it or not.

It looks like an office. The hazy flicker of bookshelves, the gleam of dark wood, shadows pooling where they shouldn't be. The image distorts, as though I'm looking through water, shifting between clarity and something else entirely. My pulse hammers, breath unsteady, body locked between the instinct to run and the pull to stay.

Julian.

I stop breathing.

Not the Julian I know. His eyes are deep red, swirling like molten fire, shifting like embers caught in an unseen wind. His features are too sharp, too sculpted, as though carved by forces older than time. Not human. Not even close. The air around him distorts, a slow ripple, like heat rising off pavement, but it's cold, the temperature in the room plummeting as though something is draining the warmth from the air itself. The shadows behind him pulse, shifting, coiling, like they have a mind of their own.

Julian Duvain. In my mirror. Watching. Waiting.

I whip around, searching the room, my breath a sharp, uneven thing scraping against my ribs. But I'm alone. No one is here. Just me. Just him. Just the impossible weight of this moment pressing into my chest. Slowly, I turn back.

He's still there.

The glass no longer looks like glass. It moves like water, shifting with the weight of something pressing against it, something stretching the boundary between his world and mine. The swirling blackness pulses, its edges curling, shifting, pressing outward, bending, waiting. My throat tightens, my stomach twists, because suddenly I know what this is.

He's mirroring me.

A tremor rolls through me, my breath unsteady as my fingers rise—hesitating, hovering—before instinct wins over reason. Every part of me screams don't, don't touch it, don't do this—but the moment my palm meets the glass, the world shifts.

The air crackles—electric, charged, alive. The mirror pulses, bending inward, not just reflecting but pulling. The weight of it tugs against me, threatening to tip me forward, and I stumble, barely catching myself before I fall through.

Heat. Skin. A grip like steel catching my wrist before I slip away.

I feel him.

The Mark flares violently. White-hot pain explodes across my chest, searing through me like fire in my veins. I choke on a cry, clutching my ribs, my vision blurring at the edges as something inside me pulls too hard, too fast. The mirror flickers, the image warping, Julian's face shifting between the man I met and something else, something darker, something not meant to be seen. The Mark ignites, burning so bright it spills light across the room, illuminating the crimson fire in his gaze as it flickers downward.

His expression sharpens. His voice is low, edged with something I don't recognize.

"A portal—" Julian breathes, and for the first time, I don't think he knows what comes next.

He's gone. The mirror ripples once, twice—before snapping back to normal, like nothing ever happened. The last thing I see before he disappears isn't a smirk. It's something else. Shock. Almost... fear.

And I know—he's coming for me. I don't need to see him to know. I can feel it in my very soul.

I turn and run out of the room. I need air. Space. The apartment is closing in on me, walls too tight, shadows pressing in. I don't stop moving. I just leave.

Emilien's gallery will help me decompress. Hopefully.

The gallery is beautiful—a tapestry of color and movement, captured in stillness. The walls are lined with carefully curated chaos, bold strokes clashing with delicate details, each piece demanding to be seen. Frames stretch across stark white walls, the scent of oil paint and varnish still clinging to the air. Conversations hum softly in the background, footsteps muted against sleek floors.

It's elegant. It's alive. It's everything a gallery should be.

Emilien is bustling around, excitedly greeting people. He sees me, and a grin lights up his face.

"Lia!" he says, running up to me.

When he wraps his arms around me, I melt into the embrace. Emilien has been one of the few I've shared my art with. He knows that it's changed. He knows it's tied to my emotions, how it basically sucks now.

"I want your pieces hanging here," he says, walking over to the empty spot on the wall. A whole section, actually.

"You know where I stand, Emilien," I say.

"I know, but you should be showcasing your work," he whines, dragging out the words with an exaggerated sigh, like the mere thought of effort physically pains him.

"Not happening."

"Come on, just think about it. It's been years. Your work deserves to be seen."

I stay firm. "No, Emilien. I told you. Not now. Not ever."

"You're wasting your talent," he sighs.

Talent. Right. I don't even know if I have any left. How can I be wasting something that isn't there?

There's no color anymore, no feeling. Just gray. Everything I try to paint looks the same—flat, lifeless, and hollow. I keep waiting for something to change, for it to come back, for that thing inside me to spark again. But it doesn't. It just sits there, locked away, out of reach.

What if it's gone completely? What if I lost it? What if I open myself up, put my work on these walls, and it's just proof that I have nothing left to give?

What if everyone sees it? What if they look at my work and feel exactly what I feel—nothing?

God, I hate this. I hate that I can't even explain it, that I can't tell Emilien that it's not about fear or rejection or even the attention. It's about the fact that the one thing I've ever been good at doesn't feel like mine anymore.

I exhale sharply, shoving the thought down.

"Not wasting it," I mutter. "Just not interested."

"You're killing me, Lia!" he exclaims. "I know that you're interested!"

"I'm really not," I say. "I like what I'm doing now."

"What? You like working for hacks who don't care about you? Who hire you and claim your work as their own?" he asks.

"That's not how being a ghost artist works, Emilien. And you know that," I admonish.

"Explain to me how it works," he counters.

I sigh, pressing my fingers against my temples. "It's not about being used. It's about not being seen."

Emilien folds his arms, unimpressed. "You think that sounds better?"

"I think it's the only thing that makes sense right now," I snap back. "You know how it works. Commission work, digital art, concept pieces—it's everywhere. Some artists put their name on everything they create. Others sell it off. No attachment, no recognition, no pressure. You think every painting in a billionaire's collection was actually painted by the guy who signed it? Or that every brand, book cover, or game concept comes from the name stamped on it? Half the time, someone else made it. Someone like me."

He exhales, shaking his head. "But that's the point, Lia. You're hiding." I stiffen. "You could have your own section in this gallery, your name up there in lights. But instead, you're letting other people take credit so you don't have to deal with it."

"It's not about credit," I mutter. "I don't care about my name being out there."

"Bullshit. It's because you don't think you deserve it."

My throat tightens.

"You don't paint for yourself anymore. You don't even try. You just bury it. You don't have to care if a commission piece has no soul, right? It's just a job. It's safe."

I swallow hard, ignoring the way my fingers twitch at my sides. He's too close to the truth, too close to touching something I'm not ready to deal with. "It's what works for me right now," I say, voice steady.

"No," he corrects softly. "It's what you think is easier."

I hate that statement, but I hate even more that he's right. It is easier. But what's worse? Doing this for a living—taking commissions, ghost painting, staying in the background where it's safe—or putting my work out there again, just to get ripped apart? I already know the answer. I don't even have to think about it.

Melanie is in the spotlight. She thrives under it, shines in it, moves through crowds like she was made for them, like she belongs. The cameras love her. People love her. She always knew how to be the person everyone wanted her to be—perfect, effortless, flawless. And me? I was always the one in the background. And when I wasn't—when my art was supposed to speak for me—it wasn't enough. It was never enough.

I clench my jaw, forcing down the lump in my throat. Emilien doesn't get it. He sees me as I was. He doesn't understand that the person who painted with color, with passion, with something real—she's gone. Because what happens if I try again? What if they look at it, tilt their heads, squint a little, and move on?

I think that would kill me more than anything, it wouldn't just be a failure. It would be proof. Proof that I lost whatever it was that made me an artist in the first place. Proof that the gray is all I have left.

The thought sinks in too fast, too heavy. The edges of my vision blur. The room starts to spin, shifting around me, tilting at the edges. I think I'm going to pass out. I may be sick. I don't know, but suddenly, I feel weak.

The lights are too bright. Voices become garbled together. The ground starts to tilt beneath my feet, and I know I'm going to go down.

Before I can reach out and catch anything, I feel Emilien's arms around me.

"Are you okay?" he asks, lifting me to my feet.

I start to regain my footing. "I'm fine," I say.

I'm starting to feel better, but his arms are still around me. I'm grateful he's making sure I don't fall, but I can't even express that.

A sudden presence presses against my back—warm, unshakable, impossible to ignore. Arms wrap around me, pulling me away from Emilien with a force that isn't just possessive—it's absolute. I don't need to turn around. I know who it is.

His scent reaches me first—dark, spiced, electric, curling through my senses, searing itself into my bones. The room doesn't just quiet, it stills, every conversation and movement dissolving into nothing.

"Don't touch her." His voice cuts through the silence, low and edged with danger. Emilien stiffens. Everyone does. The gallery feels frozen, like the air itself is holding its breath.

Julian doesn't move. He doesn't have to. His presence alone is a warning, his words sharp enough to slice through the air. My pulse slams against my ribs, my breath hitching as the Mark flares beneath my skin, reacting to him, to his fury, to the invisible force rippling through the space.

Emilien swallows hard, eyes darting to me, but he doesn't touch me again. "We're leaving, Ophelia," he says.

He pulls me out of the gallery. I only have time to give Emilien a small wave—not like he noticed. His mouth is still hanging open.

"We need to talk," I tell him.

Now where to go? I am not taking him to my apartment—my place to be me—and this conversation needs to be held on neutral ground.

The Larkspur Theater has been abandoned for at least a decade, but people come here all the time. No one really watches it, no one really cares. It's private. Hidden. The perfect spot.

The doors hang slightly off their hinges, the once-grand entrance warped by time and weather. Faded marquee letters cling stubbornly to the facade, the ghosts of old film titles barely visible beneath years of grime. Inside, dust coats the velvet seats, and the scent of mildew and forgotten memories clings to the air. The stage, though cracked and crumbling, still holds an eerie presence—like it's waiting for a performance that will never come.

We get to the middle of the theater, and I don't wait a second longer. I turn around and stare at Julian.

He's waiting, like he knows I have something to say. I can't read him at all. I'm pissed, and I want to show it. I yank my jumpsuit to the side and show him the Mark. It's glowing in all its fucking glory.

"You need to explain what the fuck you did to me!" I scream.

Wait. I screamed. I showed him emotion. But I can't think about that little revelation now.

"I don't know what you mean," he says leisurely.

"You—what?" I shout. "You know what I mean! This!" I say, pointing at the Mark, rage is burning inside me.

"I think I do," he says.

"Stop being so fucking cryptic," I snap.

"Fine, sweetheart," he starts, his lips curving into a slow, knowing smirk, eyes flickering with amusement, challenge, maybe both. "I'll tell you what that is because I have one too."

He pulls up his sleeve, and there, on his left forearm, is a Mark that looks exactly like my own.

"The Mark of Duvain," he murmurs. "You belong to me now, whether you like it or not. You're my soulmate."

Seven
Ophelia

I can't speak, can't move. Hell, I may not even be able to breathe. His words are just replaying in my head.

The Mark of Duvain. You belong to me now, whether you like it or not. You're my soulmate.

A laugh spills out before I can stop it. It's raw, jagged, almost bitter. But hell, if he gets to say insane things, I get to laugh at them.

"No," I start. "No. That's not happening. I'm not your soulmate. You're mistaken."

"It's no mistake, sweetheart," he says, leaning against a chair.

He's just sitting there. Seriously? Like this isn't a huge deal. Like he didn't just say something that tipped my entire world off its axis. He has to be lying.

"I'm not lying," he says.

Wait. I didn't say that out loud?

"Nor am I insane," he adds.

I take a step back, pulse hammering. "Okay, I know I'm not talking."

"Nope. You're thinking," he replies smoothly, leaning back like this is nothing new, like he's already a step ahead. His fingers drum lazily against his thigh, his mouth twitching—half amusement, half boredom, like he's waiting for me to catch up.

I stare at him, my skin prickling. "Thinking? What? What the hell are you talking about? Don't say that you can 'read' me, no one has been able to do that for years."

He sighs, shifts to his feet, walking toward me—slow, measured, like he has all the time in the world. "Yeah, darling. Thinking."

I swallow hard, trying to suppress the unease curling through me. "I think it's time you explain."

A ghost of a smile. "The soulmate bond," he says.

I scoff. "The what?"

His amusement doesn't waver, but there's something sharper beneath it. "The soulmate bond," he repeats, like I should already know.

I fold my arms, grounding myself. "That's not real."

"Oh, it's real," he says, voice steady. "And you're already feeling it." Julian watches me for a long moment before exhaling. His voice lowers, slow and deliberate. "The bond isn't a choice. You don't get to pick who your soul is tied to. Neither do I. It's written into existence, whether we like it or not."

I shake my head, refusing to accept that. "No. That's—no. That's not how things work."

"It is," he says, lips twitching. "A beautiful, impossible, inescapable trap."

That should be poetic. Instead, it feels like a warning.

"You've felt it already," he continues, watching me too closely. "The pull. The way your emotions spike when I'm near. The way your body reacts before your mind catches up."

I stiffen but don't answer.

"That's the Mark," he says, his gaze flicking toward it. "A physical manifestation of the bond. You can see it, but you haven't learned how to use it yet. Not fully." He watches me carefully, his voice even, measured. "It reacts—to emotions, to proximity, to supernatural forces. And when I get too close—" he takes a slow step forward, the air tightening, heat curling beneath my skin "—you'll feel it."

He steps forward, closing the space between us, and instantly, a slow, crawling heat spreads through my veins. A pulse beneath my skin that wasn't there a second ago. I jerk back, breath catching. "What the hell—?"

Julian smirks. "See?"

My hand presses against my chest, heart pounding.

"It's not just physical," he says, voice quieter now. "The bond is emotional. You'll feel what I feel. Anger. Pain. Desire. Fear. It doesn't matter if you want to or not."

"That sounds like a nightmare."

"It can be," he admits. "Especially when one of us is injured. Pain sharing is part of the deal. If I take a hit, you'll feel it. Sometimes a dull ache. Sometimes like it's happening to you."

I swallow hard. "Fantastic. What else?"

He tilts his head. "It goes deeper than that. Over time, it strengthens. If we let it."

Something about the way he says 'let it' makes my stomach tighten.

"It's why I can hear you," he adds.

A chill runs through me. "What?"

Julian's smirk deepens, like he's been waiting for me to realize. "You're not hearing me yet," he says. "But I hear you."

Dread seeps into my spine. "You—" I cut myself off, a dozen thoughts spiraling at once.

How much has he heard?

His expression answers before he does. "Everything, sweetheart."

I clench my fists, my stomach twisting. "That's—no. That's not fair."

Julian draws in a sharp breath, raking a hand through his hair, and for the first time, I see something beneath the amusement—frustration.

That throws me, I can't explain why, but it hurts far more than I'm ever going to admit.

"But it's fate," he continues. "And fate doesn't care what we want."

I let out a sharp laugh, but there's no humor in it. "I don't believe in fate."

Julian raises an eyebrow, tilting his head like I've just said something that doesn't make sense. "You will."

I shake my head, the weight of all this pressing in. "No, fate is just an excuse people use when things don't go their way. It's a crutch. A way to pretend we don't make our own choices."

He exhales, slow and measured, rubbing his fingers together like he's considering his next words carefully. He looks at me, gaze unwavering. "That's cute."

I bristle. "It's not cute. It's reality."

"No, sweetheart. Reality is this—" He steps closer, and the second he does, I feel it again—that pull, that static crawling over my skin like invisible threads tightening.

I don't want to react, but my body betrays me.

"That's reality," he says, watching me shiver. "No matter how much you fight it."

I open my mouth, but nothing comes out. My throat feels tight, my thoughts a tangled mess of denial and something dangerously close to belief.

For the first time, I ask the question I should have from the start. "What... what are you?"

His gaze sharpens, gold flecks catching the dim light.

I shake my head. "No, seriously. You're reading my mind, you're talking about fate like it's written in stone, and I—" My breath stutters. "You're not... normal, are you?"

Julian chuckles, slow and dark. "Haven't figured it out yet?"

I don't respond. I can't.

He tilts his head, watching me like he's waiting for the realization to click into place. Finally, he gives me the truth. Smooth. Simple. Unshaken.

"I'm a demon."

Something inside me goes ice-cold. My stomach drops, my skin tightens, and suddenly, it's like I can feel my own pulse too loud in my ears. I stare at him, but he doesn't waver.

No laugh, no smirk. Just fact.

"No," I say, firmer this time. "You're lying. Or worse—you're telling the truth, and you think that matters to me."

"I already told you—I don't lie."

"So now what?" I ask.

For the first time since this started, he hesitates. Just a flicker of something in his expression, gone in an instant, but I catch it. I bite back a smirk. Good. I got something over him.

"What do you mean?" Julian asks, recovering quickly. "You don't seem scared."

"Scared?" I scoff. "Please. You'd have to be scarier than this."

His eyes flicker with interest. "What do you feel?"

I exhale sharply, frustration curling around my ribs. "I can't tell you."

His lips twitch. "Can't or won't?"

"Both."

For the second time, he doesn't have a response ready. Not an easy one, at least. He studies me, gaze sharper now, like he's picking me apart thread by thread.

"Open up," he says.

I frown. "Do what?"

"Stop blocking me. Show me how you feel."

I narrow my eyes, if this is true, if he can sense me, he should know that I can't. "You can do that?"

He just waits, like he already knows I'll try. And maybe I will. Maybe it's worth a shot, just to prove something to myself.

So, I stop fighting it. Stop keeping everything buried so deep inside me that I can barely feel it myself. Instead, I push—not words, not explanations, just raw emotion, like shoving open a locked door and letting him see inside.

Julian doesn't say anything. Doesn't move.

His lips part slightly. Just for a second. A slow inhale, controlled but not entirely unaffected. "Well, I guess fear isn't your main emotion. More like determination."

I hold his gaze. "Because if this is forever, I'm not going to be the one to break first."

Something in his eyes flickers—something dark, knowing. "Careful, sweetheart. That sounds a lot like a challenge."

I don't blink. "Maybe it is."

A slow smirk stretches across his lips, like he's savoring every second of this. "But you don't like me," he says.

I scoff. "Fuck no."

His amusement deepens. "Why?"

It's the way he says it—genuine, like the idea is incomprehensible. Like no one has ever not liked him before. And maybe they haven't. He's hot, probably gets whatever he wants, whenever he wants it, especially from women.

I let the silence drag before answering, just to watch him wait. "You're arrogant. You talk like I'm supposed to just accept all of this because you said so."

His eyes show more curiosity than anything else now. "Anything else?"

"I'm sure you've used this exact thing plenty of times to get women to do what you want," I say, crossing my arms, my voice sharp, I don't want him to see the uncertainty.

Julian laughs—quiet, low, amused. "You think I need the bond for that?" His gaze rakes over me, deliberate. "I don't force. I don't chase. They come to me."

My fingers twitch at my sides, my pulse kicking up despite the flat look I shoot him. "Why are you following me?"

Julian tilts his head, considering me, his smirk never fading. "Who said I'm following you?"

"You're always there," I snap. "Always watching. Always waiting. If it's not the bond, what is it?"

That lands. Not in a way that fazes him, but in a way that interests him. Like he's just found something worth pulling apart. "And that bothers you?"

I straighten my shoulders, refusing to let him see the way my stomach tightens. "Yeah, it does. You act like this is already said and done. Like I don't have a say. But I'm not going down without a fight."

Julian studies me for a moment longer. Then his voice dips, velvet over flame. "Good. I'd hate for this to be too easy."

He makes a show of breathing out like I'm the exhausting one, then tilts his head. "You're so sure you don't like me, aren't you?"

I don't hesitate. "I know I don't."

His lips twitch like he finds this amusing. "Well, that's a relief. Because I don't like you either."

I roll my eyes, of course he doesn't, no one has in a very long time. "Good. We're on the same page."

"Hardly." His tone is silk and steel, smooth but edged with something sharp.

I fold my arms. "Oh, please. What could you possibly hate about me?"

He takes a step closer, his eyes glinting like he's been waiting for me to ask.

"You're stubborn to a fault," he says, voice quiet but carrying weight. "You refuse to see what's right in front of you just because you don't like the way it looks. You think if you ignore the truth hard enough, it'll change. It won't."

I stiffen. "That's not—"

"You push people away before they even get the chance to decide if they want to stay." His voice is softer now, and somehow that makes it worse. Too precise. Too accurate. "And you act like that's power, when really, it's just fear dressed up as control."

A slow, mocking smirk flickers at his lips as he watches my hands curl into fists. "What? Don't like hearing the truth?"

I swallow hard, refusing to let him get a reaction out of me, despite the fact that I think I'd finally be able to *have* a reaction. "You're so full of shit."

He laughs, dark and quiet. "Maybe. But I'm not wrong, am I?"

My nails dig into my palms. I hate him. I *hate* him.

He watches me for a second longer, like he's waiting to see if I'll break. With a bored exhale, he steps back. "You don't like me? Fine. But don't pretend you're the only one suffering."

I glare at him, forcing my voice to stay even. "Oh yeah? And what are you suffering from exactly?"

His smirk is slow and infuriating. "The endless misfortune of being stuck with you."

I clench my jaw as he turns, completely unfazed.

"It's a shame fate has such a cruel sense of humor, isn't it?"

I don't know who moves first.

One second, I'm glaring up at him, my pulse hammering in my ears, and the next—his hands are on me, and my back slams into the wall.

My breath catches. My body reacts before my mind can scream at me to stop.

Julian is heat and pressure and dominance, his palm flattening against my hip, fingers digging in just hard enough to make me gasp. His other hand cages me in against the wall, the heat of him pressing into me like he's trying to brand himself under my skin.

"Hate me all you want," he murmurs, his breath a whisper against my lips, "but don't lie to yourself, little fighter."

I want to shove him. I want to tear him apart. Instead, I grab the front of his shirt and yank him down into a kiss.

The second our lips crash, it's not a kiss—it's a war.

Julian doesn't hesitate, doesn't stop to breathe, doesn't give me even a second to pretend I have control. He takes. His fingers tighten around my waist, pulling me forward until I'm pinned between him and the wall, no space, no air, just heat and hunger and the suffocating weight of this bond between us.

A growl rumbles in his chest, low and rough, vibrating against my body as his mouth devours mine, all tongue and teeth and something feral. His lips move with slow, devastating precision, teasing mine apart just enough to let his tongue slide against mine—hot, claiming, tasting.

I gasp into him, my nails digging into his shoulders, and that's when he really reacts.

His hands grip my thighs, lifting me effortlessly, forcing my legs around his waist.

I moan before I can stop myself.

He smirks against my lips.

Smug bastard.

So I bite him.

A sharp nip to his lower lip, just enough to bruise, just enough to make him hiss through his teeth.

He loses it.

His hands tighten, his body pinning me harder against the wall as his mouth moves to my neck. Hot, wet, open-mouthed kisses, teeth scraping, tongue soothing, marking me as if he knows he shouldn't but can't stop.

I arch against him, unable to hold back the way my body reacts to him. It's electric, consuming, fire and friction, every part of me screaming for more, more, more.

His lips drag up, pressing against my ear, voice dark and full of pure sin.

"I knew you'd taste like this."

I shudder, my nails raking down his back, and his hips grind forward—slow, teasing, deliberate.

Fuck.

I hate him. I hate him.

But right now, I need him.

I need this.

"You think that was surrender?" His voice is steady, but his breathing isn't. His grip is still tight, too tight, like he's holding something back. Like if he lets go, he won't stop. "Try again, little fighter."

This isn't fate. This isn't magic. This is me, giving in to the one thing I swore I'd never want.

A soulmate bond is a tether. This one feels like a leash—wrapped around my throat, held by a demon who won't let go.

Eight
JULIAN

I haven't been back to Earth since I told Ophelia she is my soulmate. I've been trying to avoid her, in fact. Not that I can. Her brain never stops. I know she's exhausted. She's not sleeping. Barely eating. Just thinking.

She can't keep going on like this. Being in Hell and away from her makes me lose track of time. I think it's time I go back.

Or I could just ask Owen what's happening up there.

Julian: *Owen.*

Owen: *Yes, Julian?*

Julian: *What's going on up there?*

Owen: *Well, brother. Maybe you should come up and see for yourself.*

Julian: *I'm pulling rank. I'm the oldest. Just tell me.*

Owen: *By two and a half minutes! That doesn't even count!*

Julian: *Owen...*

Owen: *Just watch Uncensored.*

Uncensored with Ashton Pierce. The celebrity late-night show. I hate those stupid things. Pointless. Just rich people talking about how amazing they are. Why people watch that, I'll never know.

Demons love the show, though. All the lounges play it, and we get it on our personal devices. So I turn on the picture frame above the fireplace. I never use this stupid thing. I'd rather read. But my mother insisted it was all the rage on Earth. Aunt Selene told her.

The show comes on, and there he is—Ashton Pierce, draped in confidence like it's tailored to him.

Everything about him is polished, deliberate. Sharp suit, styled hair, an easy smirk that says he already knows how this will play out. He leans back in his chair, perfectly at ease, like he's the only one in the room who matters.

The show starts, and the intro music begins.

"Good evening, everyone!" he exclaims. "Welcome to Uncensored. I'm Ashton Pierce. I don't ask the questions you want. I ask the questions you need. So let's get going with tonight's show!"

"Wow. So invigorating," I mutter.

"Tonight we have Oscar-winning actor Dominic Arden-Forsythe and Melanie Arden-Forsythe with us! They're here to tell us about their upcoming movie, The Sun Will Forget Us, releasing in just two weeks!" Ashton continues.

The screen flickers, the lights in the studio dim, and the murmurs in the audience settle into silence.

"Let's take a look," Ashton says smoothly.

The screen flickers, the studio lights dimming as the audience leans in.

Dominic and Melanie fill the screen, bathed in cinematic lighting, their voices hushed, aching, meant to pull the audience into something raw and real. The score swells beneath their words, subtle but deliberate, designed to make people feel something.

I don't care.

Something flickers. A brief shift in Melanie, in the way she moves, in the way she looks at Dominic. There's something familiar there.

I recognize it instantly.

Ophelia.

It's diluted, watered down, barely there—but I feel it. And yet, even with that stolen spark, she still manages to just be mediocre.

I exhale, slow, amused. To take Ophelia's gift and still suck? That's laughable.

The clip ends. The audience erupts into applause.

"Now let's welcome Dominic and Melanie to the stage!" Ashton announces, his voice smooth, practiced.

The applause swells as they step out.

Dominic walks first, moving easily, naturally—polished, but not obnoxious. The suit fits well, the posture is effortless, and if he's tired of the cameras, he hides it well. He looks like what he's supposed to be: an Oscar-winning actor at the peak of his career.

A vision in something over-the-top, every detail meticulously planned. The dress clings just right, sequins catching the light like she's trying to blind everyone in the first row. Her makeup is too perfect, her smile too poised, her wave too rehearsed.

Dominic looks like himself. Melanie looks like a performance.

I lean back, unimpressed. She was already unbearable on-screen—this is just worse.

The screen flickers, the studio lights dimming as the audience leans in.

Ashton's smirk widens, like he's been waiting for this. "Now, I can't have you both here without asking about the wedding."

The audience erupts into applause, cheers rolling through the studio. Ridiculous.

On-screen, Melanie lights up instantly. She tilts her head just enough to catch the best angle, smile dazzling, effortless, so perfectly staged it's almost impressive.

"Oh, it was perfect. Absolutely perfect."

I barely look at her. I'm watching Dominic.

The smile is there. Thin. Forced. Just enough.

"A private ceremony, but from the pictures we've seen, it looked like something out of a movie." Ashton says.

Melanie doesn't hesitate. She never does. She lets out a soft laugh, reaching over and resting a hand on Dominic's arm—a subtle claim, meant to be noticed. "It was everything I ever dreamed of. I mean, marrying your best friend? What could be better?"

She looks up at Dominic, waiting. Expecting.

I catch the pause before he speaks. It's barely a second, but it's there. A hesitation, a flicker of something before he smooths it over.

"We wanted something intimate, just for us," Dominic finally says, voice easy, practiced.

I watch them, watch the world eat up the lie. They're so deep in it, they might actually believe it themselves.

Melanie squeezes Dominic's arm before pulling away, her voice slipping into something softer, more intimate—the actress switching scenes. "It was the best day of my life."

Ashton leans back, still grinning. "Now, let's talk about the movie."

Here we go.

The next few minutes play out exactly as expected. Ashton hypes them up, talking about The Sun Will Forget Us like it's a masterpiece. Melanie basks in it, playing the charming starlet, glowing, laughing, making everything seem effortless.

"The story is just so powerful," she says, pressing a hand to her chest. "It's about love, but also about sacrifice. And the kind of pain that stays with you forever."

I almost roll my eyes.

Dominic is more measured, he nods when he should, answers smoothly, never stumbles. But I notice the details, the way his fingers twitch against his knee, the fraction-of-a-second slip in his smile before he corrects it. He's playing the part, but something in him isn't as comfortable as Melanie.

Ashton leans forward, smirking. "Of course, the chemistry between you two is undeniable."

Melanie's already nodding before he's finished the sentence. "Oh, absolutely."

She reaches for Dominic's arm again. She's selling it. Hard.

"Did that connection come naturally?" Ashton asks, eyes gleaming with something sharp.

Melanie doesn't hesitate. "When you work with someone as talented as Dom, it's effortless."

Dominic nods, easy, agreeable, but I see it. The slight shift in his jaw. The faint tension in his shoulders. The audience doesn't notice. But I do.

"It really does feel like magic on screen," Ashton continues, glancing between them. "Which, of course, makes me wonder... was any of that magic still lingering off-screen?"

The audience erupts with laughter and whistles.

Melanie lets out the perfect laugh—light, teasing, not confirming, not denying. "I mean, we do play soulmates."

And there it is. The word.

Dominic's reaction is so quick most people wouldn't catch it. The way his breath shortens, the way his eyes flicker, just for a second, toward the camera.

I exhale, slow.

Melanie keeps talking. "Obviously, we poured everything into these characters. The emotions, the intensity—it's all real in the moment."

Ashton nods along, eating it up. "And people are already saying this could be one of the most romantic films of the decade."

Melanie beams. "That's incredible. It's truly an honor to be part of something so special."

Dominic doesn't speak this time.

Ashton leans back, his smirk shifting just slightly. A change in rhythm. A new game to play.

"Of course, I can't bring up soulmates without touching on a certain past connection," he says smoothly. "Dominic, this is your first big romance role since... well, since Ophelia."

The studio goes still.

For the first time, Melanie's polished veneer falters. Her fingers twitch in her lap, her smile slipping just a little before she forces it back into place.

Dominic doesn't move. Doesn't blink.

The audience shifts, murmurs rising. This wasn't part of the script.

Ashton tilts his head, watching them both carefully. He's not done. "Your team has done a great job keeping this under wraps," he continues casually, "but my team? We like digging up the good stuff."

A pause. A deliberate breath. "Not everyone knows that before Melanie, Dominic was actually with her sister."

The audience gasps. A few hushed whispers ripple through the studio. Melanie's head snaps toward Dominic. That wasn't supposed to come out. Dominic's jaw clenches. A warning. Don't.

But Melanie isn't one to sit in silence. She exhales sharply, tilting her chin up, voice dripping with false sweetness. "Oh, Ashton, really? I thought we were here to talk about the movie."

"We are," Ashton replies, all innocence and charm. "But it's such an interesting coincidence, don't you think? A film about soulmates, and now you two are married. But before that—well, let's just say the story had a different lead."

Melanie lets out a laugh that doesn't quite land right. She shakes her head, glancing toward Dominic as if expecting him to clean up the mess. He doesn't.

Ashton leans forward slightly, his smirk widening. "In fact, the last time Ophelia was seen in public was at your wedding, wasn't it?"

Melanie stills.

The audience reacts instantly—gasps, murmurs, a new buzz of excitement.

"It's funny," Ashton continues, "because when those wedding photos were released, people started asking, 'Wait, who's that in the background?'"

The screen behind them flashes to one of the widely shared images of Dominic and Melanie's wedding.

I watch as the pristine, romantic shot is overtaken by one detail—Ophelia, caught in the frame, just behind Melanie's shoulder.

She's not smiling. She's not front and center. She's just there.

And it's enough.

The murmurs grow louder. Melanie laughs, forced and bright. "Oh, come on, Ashton. You're really reaching now."

"Am I?" Ashton tilts his head. "I just think it's interesting that, for someone who stays so far out of the public eye, that was the last place she was seen. You and Ophelia must be close?"

Melanie stiffens. It's slight, but I see it.

She exhales, rolling her shoulders back, her expression smoothing into something confident. Composed. Ready to burn. "No, Ashton, we are not close." She lets the words hang there for a second, making sure the audience feels it. "Look, I know the internet loves their little theories, but the truth is, Ophelia has always been... different. She's never really been interested in what the rest of us do. She's never tried. Never fit in."

I drag in a breath, steadying what little I can.

"She's quiet. Awkward. Always lurking on the sidelines. And, honestly?" Melanie shrugs, like she's being generous. "She's just not that interesting."

A few chuckles from the audience. Some laughter.

Melanie smiles wider, emboldened.

"I mean, come on. Let's be real. We all knew Ophelia wasn't going anywhere. She never had the drive. Never had the talent. She barely lasted in Dominic's world, and when it got too hard? She disappeared. That's what she does."

I watch Dominic's hands press against his knees, tension radiating off him like heat.

Melanie isn't done. "I mean, we're talking about someone who used to get anxious just ordering her own coffee. Someone who was never comfortable in her own skin. It was embarrassing watching her try to belong." The laughter grows. Melanie keeps going. "Honestly? I don't know why people even remember her. She's forgettable. She always has been."

The words settle like dead weight.

Dominic moves before he speaks. Just slightly. His jaw tightens, his fingers curling into fists. "Stop."

It's not loud. But it cuts through the noise like a blade.

Melanie freezes, her lips parting slightly like she hadn't considered that he might actually push back. Dominic turns toward her fully now. His face is neutral, but there's something cold in his eyes. "Don't."

Melanie scoffs, feigning amusement. "Oh, come on, Dominic, don't act like—"

"I said stop." His voice is sharper this time. Unmistakable. Silence.

Melanie swallows, her face smoothing over as if nothing happened. But it did. Everyone felt it. Ashton leans back, watching them both like a man who just set fire to a room and is waiting to see how far the flames will spread.

Just as the argument is about to break open completely, the screen glitches and cuts to black. I don't know who cut the feed. Maybe the network. Maybe Dominic's team. Maybe someone decided this mess had gone on long enough.

It doesn't matter. I'm already laughing.

I turn the TV off and I feel it. A pull. A call. My mind starts to hyper-focus on where it is coming from.

Once I pinpoint it, I know it's not where. It's who.

Ophelia: *Julian! I—I can't move—I can't—*

Nothing more needs to be said because I will myself to where she is.

She twists against the sheets, her breath coming in sharp, uneven gasps. Her fingers clutch at the blankets, as if trying to hold onto something just out of reach.

"Ophelia, wake up!" I call.

No answer. She's stuck wherever she is.

"Lia, baby, I'm here. You can relax," I say, putting my hand gently on her shoulder.

She exhales sharply, her body going still. The tension seeps out of her limbs, like the nightmare has been drained from her all at once.

Her lashes flutter. Slowly. Like she's surfacing from somewhere deep, heavy.

When her eyes rise to meet mine, I freeze. They aren't the same. At first, I think it's a trick of the light, the dim glow casting strange shadows over her face. But no—it's real. It's happening.

The color shifts, deepens. Her once crystal-blue irises darken as deep red swirls bloom within them, curling at the edges like ink spreading through water. Like mine.

Something shifts. Something primal. Deep. Ancient. It slams into me like a force I can't fight, it's older than thought, stronger than reason.

I move before I can stop myself. My body, my instincts—they decide before my mind does.

I grab her, my grip is hard and desperate. My fingers dig into her waist like she's the only thing anchoring me to reality.

I'm kissing her. Hard. Fast. Devouring. She tenses beneath me, stiff—but I don't stop.

I can't. She's my soulmate. My mate. It's all I can feel. All I can see.

She exhales sharply against my lips, her breath stuttering, caught between shock and something else. Finally, she moves, not a push or a resistance, but something between hesitation and response.

My grip tightens. A growl builds low in my throat, primal and possessive. I tilt my head, deepening it, tasting her, needing her in a way I can't name.

The bond pulses between us, thick and undeniable. She's here. She's mine. She's pulling away.

I jump back and hit the wall. *What the fuck am I thinking?*

She called me. She wanted me to come. Protect and save her. She wants me, I think to myself.

But she isn't ready for this. Not yet. But soon.

Julian: *Owen! I need you! Now!*

Owen: *What?*

I think to myself, *screw it.* I open the link to all the guys.

Julian: *Please! I need help!*

No one responds.

Seconds later, they're all there.

I make a mistake, though. I look into Ophelia's eyes again. I can't stop myself from lurching toward her, my body moving before my mind can catch up. Every cell in me screams to go back. To touch her. To pull her into my arms.

But arms clamp around me, dragging me back.

I snarl, fight, push forward—but they don't let go. My legs still move, but I'm barely making ground.

Her name rips from my throat, a sound I don't recognize, something between a plea and a demand.

"Julian, stop." A voice—distant, steady, barely cutting through the chaos.

Hands grip tighter. A force stronger than me, stronger than the bond, pulling me away.

"I got you. Let's go." Damian.

No. No, no, no. I twist, fight harder, but they're too many. The bond pulls like a noose around my ribs, tightening, burning, clawing at my insides.

"Ophelia!" The name rips from me like it's the only thing I have left.

Darkness crashes down, swallowing me whole.

Nine
Ophelia

Julian is gone. One second he was here, the next—nothing. Like he was never here at all. I knew he wasn't human. Knew he had power. But knowing and seeing are two different things.

Now, I'm alone in my tiny studio. Well, not alone.

Five other guys stare at me, watching, waiting. One of them looks almost exactly like Julian, but I know immediately that he's not. I don't just see it—I feel it. Something in my gut tells me this is someone else entirely.

I don't know what to say, so I say nothing.

"So, you're Julian's mate," the lookalike says, his voice steady, almost bored.

My fingers twitch at my sides, uneasy, and that's when I notice—my shirt has shifted. The mark is showing.

A sharp pulse of embarrassment crawls up my spine as I grab the fabric, pulling it closed, but it's too late. They've already seen it. We all know they've seen it.

I press my fingers against the hem of my shirt and lift my chin, locking eyes with the one who spoke. "So what if I am?"

A low chuckle rolls through the room, deep and edged with amusement. The stranger smirks, tipping his head toward me. "Feisty. I like her."

I turn toward the voice. Another guy, taller than the rest, leans casually against the wall like he has all the time in the world. Dark hair, messy in a way that looks too effortless to be accidental. His smirk lingers, widening slightly when I glare at him, like I'm the most interesting thing in the room.

Their stares pin me in place, heavy with something unreadable. Five strangers. Five men who clearly know more than I do about what's happening to me.

"Owen," he says, his voice similar to Julian's but flatter. Less emotion, less edge. Like he's not interested in playing whatever game his brother seems to enjoy.

I grip the hem of my shirt a little tighter. I don't like that they look so much alike, but they don't feel alike at all.

To his right, another one sighs, crossing his arms over his chest. Broader, heavier presence, already over this conversation.

"Lucas," he says. He doesn't smirk like Owen. Doesn't watch me like he's weighing my worth. Just looks me over, unimpressed. "Before you ask—no, I'm not the friendly one."

"That would be me."

I turn toward the voice. Another one speaks up, leaning against the chair behind me. Not close enough to touch, but close enough that I know he's there.

His grin is easy, unbothered, like this is all some inside joke I'm not in on.

"Seth," he says, flashing a smile like he expects me to remember it. "And don't let these guys fool you—I'm the favorite."

Lucas scoffs. "No, you just think you're the favorite."

Seth shrugs. "Same thing."

The tension shifts, not gone, but redirected for half a second. He's testing me, baiting me, waiting to see if I'll push back, if I'll play along.

But before I can decide, another voice cuts through the space—softer than the rest. He's been watching me the entire time, but not like Lucas or Owen. More neutral, deliberate, like he's measuring me.

He's been watching me the entire time, but not like Lucas or Owen. More neutral. More deliberate. More careful. Like he's waiting to decide something.

A sigh escapes him. "Adrian."

I flick my gaze toward the last one. He stands like he's part of the background, like he'd rather be anywhere but here. But there's something sharp in his stillness, something contained.

His voice is low. "Caleb."

No smirk. No reaction. Just a name. A look. And his presence—silent, unmoving—settling into the room.

I take them all in again, pulse steady, expression blank. None of them seem as cold as Damian, but I don't trust them either.

Owen doesn't take his eyes off me. Julian's face, but not Julian.

Lucas exhales, sounding like this has all been a waste of his time. "Alright, now that we all know each other—" he gestures vaguely toward me. "How much do you actually know about the bond?"

I hesitate, grip tightening on the hem of my shirt. "Only what Julian told me." The words feel too thin, too uncertain.

Owen watches me, unreadable, his eyes never leaving mine. "And what is that?"

I shift my weight from one foot to the other, resisting the urge to cross my arms again. "That the bond is something I can't control. That it binds our souls or something like that."

Seth—I think it's Seth—lets out a low laugh, leaning back like this is the most entertaining thing he's heard all night. "Yeah. Something like that."

My patience snaps. "What the fuck happened tonight?" My voice is sharp, cutting through whatever quiet amusement lingers in the air.

Silence.

A shift. Something unspoken pressing against the space between us.

Owen is the one who answers, his tone matter-of-fact, like he's explaining something inevitable. "That would be the mate bond. Except on steroids."

Caleb exhales through his nose, shaking his head slightly. "Fun most of the time. Right now, not so much."

Owen shoots him a look before turning back to me. His gaze is steady, too steady. "Besides, you called him."

My stomach twists. Something cold and sharp presses against my ribs. I freeze, shake my head, and step back slightly. "I did not. No way."

Adrian shifts, arms crossed as he leans against the wall. His expression doesn't change, but there's something certain in his tone. "Not on purpose. But you're tied together by the thread of your very soul. You called. He came. Simple as that."

A hollow feeling spreads through my chest, heavy and unshakable. The truth settles in my bones before I can even fight it.

"So that's it?" I say, my voice sharper now, edged with something close to panic. "I just have to accept that I have no control over my own body? Over my own damn mind?"

Owen tilts his head slightly, still calm. Too calm, it's the same way the world sees me, emotionless. "You have control. But the more you resist, the harder it pulls."

I exhale slowly, pressing my fingers to my temples. I don't want it to make sense. I hate that it does. "So you're saying I have to give in to this bond?" My voice is quieter now, but no less tense.

Owen shakes his head, his gaze locked onto mine. "Not give in, per se. But you need to make a decision. Or at least hear him out."

The words hit harder than they should. Because I know. I've known. I already know I can't ignore this forever.

I throw the covers off, barely feeling the cold air as I swing my legs over the edge of the bed. My body still aches—not from exhaustion, but from something deeper, something I don't have the energy to name. The bond hums faintly beneath my skin, not as intense as before, but there. Lingering. Waiting.

I shove it aside, and head toward my closet without a word.

I don't care what I put on—just something comfortable, something that doesn't make me feel like I'm sitting here waiting for answers I don't want to hear. I grab the first hoodie I see, tugging it over my head before shoving on a pair of leggings.

When I step back out, they're all still there. Lounging. Waiting. Like this is just another night, like my entire world hasn't shifted underneath me.

I grab my keys.

"Where are you going?" Lucas asks, sounding entirely too casual, while I'm planning my escape.

"On a walk. Enjoy yourselves."

I don't stop. I don't wait for their response. I just move toward the door because I need air, need space, need to clear my head before someone else tells me what I don't want to hear.

"Sit down," Adrian says, his voice calm, even, but laced with a quiet certainty that makes me grit my teeth. It's not a demand, not a request—just something final, something that tells me arguing would be pointless.

I don't turn around.

"We called someone that may be able to help you. To read you. See why your bond is so strong and why things moved so fast."

I exhale sharply through my nose, gripping my keys tighter before finally turning back. "Fine."

I plop down onto the couch, crossing my arms, tapping my fingers against my knee. If they want me to sit here and wait for some supernatural diagnosis, fine. It's not like I have much of a choice.

The air shifts. It's subtle at first. A hum beneath my ribs, vibrating just under my pulse. The lights dim—not flickering, just... adjusting, like the room is making space for something else. A breeze stirs the air, carrying the faintest trace of something unfamiliar.

Without warning, they've arrived.

Not appearing in a dramatic flare of shadows like Julian and the others. No overwhelming force pressing into my chest. This is different. Like reality bends around them, like the space simply allows them in without a fight.

And still, I scream.

Not a cute, startled gasp—an actual, full-bodied scream, instinct launching me off the couch.

Seth barely holds back laughter. "Oh, she's awake for this one. That's new."

I glare at him, heart slamming against my ribs. "You think this is funny?"

"A little," Lucas mutters.

I turn back to the intruders.

The woman stands effortlessly poised, barefoot on my living room floor, the hem of her dark silk dress swaying slightly as though touched by a breeze only she can feel. Her auburn curls spill freely over her shoulders, wild but deliberate, untamed but not careless. Silver eyes—hypnotic, too sharp, too knowing—take me in all at once, as if she's already figured me out.

Beside her, the man leans lazily against the arm of a chair, smirking like he's been here the whole time, watching, waiting for the perfect moment to say something just to get under my skin. Dark tousled hair, an unbuttoned collar, red-and-gold eyes gleaming with amusement and absolutely no urgency.

Adrian exhales like this is a formality at best. "Selene and Theron." He glances at me. "Our parents."

My head jerks toward them, eyes narrowing. "Parents?"

Selene tilts her head, silver gaze flicking to the Mark on my skin before returning to my face. A soft hum leaves her lips, not in surprise. or concern—in interest.

"She's destabilizing," she murmurs, her voice smooth, warm. She lifts a hand, the delicate rings on her fingers catching the light as if the gesture itself means something. "I can feel it."

My skin prickles at the certainty in her voice. "You want to explain what the hell that means?"

Theron exhales, shaking his head, the smirk still there but softer now, edged with intrigue. "It means we need to know exactly what's happening to you. And for that, you need to stop fighting it long enough to listen."

I cross my arms, narrowing my eyes. "Right. Because I should just take the word of two people who walked through my living room like reality doesn't apply to them."

Selene's lips twitch. "That's fair. Let's make this easier. You ask the questions first."

I glance between them, skeptical. "Really?"

Theron shrugs, settling into a chair like he's been here the whole time. "Why not? I'd want to know who was screwing with my life too."

I inhale sharply through my nose, already regretting this. "Fine. What are you to Julian?"

Selene leans back slightly, resting her weight on one hip. "His aunt. And before you say anything—yes, I know. I don't look it. Demonic blood has its perks."

My eyes snap to Theron. "And you?"

He smirks. "Uncle. Younger than his father, but infinitely more charming."

"That's debatable," Selene mutters under her breath.

Theron places a hand over his chest in mock offense. "You wound me."

I roll my eyes. "So, Julian's entire family is a supernatural mess, and now I'm tangled in it because of some cosmic matchmaking glitch?"

Theron laughs, tipping his head back like I'm the funniest thing he's heard all day. "Oh, I like her."

Selene's expression is more measured, but her amusement is obvious. "It's not a glitch. It's a design."

I shake my head. "No, it's a mistake."

Her expression doesn't waver. "You think that because you're fighting it. But let me guess—despite how much you resist, despite how much you tell yourself you don't want this, the bond is still pulling. You still feel him, don't you?"

The question lands like a rock in my chest. My jaw tightens, but I say nothing.

Theron drags a breath through his nose, clearly unimpressed. "Look, we can get into all the poetic fate stuff later. Right now, the problem isn't whether or not you *like* this bond. It's why it's moving so fast."

I grab onto that immediately. "Yes. That. Why is this happening so quickly? And Julian looks like he's one second away from completely losing it. Is that normal for him? I don't know. Maybe it is. Maybe this is just who he is."

Selene and Theron exchange a look—one of those silent conversations that makes my stomach tighten.

Selene sighs, finally moving to sit, her posture still too effortless, too composed for someone delivering what I assume is about to be bad news. "Your bond isn't just strong. It's unstable. It's reacting faster than it should, and Julian..." She pauses, her lips curving slightly. "Well. He's taking the brunt of it."

I straighten slightly. "What do you mean?"

Theron rests an elbow on the arm of his chair, watching me. "Your bond should be like a slow-burning fire, right? Controlled. Gradual. Except yours? Someone doused it in gasoline and lit a match."

"Great. Super helpful. Thanks."

Selene ignores my sarcasm. "Julian is feeling the full weight of it, more than you are. Probably because—" she waves a hand in my direction, as if gesturing to my entire existence "—you're resisting."

I scoff. "So what, this is my fault? He's turning into a possessive psychopath because I'm not swooning into his arms?"

Theron grins, clearly enjoying this too much. "Not your *fault*, exactly. But let's just say, the more you fight, the worse it gets for him."

I exhale sharply, resisting the urge to throw something at his smirking face.

Selene tilts her head slightly. "You feel it too, don't you? The way it's pulling, the way it's waiting for you to make a choice."

My fingers twitch at my sides, my breath feeling just a little too uneven.

"And if I don't?"

"You'll keep fighting it. He'll keep feeling it. And eventually?" Theron shrugs. "Something's going to break."

Theron's words settle in the air between us, thick and unshakable. *Something's gonna break.* I hate how much sense that makes.

Before I can push back, Selene exhales through her nose, a quiet, knowing sound that immediately puts me on edge. She shifts slightly, brushing a stray curl behind her ear, adjusting the stack of rings on her fingers like she's working up to something.

"That's not the only thing we need to talk about."

I blink, stomach twisting at the sudden shift in her tone. "What now?"

Selene leans forward, resting her elbows on her knees, silver eyes meeting mine without hesitation. "Your family."

My fingers twitch, curling against my thigh. "What about them?"

Theron snorts, shaking his head. "Oh, come on. You had to know this was coming. It's not just Melanie running her mouth on national television. It's your entire bloodline, sweetheart."

Selene hums, tapping a ring against the arm of her chair. "Cassius Arden. Your father. The real question is: how much do *you* know about him?"

I scoff, rolling my shoulders back. "Enough to know I don't care."

Theron smirks. "That's the thing about Cassius. Even when you don't care, he still finds a way to make himself *very* relevant."

I clench my jaw, refusing to rise to whatever bait they're dangling. "I know what I need to. He's a businessman, he's powerful, and he only cares about himself. There. Covered it."

Selene watches me too carefully. "And Calliope?"

The name hits like ice water down my spine. My stomach twists, my nails digging into my palms before I can stop them.

"She's dead," I say, voice tight. "Not much else to say."

Theron exhales dramatically, shaking his head. "See, that's what I *was* hoping you'd say. But it's not true, is it? There's plenty to say about Calliope Arden—if you ever bothered to listen."

A slow ache blooms in my chest, the kind that never really goes away, the kind that lingers no matter how much time has passed. I should be used to it by now.

I wanted to listen. I wanted to know her.

But she died before I ever really got the chance.

"I don't need a history lesson," I snap.

Selene tilts her head, studying me like she already sees through my defenses. "No, I suppose you don't. You already know the important parts, don't you? You just don't like to talk about them."

I press my lips together, refusing to let them see how much this conversation is digging into something raw.

Theron leans forward, resting his arms on his knees, his smirk softening just slightly. "You miss her."

It's not a question.

The air feels too heavy, my throat too tight. I exhale sharply, shaking my head. "What does it matter?"

Selene's voice gentles, but it doesn't waver. "Because your mother was important, Ophelia. And not just to you."

I swallow, looking down at my hands, fingers twisting together. "She wasn't even married to my father that long. He had an affair. Rosalind was already pregnant with Melanie before my mother even died."

Theron exhales through his nose. "Cassius never wastes time, does he?"

I shake my head, jaw tightening. "No. He doesn't."

Selene leans back, watching me carefully. "And yet, despite all of that, Rosalind still raised you like her own."

My stomach twists, and suddenly, this conversation feels even more exhausting than before.

"She did," I say, quieter now. "She made sure I remembered my mother. She talked about her like she was still here, like she wasn't just a name in a family history book." I pause, pressing my nails into my palm, focusing on the sting. "But she was still my mother, too. Rosalind. She never made me feel like I didn't belong."

Theron whistles, shaking his head. "So let me get this straight. You've got an angel for a stepmother, a power-hungry father, and a dead mother whose name still carries weight. Yeah, you're definitely in the clear."

Selene ignores him. "And yet, Rosalind wasn't at Melanie's wedding."

I go still.

Selene raises a brow. "Why is that?"

I exhale sharply, crossing my arms tighter. "She wasn't invited."

Theron lets out a low whistle. "Oof. Cold."

"Melanie made sure of it," I continue, jaw tightening. "She never wanted Rosalind to be part of our lives after she left our father. She spent years making sure we knew she wasn't an Arden anymore. That she wasn't family. When she married Dominic, it was her chance to erase the last thing tying her to Rosalind."

Selene hums in thought. "And how did Rosalind feel about that?"

I hesitate, the memory hitting me all at once. The way Rosalind smiled, soft and warm, like it didn't hurt at all. Like she understood. Like she always understood.

"She didn't fight it," I say after a long moment. "She never fought Melanie on anything."

Theron raises a brow. "And you don't think that's strange?"

I shake my head. "She's not like you. She's not like any of you. She doesn't want power, she doesn't play games, she—"

"Kept you hidden," Selene finishes. "Kept you safe. Which is exactly why this might be a problem now."

A lump lodges itself in my throat, cold and solid.

"What are you saying?"

Selene leans forward, eyes sharp, voice softer now. "I'm saying that whatever happens next, you need to be prepared. Because if you don't act first, someone else will. And Julian?" Her lips curve, not quite a smile. "He's not the waiting type."

Theron stretches his arms behind his head, still smirking. "And considering he's already barely holding it together, I don't think you want to see what that looks like."

They leave, and I open my laptop, pulling up the interview.

I don't know why I do it. Maybe I need to see it for myself. Maybe I need proof. But the second it starts, I know. They're right. This is a problem.

Melanie's voice is perfectly measured, perfectly cruel, designed to cut without leaving a mark. And the world eats it up—the audience, the headlines, the people who will never know me but will believe every word of hers. My chest tightens, a slow, sinking weight settling inside me.

I'm so unhappy in my life. Why? Why can't I be happy? Why can't I just let someone make me happy? My fingers twitch against the keyboard. Maybe Julian could do that.

The thought hits too fast, too hard, and I swallow it back just as quickly. But first—first, I need to do something.

I click on my email, scanning the name I haven't been able to stop thinking about since it arrived.

Rhys Westwood. Investigative reporter.

I want to do a story on the Arden and Arden-Forsythe families. I have reason to believe that Melanie Arden's success wasn't entirely earned. If you're interested in helping, let me know.

Underneath, he left his phone number. I don't hesitate. I type out a message and hit send before I can second-guess it.

> Hi Rhys. This is Ophelia Arden. Let's talk.

Ten
Ophelia

I'm anxiously excited to meet Rhys in person. We've spoken a few times on the phone. He's investigating my family. He said he wants to talk face-to-face.

Not going to lie, that freaks me out.

I don't love the idea that there is actually something for him to find.

The coffee house he picked is tucked between two brick buildings, the kind of place you'd only notice if you were looking for it. Dim lighting, scratched wooden tables, the air thick with espresso and something sweet baking in the back. It doesn't draw attention, which I guess is the point. Far enough that I won't get caught. Close enough that I can disappear if I have to.

Rhys is already here, seated near the window, fingers drumming idly against a ceramic mug. His eyes scan the room like he's expecting to be caught—or like he's the one doing the catching.

He looks just like his byline photos—dark, unruly hair, sharp blue eyes that miss nothing, a posture that says he's listening even when no one's speaking. He doesn't just observe stories; he unravels them, pulls them apart until there's nothing left hidden. And now, for whatever reason, I'm the story he's waiting for.

I walk over and slide into the seat across from him.

"Hi, Rhys," I say.

"Ophelia," he acknowledges, his gaze assessing, scanning, filing me away like evidence.

A beat of silence stretches between us. Not uncomfortable—just measured.

"You always meet your sources in places like this?" I ask, glancing around at the nondescript coffee shop.

"Safe. Public. Neutral," he replies easily. "Harder for someone to disappear without a trace."

I raise a brow. "Reassuring."

"Depends on who you are."

"And who am I?"

He takes a slow sip of his coffee, eyes flicking back to me. "That's what I'm here to find out."

I lean back, crossing my arms. "Actually, you said you have something for me."

"I do." He sets his mug down, fingers tapping lightly against the ceramic. "I found something about your sister. And your father."

That surprises me.

I mean, I know they're cruel, calculated, and incapable of empathy. But they actually did something? No way. That's not how they operate. They don't get their hands dirty. They manipulate, they push, they ruin people from a safe distance. *That's* how they work.

So if Rhys has something—something real—that means...

No.

It's probably nothing. Some shallow, tabloid-level scandal, the kind that makes headlines for a week and disappears. Maybe another affair. Some money laundering. A quiet little bribe.

Bad? Sure. Unexpected? Not even a little.

What if he knows something bigger? What if he knows something about Julian? No, that's impossible. There's no way he could have dug that deep. Right?

"So," Rhys starts, fingers drumming against his cup, gaze sharp. "Melanie Arden. Hollywood's golden girl. Critics call her a once-in-a-generation talent. Directors say she's transformative. Fans swear she feels real in every role."

He pauses, watching me, waiting for a reaction. I don't give him one. "But here's the thing," he continues, his voice measured. Too careful. "She wasn't always like that. Ten years ago, she was just another struggling actress. No connections. No famous last name. Just another pretty face trying to make it."

I swallow hard. I know this.

"She wasn't bad, exactly," he says, tilting his head slightly. "But she wasn't good, either. Forgettable, at best. Casting directors passed her over. Directors called her stiff. She could hit her marks, say her lines, but she couldn't feel them. Couldn't make anyone believe her."

I remember. I remember the way she used to force emotion, how nothing ever quite landed. And I remember how I used to feel everything too much—how my emotions bled into everything I touched.

Rhys leans forward, his voice as smooth as it is deliberate. "Something changed."

My stomach twists.

"She started getting better. Not all at once, not overnight—but suddenly, it clicked. She started landing roles. Small ones at first. Indie films. Side characters. And people started paying attention."

At the same time, I was losing something. It was slow, subtle, like a leak I couldn't find. My paintings still looked like mine, but they felt hollow. Like I was mimicking myself instead of creating something real.

But Melanie? She was gaining something.

"She worked steadily for a few years," Rhys continues, fingers tapping lightly against the table. "She was solid. Good, even. But five years ago? She wasn't just good anymore. She was extraordinary."

A tight knot forms in my stomach.

"She didn't just improve," he says, his voice dropping slightly. "She became the best. Directors called her a once-in-a-generation actress. Critics swore her performances were visceral. She could cry on cue, break down in ways that felt too real. No one could touch her."

I stare at the table.

I know. I've seen it. I've felt it. That thing inside her—that ability to pull emotion from nowhere, to make every moment raw. It used to be mine.

Rhys keeps watching me. "It's weird, right? People don't just become that good. Not like that. Not after years of being fine at best."

I don't answer. Because no one questions it. No one remembers how she used to struggle. There are no bad reviews. No clips of awkward performances. No proof that there was ever a time when she wasn't brilliant.

It's like that version of her—the one who failed, the one who tried and fell short, the one I grew up with—never existed.

I press my nails into my palm, grounding myself. Quiet. Steady. Keep it together.

Rhys tilts his head, his voice lowering. "You ever wonder how she did it?"

I force a shrug, even as my pulse hammers. "Not really."

Rhys doesn't buy it. He knows I'm lying. But he doesn't call me on it. He just watches, his blue eyes too sharp, too focused—like he's waiting for me to slip.

I shift in my seat, resisting the urge to look away. I don't like the way he's looking at me. Because he's right. Something isn't normal. Something isn't natural. Maybe this is something I should talk to Julian about.

No. What am I saying? I don't want to talk to Julian. I don't want to go to him for anything. It's better if we keep our distance.

I push back my chair abruptly, the legs scraping against the floor. Rhys doesn't react, just watches as I stand, his expression unreadable.

"I'm done with this," I say, my voice sharper than I intend. Too raw. Too fast. But my thoughts are racing, tangling together in ways I don't want to untangle. "I don't care if you keep looking into Melanie. Or my father. But I'm not helping you."

Rhys exhales through his nose, his fingers curling around his coffee cup. He studies me, considering. "You sure about that?"

I hesitate. Just for a second. I nod once. I turn and walk out before he can say anything else.

I need to think. I need time. I can't let myself get sucked into this.

I glance at my watch—almost time for lunch with Bella and Rosalind. We try to meet once a month, but Bella's been buried in work, and Rosalind's been running a charity event. I'm the only one with time to spare. So I work around their schedules.

The rain picks up as I step outside, slicking the pavement, soaking into the fabric of my jacket. Perfect. Like I wasn't already annoyed enough. I climb into the cab, pressing my forehead against the cool window as the city blurs past.

The restaurant is small, family-owned, the kind of place that doesn't change. No gimmicks, no overpriced nonsense—just food people actually want to eat. The air is charged with the scent of fresh bread and garlic, something simmering on the stove.

A few families sit in booths, voices low but comfortable, silverware clinking against plates. Nothing fancy. Nothing that demands attention. Just a place to exist for a while.

I spot them in our usual booth and slide in, cutting off their conversation.

Rosalind looks up. For a second, she just stares—like she's trying to read me.

She still carries herself with the same quiet grace, but there's something softer about her now. Her honey-blonde hair is still styled, but not in that perfect, untouchable way it used to be. A few strands fall loose around her face, brushing against the faint lines near her green eyes—the kind carved by years of worry, but never bitterness. The elegant dresses and pristine makeup she once wore have given way to a more effortless beauty—simple gold earrings, a warm-toned sweater, barely-there lipstick.

She smiles at me like I am her biological daughter. And in every way that matters, she is my mother.

My mother, Calliope Arden, died when I was five. I don't remember much—just flashes. The sound of her laughter. The smell of oil paints and lilacs. The way she used to cup my face in her hands, pressing a kiss to my forehead like she was imprinting something onto my skin.

Six months after she was gone, my father married Rosalind. I was too young to understand what it meant, but I learned quickly. He had been having an affair. Rosalind got pregnant while my mom was still pregnant with me. That's how I ended up with a half-sister only six months younger than me.

But I never blamed Rosalind. Even when I wasn't hers, she treated me like I was. She combed through my hair after ballet class, packed my lunches, tucked me into bed. She never tried to replace my mother, but she never let me feel like I was alone.

She stayed until Bella turned eighteen, until she was off to college. The day after graduation, she finally walked away from the life my father had built for her. But she never walked away from me.

We kept in touch. We stayed close. We never had to question whether we were still family.

I feel lucky to have her. And that smile—God, that smile—makes me want to cry.

"Lia! You made it!" Bella exclaims, grinning.

"I wouldn't miss it," I say, forcing my voice steady.

Rosalind's eyes stay on me. Still searching. Still soft. "Hi, honey."

"Hi, Rosalind." I say it casually, like it doesn't feel like something big. But my smile is huge, and I don't try to stop it.

"How was your meeting with Rhys?" Bella asks.

The waitress drops off our food. We don't even have to order. They know us here.

I take a bite of my salmon Cobb salad, the flavors hitting all at once—fresh, bright, perfect. I groan, closing my eyes for a second.

"He figured out Melanie was average at best and suddenly, she's amazing." I shrug.

"I mean, we all knew that." Bella rolls her eyes, stabbing her fork into her pasta.

Rosalind stays quiet. I glance at her, and there it is—that flicker of sadness. She hides it well, but I know what it's about.

Melanie disowned her. Pretends she doesn't exist. I don't say anything. What would I even say? I just let the silence stretch between us.

"Well, ladies, I hate to eat and run, but my lunch hour is pretty much up, and I have to stop at the store before I head back," Bella says, wiping her mouth with a napkin.

Rosalind smiles softly, standing to kiss her cheek. "It was good to see you, honey."

"Please be safe," I say.

"Always." Bella grins before pressing a quick kiss to my cheek and waving at the staff before heading out.

I watch her go, twisting my fork between my fingers.

Bella got a job running a program for women who've been trafficked. She's doing a lot of good. Helping them get back on their feet.

She's incredible at it. But it's dangerous. And I can't shake the feeling that one day, we're going to lose her to it.

Rosalind hums in approval, her fingers circling the rim of her glass. "I'm so proud of her." Just as I take a sip of water, she switches gears completely. "Speaking of which... Bella told me about the man you were dancing with at Melanie's wedding."

I choke. Actually choke. The water goes down wrong, and I have to press my fist against my chest to clear my throat. "Excuse me?"

Rosalind grins like she's been waiting for this moment. "Oh, don't act like you don't remember."

I do remember. Unfortunately. The way Julian held me, the way his voice curled around my name, the way my pulse betrayed me every time he looked at me. But I am not talking about this. Not here. Not now. Not ever.

"It was just a dance," I say, forcing my voice into something neutral.

Rosalind's brows lift, sharp and knowing. "Bella said it didn't look like 'just a dance.'"

Of course she did.

"Was he a friend of Melanie's?" Rosalind asks, like it's an innocent question.

I should lie. I should give her a simple answer and move on. But the truth presses against my teeth, and the way she's looking at me—like she actually cares—unsettles me more than the question itself.

"No," I say. And that should be the end of it. "He's not. Just a guest, though."

Rosalind doesn't even hesitate. "I don't believe you. He's someone to you."

I scoff, reaching for my water. "Why do you say that?"

She tilts her head, like she's studying me, like I'm a painting she's trying to decode. "Because, honey, if he wasn't, you would've just said no to the dance."

I freeze. She's right.

If I hadn't wanted to know him—even subconsciously—I would've just walked away. That's what I do. I shut people out, push them away before they can hurt me. But that night... I didn't.

I don't like what that says about me.

Before I can shut this conversation down, she shifts again. "I know something happened with Melanie, and that reporter is onto something."

My stomach tightens.

Rosalind isn't one to pry. She barely talks about Melanie at all. She's spent years avoiding it, staying out of the mess, out of the conversations, out of the headlines. And yet, she's bringing it up now.

I force my expression into something neutral. "What do you mean?"

She exhales, slow and measured, studying me like she's choosing her next words carefully.

"I mean," she says, voice cooling, "she's involved in something. And I think you know exactly what I mean."

I don't answer. Because answering means acknowledging it.

Rosalind shakes her head. "I may not have been there, but Bella told me everything."

My stomach tightens.

"She told me about the guy you danced with. About the way Dominic watched you the whole time." She pauses, searching my face. "And about how Melanie lost her mind over it."

I force a small scoff. "Melanie loses her mind over everything. This is hardly special."

"Is it?" she challenges. "Because what I heard is that Dominic couldn't stop looking at you, and Melanie could barely stand it."

I stare at the table.

"She stole him, and she's still insecure."

I scoff, shaking my head. "She has nothing to be insecure about."

Rosalind doesn't blink. She just waits.

I hate that.

I grab my glass of water, taking a slow sip like I can drown out the conversation, like the weight in my chest isn't growing heavier. She has nothing to be insecure about. She won. She has him. She has everything. So why does it feel like I lost more than just him?

I place the glass down carefully, too carefully, like I need control over something. "Melanie always thinks someone is out to take what's hers. It's a personality trait at this point."

Rosalind hums, unconvinced. "And Dominic?"

I swallow hard. "She already has him."

Rosalind scoffs. "Why does he keep looking at you like he doesn't want you to move on?"

The words land like a slap. "I—" I start, but I have nothing to say.

Because I feel it too. I feel it when his gaze lingers too long, when his expression tightens just enough to make me wonder if he regrets it. And I know—I know—that he doesn't want me to move on. Not really.

Rosalind exhales sharply, shaking her head. "He made his choice, Ophelia. And now he's sitting in it. You don't owe him anything."

I press my lips together. I didn't push him away. I didn't betray him. He made that decision all on his own. And now, I can make mine.

Lunch winds down after that, conversation shifting to lighter things—Bella's work, the restaurant's incredible dessert, Rosalind's insistence that I take some leftovers home. But the weight of our discussion lingers, threading through my thoughts as I step outside.

The rain hasn't let up. It's a steady drizzle now, soft but relentless, seeping into my clothes and clinging to my skin as I walk to the curb. I pull my coat tighter around me, but it does nothing to shake the chill creeping up my spine.

By the time I slide into the backseat of a cab, my fingers hover over my phone, hesitating. The city blurs behind streaks of water on the window, headlights glowing against the wet pavement. I could go home, pretend none of this is gnawing at me, let it all settle into the pit of my stomach like it always does.

Or I could do something I'll regret.

I don't know if this will work. I don't even know if he'll answer. But I try anyway.

Ophelia: *Julian? Can you hear me?*

Julian: *Ophelia? Is that you?*

Ophelia: *Yeah. I thought that we should maybe talk.*

Julian: *Of course. Where?*

Ophelia: *Do you think you could come to my apartment? I should be home soon.*

Julian: *Meet you there.*

I get home and before I even unlock the door, I know that he's in there. I can feel him. So I decide to just go in and talk to him.

When I open the door, my breath catches.

He's handsome—undeniably so. But something is different. The effortless composure he always carries feels frayed at the edges, like a thread pulled too tight, ready to snap. His red eyes, flecked with gold, don't burn with their usual sharp amusement or quiet arrogance. Instead, they seem dimmer, shadowed by something I can't quite place.

He looks drained. Not in the way mortals do—no dark circles, no signs of wear—but there's something weighted in the way he stands, something restless in the way his fingers twitch at his side, like he's holding something back. His jaw is tight, his usual smirk absent.

It's subtle, but I notice. And for some reason, that unsettles me more than anything else.

"Are you okay?" I ask, setting my things down.

Julian exhales slowly, rolling his shoulders like he's trying to shake off something heavy. "I've been better," he says. His voice is quieter, rougher, like he's been carrying something that even he can't quite disguise. "You wanted to talk?"

I nod. "Yeah. About us."

His gaze locks onto mine, unreadable but unwavering. He doesn't look surprised. He never does. But it's clear that he's been expecting this.

I sit on the couch, and he moves with me, effortless and instinctual, settling beside me without hesitation. Julian never keeps his distance, never shies away. He's always there, always steady, always close enough to remind me that this—whatever *this* is—exists whether I want it to or not.

But for the first time, I'm not trying to shove it aside.

For the first time, *I* am the one choosing to be here. To talk. To figure out what this thing between us is, even if I'm not ready to surrender to it.

I exhale, pressing my fingers against my palms, grounding myself in the reality of this moment—one I never thought I'd allow myself to have.

Julian doesn't speak. He waits. Not with impatience, not with expectation—just with the kind of certainty that says he knew I'd get here eventually.

I've spent my whole life losing—pieces of myself, my art, my choices, my future. But this? This is mine.

"I don't want to just accept this." The words come slow, deliberate. "I want to choose it." I swallow hard, fingers curling against my knee. "I want to try. Us. Not just the bond. Not just fate. I want this on my terms."

The words feel foreign. But not wrong.

Julian tilts his head, studying me like I'm a puzzle he's finally seeing all the pieces of.

"Your terms." His voice is smooth, quiet, like the weight of those words is something he's turning over in his mind, letting settle.

I nod. "No more hiding. No more pretending. I have a chance at something real. And for once, I'm taking it."

A slow inhale. A longer exhale. Julian watches me like he's waiting for something—or maybe savoring it. "Good."

Just one word. One that settles into my bones, anchoring me.

I exhale, tension unraveling from my spine.

He moves, slowly, testing, just close enough that my breath catches, fingertips grazing my jaw, his touch featherlight, tilting my chin just enough—

My phone rings.

The moment snaps like a thread pulled too tight. I flinch. Julian stills. His gaze flickers to my phone, eyes glinting with something wicked and unsatisfied.

"Fate," he murmurs, "has a terrible sense of timing."

I glance at the screen. Melanie. Of course.

Pressing my lips together, I answer. "What?"

"You need to be at the premiere tonight," Melanie says smoothly, skipping over any form of greeting.

I scoff, shifting my weight against the couch. "Not interested."

A sharp sigh crackles through the phone. "Oh, come on, Ophelia. Don't be childish."

The audacity. I almost laugh. "Childish?"

"It's important," she insists, her voice dripping with manufactured patience. "To all of us."

"To all of us?" I repeat slowly.

There's a shuffle on the other end, followed by a muted exchange I can't quite make out.

"Ophelia, please." Dominic. I close my eyes for a second, dragging in a breath before opening them again. Of course he's involved.

"You don't have to do this," I mutter, rubbing my fingers against my temple. But we both know he will.

"I'm not asking for much," he says, his voice softer now, edged with something that almost sounds like regret. "Melanie's right. This could be huge—for all of us. It's a big night."

"For her," I correct flatly, my nails digging into my palm.

A pause. No argument. No denial. Just silence.

Julian watches me, eyes sharp and his eyes turning to liquid gold. I can feel it—the choice settling in my hands. For the first time in my life, no one gets to decide for me.

"Fine," I say, my voice steady. "But I'm bringing a date."

The silence that follows is thick, heavy.

"No." Dominic's voice is sharp. Immediate.

But Melanie, sounding almost amused, overrules him. "Yes."

Julian exhales dramatically, shifting against the couch like this is the most entertaining conversation he's ever heard. His arm stretches along the back of the couch, his hand grazing my shoulder in a way that's almost absentminded—like it's second nature, like he belongs there.

"You know," he muses, voice smooth and tauntingly casual, "I've always wanted to walk a red carpet."

Dominic is the first to react. "Who's—"

Melanie speaks at the same time. "Who—"

I don't let either of them finish. "My boyfriend."

Julian lets out a quiet chuckle beside me, the sound curling around the room like smoke. His fingers trace the curve of my shoulder before his palm settles against the nape of my neck.

He leans in slightly, his voice brushing against my skin.

"Oh, sweetheart," he murmurs, low and amused, "we're much more than that."

Dominic inhales sharply, the sound picked up by the speaker. "You're—?"

I glance at Julian. His red-gold eyes meet mine. Waiting. My decision. My choice.

I let out a breath and turn back to the phone.

"We'll be there."

Another pause.

Dominic's voice is tight when he speaks again. "We?"

I don't hesitate. "I'm not going without him."

The silence is deafening, stretching longer than before.

Unexpectedly, Melanie laughs—a quiet, satisfied sound that unsettles me more than it should. "Fine," she purrs, like she's just won something I don't understand yet.

The call ends with a sharp click. I drop my phone onto the couch and turn to Julian. He watches me with a slow, lazy grin.

"How do you feel about a movie premiere?"

Julian hums, tilting his head like he's considering it, but his grin only deepens. "Oh, darling. You have no idea what you've just started," he says smoothly, deep red flashing in his eyes. "Let's give them a show."

Eleven

JULIAN

T he limo rolls to a stop, and I step out first, greeted by a blinding storm of camera flashes. The red carpet stretches ahead—a sleek expanse of deep sapphire and silver, banners emblazoned with *The Sun Will Forget Us*, the title glowing under the lights like a prophecy. Reporters hover at the edges, celebrities move with calculated grace, and the air hums with the kind of anticipation that only exists in places built on illusion.

I turn back, offering my hand. Ophelia hesitates for a heartbeat before taking it.

The moment she steps out, the cameras shift. The attention is hers. And for once, she doesn't run from it.

I watch her, and for a second—just a second—I forget where we are.

She is stunning. Not in the way Hollywood expects, all artifice and pretense, but in a way that demands to be seen.

Her dress is dark as ink, sleek as liquid shadow, reflecting the lights in a way that makes her look untouchable. The fabric molds to her, elegant but effortless, as if it was made for her and no one else. Her skin glows beneath the lights—bare at the shoulders, radiant beneath the camera flashes, like she's something more than mortal.

Her hair is swept back, exposing the delicate curve of her throat, the sharp angles of her jawline. Minimal makeup—except for her lips, painted in a red so dark it borders on sinful.

I smirk.

A contradiction. Always. Sharp edges wrapped in something deceptively soft. A work of art that no one else is allowed to touch.

I tighten my grip on her fingers, drawing her just close enough that she knows she belongs to me. And tonight, the world will know it.

I look over to my left and I see Dominic posing alone on the carpet. It looks like Melanie already walked, probably wanting to go first. Now he is there, by himself, but he isn't looking at the cameras. He's looking at us.

He finishes with the reporters and walks over.

"Ophelia," he says, voice clipped. "Really? The guy you danced with?"

I smirk, but I don't say anything. Not yet. Ophelia, though—she doesn't hesitate.

"Yeah," she says, sweet as poison. "At your wedding. Remember, Dominic?"

Dominic's jaw tightens. Good.

"This isn't a game," he mutters.

"Oh, trust me. I know. You made that pretty clear when you married my sister six months after we broke up."

The words land like a blade, and he exhales sharply—like she's being cruel, like he has the right to be angry.

"I didn't think—"

"No, you didn't," she cuts in smoothly, tilting her head. "And now you don't get to think about me at all."

Dominic's fingers flex at his sides. He's losing control.

"I don't even know him," he says, frustration bleeding into every word. "He doesn't run in our circles, Ophelia."

"And that matters?" she scoffs.

"It matters because you don't know him either."

Her expression hardens. That hits a nerve.

"That's funny," she says, voice like steel wrapped in silk. "Because I could say the same thing about you."

That's when I decide I've had enough.

"Lia," I say smoothly, drawing her attention, letting the name roll off my tongue like it belongs to me.

She looks at me immediately. Soft, unguarded.

Dominic stiffens. I watch it happen. The moment he realizes I called her that. The moment he realizes she let me. The moment he realizes I have something he lost.

Dominic's eyes snap to mine, rage igniting behind them.

"Don't call her that," he grits out.

I tilt my head, amused. "Why not? It suits her."

"Stay out of this," he snaps.

"Oh, Dominic," I sigh, mocking pity dripping from every syllable. "You seem to have forgotten something important. You don't get to dictate who Ophelia stands beside anymore."

Ophelia glances at me, her lips twitching in amusement. Dominic looks ready to kill me. And I'd love to let him try.

But before he can, Melanie calls for him.

"Dominic," her voice rings out, smooth, impatient, practiced. "Come on. We need couples shots."

Ophelia exhales sharply, shaking her head. She is done.

"Your wife, remember her?" she says, gesturing toward where Melanie waits, already smiling for the cameras. "She's calling."

Dominic hesitates. Too long. Ophelia doesn't.

"Oh, and Dominic?" she says, her voice calm but cutting like glass. He looks at her. That was his first mistake.

"You left me. I'm moving on." Her expression doesn't waver. "Stay the fuck out of it." She doesn't wait for a response before turning, lifting her chin, and sliding her hand into mine.

"Ready to walk the carpet?" I ask her.

"No," she says. "I never walk the carpet. Usually, I just go in and watch the movie and leave."

"Times have changed, Lia," I say. "We can walk it together, but you are beautiful. And I want to show that off."

"Okay, let's do this," she says.

We go to the carpet, and I wrap an arm around her, drawing her close. The cameras go crazy, and I hear people calling her name. We take the attention from Melanie and Dominic.

I have to try to keep my composure as they stomp away, their frustration practically vibrating in the air behind them. I could gloat. I should gloat. But right now, I have something more important to focus on.

Ophelia.

We step forward, moving toward the reporters, the flashing cameras, the endless noise of the red carpet. This is where the real game begins.

That's when I feel it. The nerves roll off her in waves.

I don't hesitate. I pull her closer. My hand finds the small of her back and I hold her to me. Leaning in, I take my chance and press a slow, deliberate kiss to her temple, letting my lips linger against her skin just long enough that I feel the tension in her shoulders start to ease.

"It's okay, darling," I murmur, my voice low, smooth, meant only for her. I turn my head slightly, just enough for my breath to ghost against her ear. "I got you."

Geneva Fox is smirking before she even speaks, and I already know what's coming.

"Ophelia," she starts, "I know you've heard the latest buzz."

Ophelia lifts a brow, unimpressed. "You'll have to be more specific."

"Oh, come on," Geneva presses, tilting her microphone just a little closer. "Ashton Mercer had Dominic and Melanie on his show last week. It was quite the moment."

Ophelia exhales through her nose, but she doesn't shift, doesn't flinch. "I'm sure it was."

I grin. Oh, I love this.

Geneva tilts her head, eyes narrowing slightly. She knows Ophelia is a tough nut to crack.

"Ashton was quite bold, though," she continues, lips curling. "He said—what was it again? Oh, right. Before Melanie, Dominic was actually with *you*."

The words hang between them. Geneva's microphone is poised, ready for the fallout.

Ophelia gives her nothing. Just a slow, measured stare—cool, unreadable.

"That's not exactly a secret, Geneva," she says calmly. "But I do appreciate Ashton reminding everyone."

Geneva was expecting denial. A flustered backpedal. She didn't expect ice. She didn't expect *Ophelia*.

I decide to make this even more fun.

"You know," I muse, slipping an arm around Ophelia's waist, pulling her just a little closer. "I quite liked Ashton's delivery. He really knows how to command a room."

Geneva turns her attention to me, curiosity piqued. "You watched it?"

"Of course," I say smoothly. "I love comedy."

Ophelia lets out a quiet laugh, shaking her head.

"So you don't mind being part of this story?" Geneva asks, watching me carefully.

I tilt my head, pretending to think. "Why would I?"

I glance at Ophelia, running my thumb along the curve of her hip, just enough to make sure Geneva—and everyone else—sees it.

"I know exactly where she stands," I say, voice silky, taunting.

Geneva hums, watching us. "Dominic might have something to say about that."

"Oh, I hope he does," I murmur, smiling. "It's been far too long since anyone put him in his place."

Ophelia laughs at that, fully and unapologetically.

Geneva's eyes flicker between us. She knows she's not getting anything more.

"Well," she says finally, "this is definitely the most interesting story on the carpet tonight."

"I do try," I reply with a smirk.

Geneva shakes her head, amused, intrigued, and maybe a little frustrated. "I'll be keeping an eye on you both."

"I'd be offended if you didn't," I say easily.

She walks away, already setting her sights on her next target.

Ophelia turns to me, exhaling. "You are impossible."

"And yet," I murmur, pressing a soft kiss to her temple, "you're still here."

She sighs, dramatic, exasperated—but she doesn't pull away.

All attention shifts again as Dorian Castellano and Harrison Drake step onto the carpet.

I barely flick my gaze toward them.

Dorian, the director—pretentious, chaotic, all disheveled charm and artistic torment. Harrison, the producer—polished, calculating, probably already thinking about how this premiere translates into box office numbers.

They move like they expect the world to bow. And, to be fair, most of it does.

I don't care. But I do notice when their attention flickers toward us. Interesting. I smirk, brushing my fingers over Ophelia's back. Let them watch.

I don't bother turning as the two start making their way toward us. Figures.

Dorian isn't too bad. Annoying, sure. A little too self-important. But he's an artist, which means at least half of his arrogance is earned. He makes films that people don't forget, and he knows it.

Harrison, though? Harrison is worse. The kind of man who smiles just a little too long, stands just a little too close, touches just a little too easily. He plays power games in every room he enters—and in his mind, women are just another piece on the board.

And right now, his eyes are locked on Ophelia.

I already don't like him.

"Ophelia," Dorian greets smoothly, his voice carrying the effortless charm of someone who expects to be listened to. "You clean up well."

Ophelia tilts her head, unimpressed. "You say that like I'm usually a disaster."

Dorian chuckles, unbothered. "No, darling. Just unseen."

Ophelia's lips press together. I watch her fight the urge to roll her eyes.

"Dorian, you're wasting time on pleasantries," Harrison drawls, his gaze dragging over Ophelia in a way that makes my fingers twitch. He steps closer, smiling in a way that shows he thinks he's charming. He's not.

"Ophelia Arden," he muses, slow and indulgent, like he's tasting her name. "You know, I always wondered why you hid behind your sister's shadow."

Ophelia doesn't flinch. Doesn't shrink. "I wasn't hiding," she says flatly. "I was avoiding people like you."

I grin. That's my girl.

Dorian snorts, amused. Harrison, though—he smirks. "I see you've got a sharp tongue," he murmurs, taking another slow step forward. Too close. "I like that."

I move before I even think about it, shifting just slightly, stepping between them, my hand settling low on Ophelia's waist. Not possessive. Just undeniable.

Harrison's eyes flick to me, and his smirk falters.

"And you are?" he asks, mildly irritated.

I smile, slow and sharp. "Julian."

His brows lift slightly. "No last name?"

"None that you need."

Harrison looks me over, assessing. I don't react. I don't blink. And he doesn't like that.

"So, Ophelia," he continues, clearly deciding I'm irrelevant. "Are you here to celebrate your sister? Or steal the spotlight?"

Ophelia finally smiles, slow and razor-sharp. "Funny," she says. "I was just about to ask you the same thing."

Dorian laughs outright, clapping Harrison on the back. "I like her."

I smirk, brushing my fingers along Ophelia's spine. "You should," I murmur. "She's unforgettable."

Ophelia tilts her head, eyes steady, lips curving into something that might be a smile. Or a warning.

"Enjoy your night, gentlemen," she says, all sugar and steel.

And just like that, we walk away.

The red carpet is a storm of flashing cameras and murmured conversations, but there's a shift—a sharp, cutting wave of laughter coming from the barricades.

"Wow. She really showed up with him."

"I guess desperate times call for desperate measures."

"You think she's trying to make Dominic jealous? Because it's not working."

"Please. She's just pissed that Melanie got everything and she got him instead."

The laughter ripples through the group, loud enough to be heard, loud enough to be intentional.

Ophelia stiffens—not noticeably, not enough for the cameras to pick up on, but I feel it. The smallest hitch in her breath, the way her fingers curl into the fabric of her dress before she forces them to relax.

I turn my head slightly. Just enough to look at them.

Five of them, clinging to the barricades like leashed animals let out to bark for the night.

They look exactly how I expected—too much foundation, too much entitlement, too much time spent living through someone else's success.

"She's so embarrassing," one of them scoffs. "Like, we get it. Dominic left you. Move on."

"She's not moving on. She's acting like she is."

"Right? And we all know why. Melanie said it herself—Ophelia was always a shadow. She doesn't fit in. She never did."

A smirk.

"I mean, even Ashton Mercer was shocked Dominic was with her first. He couldn't believe she had him before Melanie."

More laughter.

"And now look at her—desperate for attention, trying to make him jealous. It's pathetic."

They still don't see me. They will.

The blonde in the center— the leader, the one who thinks she's untouchable—keeps going.

"Melanie is the reason Dominic is successful. Ophelia is the reason she's miserable."

That's when Ophelia reacts. Not much. Just a tiny, sharp inhale. And that's all it takes. I turn fully now, slowly, deliberately, letting my gaze drag over them like I'm peeling back their skin.

The blonde notices first. She falters.

"You know," I murmur, voice low and cutting, "I find it fascinating how much time you spend talking about someone you claim to have forgotten."

The laughter stops. Blondie stiffens, blinking rapidly like she's recalibrating.

I take a step forward. They instinctively shrink back.

"I mean, really," I continue, still soft, still pleasant, still dangerous. "Do you think about her before bed? Whisper her name to each other when the lights go out? I can't imagine another reason you'd be so obsessed with someone who has never once spared you a thought."

One of the brunettes glares, trying to act brave. "We were just stating facts."

"Oh?" I arch a brow. "And which part of your screeching was factual? The part where you pretended Dominic wouldn't snap his own spine trying to get another glance at her? The part where you conveniently forgot that Ashton Mercer—the king of media's bullshit circus—was the one who dragged your queen into the spotlight and reminded the world that Ophelia was there first?"

The brunette's lips press together. I tilt my head, amused. "Or was it the part where you reduced a woman's worth to the man she did or didn't end up with?"

They say nothing.

I take another step forward, just enough that they realize how close I could get if I wanted to. "Here's the real fact," I say, my voice smooth, patient, wrapping around them like a noose. "You're nothing more than a mouthpiece for someone else's words. You repeat Melanie like scripture because it makes you feel important. But tell me—does she even know you exist?"

The blonde flushes red. She does now. They all do.

"So," I say, suddenly cheerful, smiling wider, sharper, "why don't you do something useful and run along before I really start having fun?"

The others flee. She stays. The blonde squares her shoulders, lifting her chin just enough to pretend she isn't trembling, as if sheer will alone will protect her. She wants to prove something—to herself, to me, to the cameras that might still be lingering. But she doesn't realize she's already lost.

"Not scared of you," she mutters, the words barely above a breath, like saying them out loud will make them true.

I let a slow, amused smile spread across my lips, studying her with the kind of patience that makes lesser creatures crumble. She's not special. Just another person who thinks they can spit venom without ever feeling its sting.

"Let's fix that."

The shift is imperceptible to the crowd, but I feel it hum through the air, wrapping around her like an unseen current, pulling her under. Her breath catches, pupils dilating as the world tilts. She takes a step back, another—confusion flickering across her face before panic sinks in.

I watch as the vision takes hold.

She tries to move, to speak, but she can't. Her voice is stolen, her body locked in place as the nightmare unspools inside her mind. It's different for everyone, uniquely crafted from the deepest fears they try to bury. And her fear? It is so very simple.

She is nothing.

The world moves on without her.

People walk past without seeing her, their gazes sliding over where she should be. She screams, but no one turns. She reaches for someone, anyone, but her fingers slip through them like smoke. The noise of the world dims, fading into a quiet that stretches endlessly, a silence that confirms what she has always feared—she doesn't matter.

She is a shadow in the background of someone else's life, a ghost before she has even died, screaming into the void, drowning in irrelevance.

A strangled noise rips from her throat as reality bleeds back in. She stumbles, gasping, her hands flying to her chest as if she can force air into her lungs, as if she can shake the feeling of emptiness that will haunt her for far longer than this moment.

She looks at me, eyes wild, face pale, horror etched into every inch of her expression.

"What's wrong?" I murmur, my voice velvet-smooth, mocking in its gentleness. "Not as fun when you're the one being forgotten, is it?"

She stares, unable to form words, the bravado she wore moments ago shattered beyond repair.

I take a slow step forward, and she flinches, breath hitching like she expects me to pull her under again.

"If you say her name again," I continue, watching her closely, "I'll make sure you feel that every time you close your eyes."

Her lips part, but no sound escapes.

I release her completely.

Her knees buckle, and she catches herself on the pavement, nails scraping against the ground, body trembling as she gasps like she's just surfaced from drowning.

Crouching down, I tilt my head, letting the silence stretch between us, letting her sit in the terror still clinging to her bones. She knows now. She knows exactly what I am.

"Run along," I murmur, my voice softer now, but no less dangerous. "Before I decide you're worth my full attention."

She doesn't hesitate. She stumbles to her feet, nearly tripping over herself as she turns and flees, disappearing into the crowd.

I don't watch her go. I already know—she won't open her mouth again.

The world around us keeps moving—the bright flashes of cameras, the low murmur of conversations, the hum of a night too loud to be real—but Ophelia is focused, turning over what just happened, the weight of it settling into her thoughts.

I feel it before she even speaks, the way her fingers twitch at her side, the way her breath comes slow and measured, like she's deciding whether she wants to know the answer or if she already does.

Finally, she asks, voice even, deliberate. "What was that?"

I glance at her, my smirk sharp, intrigued by the lack of fear in her tone. "Which part?" I tease, though we both know what she means.

She exhales, shaking her head, not quite an eye roll, but close. "Julian."

I chuckle, tipping my face down to look at her, studying her. "It's a gift, really. I can make people see their worst nightmare. Not illusions. Not tricks. Real fear. The kind that sits in their bones long after I've let them go."

She takes that in, lips pressing together, but she doesn't recoil. Instead, she tilts her chin slightly, looking up at me, her gaze clear, searching.

"And you just—decide what it is?"

"No," I murmur, watching her carefully. "They decide. I just let them drown in it."

She nods slowly, absorbing that, her fingers tapping lightly against her dress like she's testing the weight of my words.

She should be horrified. She should be unsettled.

Instead, she holds my gaze, blue eyes flickering with something unreadable before she exhales, her voice steady. "That's terrifying."

I grin, slow and easy, the kind that makes people uncomfortable, but she's still looking at me like she's trying to figure something out.

"And you?" I murmur, my fingers brushing lightly against her waist, just enough to feel her skin beneath the fabric. "Do you have something to fear, Ophelia?"

Without looking away, without hesitation, she says, "I've already lived my biggest fears, Julian."

I still.

"Being abandoned. Losing my ability to show emotion. My painting." She inhales, slow, like the weight of those words alone could crush her if she let them. "I'm living it."

I don't breathe. Because it's not a dramatic confession. Not a plea for sympathy. She's just... saying it. Like it's a fact. Like it's a truth she carries, something so ingrained into her that it doesn't even feel like something worth breaking over anymore.

That's worse than fear. It settles into my chest like something sharp. This has all been fun and games.

Until now.

Because she's right. She is living her worst fear.

And I am the reason why.

For the first time tonight, I don't have a clever response. I don't have a smirk, or a sharp-edged comment, or a teasing quip to pull her out of it.

I just look at her.

And she? She just looks right back.

Twelve
Ophelia

I get about halfway through this damn movie and I can't do it anymore. It's really uncomfortable. Not seeing intimate scenes with Dominic. Unfortunately, I've seen some before. It's with Melanie that's horrible. Not because I still love him. I don't. Really it's just gross as hell.

I look at Julian sitting next to me. His face makes it almost impossible not to break into a fit of laughter. I can tell that he's trying to watch it, but he looks like he's in pain.

I lean in close, my voice low so only he can hear. "Hey. Want to get out of here?"

Julian exhales like I've just handed him salvation. A slow grin spreads across his face as he turns toward me. "I thought you'd never ask, sweetheart."

His fingers tighten around my wrist, firm and inescapable, his grip humming with something just shy of a promise. He lifts my hand, pressing a deliberate kiss to my palm before rising to his feet. In one smooth motion, he helps me up.

We barely take three steps before—

"Ophelia!"

The sharp whisper-yell cuts through the theater, frantic and full of disbelief.

I glance over, unbothered. Melanie has fully turned in her seat, her manicured nails gripping the armrest like it's the only thing keeping her upright. The fact that half the audience is now watching us? Not my problem.

"Where are you going?" she demands.

I shrug, keeping my tone light. "We're leaving."

Melanie blinks at me, her mouth parting in pure horror. "You're leaving?"

"Yup." I pop the p just to drive it home.

Her whole body jerks forward, as if physically wounded by my audacity. "How could you? It's my big night!" She gestures wildly around her, like I should be taking in the sheer magnitude of this event. "You should at least try to fit in! Be normal! For once!"

I tilt my head, smiling sweetly, letting the moment stretch just long enough to make her squirm. With practiced ease, I throw her own words right back at her.

"Oh, dear sister. Remember?" I mimic her exact tone—that perfect, condescending, media-trained delivery. "She's never really been interested in what the rest of us do. She's never tried. Never fit in."

Julian laughs—loudly, unapologetically. A real, deep burst of amusement that turns more heads than Melanie ever could.

Still chuckling, he slides an arm around my waist, guiding me toward the exit like he's thoroughly enjoying every second of this.

As we push through the doors, I swear I hear a round of applause. And considering how boring this movie is? It's definitely not for that.

"I'm so proud of you," Julian says while lifting me up and twirling me around.

I look at the marquee above the theater. The Eclipse Theater. That makes me laugh. Melanie always thought she was the sun, but even the brightest star can be eclipsed when something stronger steps into its path.

I hate being complimented. It always makes me feel weird, so I do what I do best—I change the subject.

"Well, what now? I can grab us a cab, and we can head back to my place."

Julian exhales, dragging his gaze over me with slow amusement. "Or..." he starts, a smirk curling at the edge of his lips. "I can give you a taste of my world."

I narrow my eyes. Never trust a demon when he sounds too pleased with himself.

"Your world?" I ask, skepticism laced through my voice.

Julian spreads his arms in an easy shrug. "You don't think demons use cabs, do you?"

"I guess I never really thought about a demon's mode of transportation," I admit, crossing my arms. "Not like I ever expected to meet one."

His smirk deepens. "A tragic oversight."

I huff. "I'm assuming you don't drive?"

"Not when I have faster options." His gaze gleams with something wicked, something undeniably entertained.

"Right, so what do you do?" I ask dryly. "Just snap your fingers and appear places?"

Julian steps forward, deliberate, his presence pressing into mine just enough to steal the air between us. "Something like that," he murmurs.

I tilt my head. "So what? You're going to teleport us?"

His eyes glint. "No, darling. I'm going to fly us."

I freeze. My lips part, words failing me for a solid five full seconds before I manage to spit out—

"I beg your fucking pardon?"

Julian laughs, low and amused, as if this is the best part of his night. "Oh, come on. Where's your sense of adventure?"

I throw my hands in the air. "I left it back at the theater, right around the time you started calling me darling."

"Lia, Lia, Lia," he tsks, shaking his head, all smooth arrogance. "You wound me."

I arch a brow. "You'll live."

"I will," he muses, stepping closer, his fingers brushing against my wrist, light but intentional. "After I take you for a little ride."

I glare at him, watching the way his eyes gleam—too entertained, too sure of himself.

"Unless you're scared?" he adds, the words a taunt wrapped in honey.

I inhale slowly, steadying myself before narrowing my gaze. "I hate that you know exactly how to push my buttons."

Julian chuckles, tipping his head, looking far too pleased. "A gift."

"A curse," I mutter.

"Semantics," he says with a lazy shrug. His expression shifts, sharpening like a blade, all challenge, all temptation. "So? Do you trust me?"

I hold his gaze, searching his face for any trace of deceit, any flicker of something insincere. But there's nothing.

Just him.

And the truth I already know.

I exhale, shaking my head. "Don't drop me, demon."

Julian smirks, stepping in closer. He lifts my hand again, bringing it to his lips, his breath warm against my skin as he murmurs, "I'd never let you fall, sweetheart."

And suddenly—

The world disappears.

Not in pieces. Not in stages. All at once.

A rush of air steals my breath as reality bends, stretching into something vast, untethered, impossible. It's not falling. Not flying. It's both—weightless and electric, like being yanked through space by something too big to fight.

Colors blur—streaks of silver and violet folding into themselves, warping into something that doesn't belong to this world. The shift is sudden, dizzying, exhilarating.

My first instinct is to panic. My second is to hold onto Julian.

I don't think about it—I just grip his jacket tighter, my fingers curling into the fabric like an anchor. And that's when I realize...

I'm not afraid.

Adrenaline pulses through me, sharp and heady, but there's no fear. No hesitation. Because he's here.

His hands don't waver. One stays firm on my waist, the other curves over the small of my back, pressing me closer. His warmth bleeds into my skin, steady and deliberate, grounding me even as the world bends.

I feel his presence everywhere.

Not just his touch. Him. The space between us hums primal, ancient, like a thread connecting us to something bigger than either of us. Something that has waited too long to be acknowledged.

It's too much. It's not enough.

The movement slows—just enough for me to register the shift. Suddenly, the world snaps back into focus.

My feet slam onto solid ground, my balance wrecked, breath dragging in sharp. The contrast is jarring, my body struggles to adjust to stillness after the breakneck speed of whatever the hell just happened.

Julian doesn't let go.

His grip tightens slightly, fingers pressing into my waist before trailing upward, slow and deliberate, like he's testing me. Like he's waiting to see how I'll react.

I inhale, but I'm still buzzing, it's too hot under my skin. The feeling lingers—not just from the teleportation, but from him.

Julian smirks, amusement flickering in his gaze. "Well?" His voice is smooth, satisfied.

I force a breath, willing my pulse to settle. "That was—"

His thumb grazes my hip, a whisper of contact that sends a sharp jolt through me.

Damn him.

"—unnecessary," I finish, ignoring how my voice betrays me—rougher, more breathless than it should be.

Julian hums, tilting his head, gaze dropping to my lips for just a second before flicking back to my eyes. "Liar."

I roll my eyes and really look around for the first time.

The world is no longer spinning, but the pulse of magic still lingers, clinging to the air. I realize we're home.

I'm in my apartment.

The lights are low, it's familiar, but something feels different. Like the space has shifted, like it recognizes the change in me. Maybe because it's not the same place I left earlier tonight.

Maybe because I'm not.

Something unspoken simmers between us, stretching the space, coiling tight like a wire. I should step away, create distance, regain my footing, pretend this isn't affecting me the way it is. But I don't. And neither does he.

His hand remains on my waist, casual but deliberate, like he knows exactly what he's doing. Like he's waiting for me to acknowledge that I felt it too. Because I did.

Julian lifts a brow, his smirk slow and knowing. "You're thinking about it, aren't you?"

My stomach tightens, a flicker of something dangerous curling low. "About what?"

His thumb moves again, tracing a slow, lazy circle against my hip, sending a sharp thrill down my spine that I refuse to react to. "Doing that again."

I inhale deeply, steadying myself, ignoring the way my pulse jumps beneath my skin. "You wish."

Julian chuckles, the sound dark and rich, leaning in just enough that his breath ghosts against my skin. The warmth of it, the closeness, him— it's all too much, and yet not enough.

"You don't need to say it, little artist." His grip tightens, subtle but certain, the pressure enough to remind me of exactly where I am. Of exactly who I'm with. His voice dips lower, just for me.

"I already know."

There's something about the way he looks at me; like he sees me. Not just the way people think they do—reading body language, searching for reactions. He doesn't need any of that.

He just knows.

I used to think the Mark was the reason. That it was the thing pulling us together, making me feel like I couldn't breathe when he wasn't near, making me want him before I even understood why.

But it's not. Not anymore.

Because it wasn't the Mark standing beside me at the premiere, keeping me steady. It wasn't the Mark letting me take control, letting me fight my own battles while knowing, without question, that he would step in if I needed him.

That was him.

And it's easy with him. Instinctive. Natural. He doesn't need me to explain things I don't know how to say, doesn't need me to force emotions I can't show. He feels them anyway. Understands them without asking.

And I don't care how he does it. Because it's enough just to be understood.

I pull him in, crush my lips against his, and he doesn't just respond—he takes.

His hands lock around my waist, dragging me flush against him, and the moment our bodies connect, heat erupts between us. There's no slow build, no teasing—just raw, unrestrained hunger.

His lips move against mine with a possessive intensity, his grip tightening like he's afraid I'll pull away. I won't. I press closer, fingers threading into his hair, tugging, needing more.

He groans, deep and low, a sound that sends a shiver straight through me. His hands wander, trailing fire down my spine, his touch just rough enough to leave me breathless.

The kiss deepens, darkens, devours.

His teeth graze my lower lip, teasing, punishing, and when I gasp, he seizes the moment, claiming my mouth completely.

The room spins, my skin burning where he touches me. Everything else disappears. It's not just a kiss. It's a storm, a collision, a promise.

He breaks away just far enough to piss me off. I want to stomp my foot. I want more. "Bedroom?" he murmurs, voice smooth, teasing.

I blink at him. "Julian. It's a studio apartment."

He tilts his head, completely unbothered. "And?"

I gesture vaguely behind me. "It's literally right there. We don't have to go anywhere. We could blink and be there."

His lips curve, delighted. "So what you're saying is... efficiency."

I roll my eyes, patting his chest like I'm proud of him for putting that together. "Wow. Yes. Incredible deduction skills. Really putting that big, immortal brain to use."

He grins, not even a little offended. "I do my best."

I shake my head, laughing—but before I can say another word, he moves.

One second, I'm standing. The next, I'm flying.

Julian moves effortlessly, lifting me like it's nothing, his hold firm and unapologetically possessive.

"Julian!" I yelp-laugh, gripping his shoulders. "I can walk!"

His smirk deepens. "I know."

The mattress meets my back before I can argue, soft but jarring enough that my body bounces slightly. I barely have time to react before he follows.

He doesn't pounce, doesn't rush—just shifts over me in one smooth, devastatingly controlled motion.

My breath catches.

Julian rests on his forearm, his body aligning with mine, his presence impossibly close. Heat rolls off him in waves, sinking into my skin, seeping into every breath like something I'll never shake.

His free hand drifts lazily down my arm, his fingertips barely grazing, sparking little jolts of electricity in their wake. Not demanding. Not teasing. Just a deliberate, lingering touch, like he's waiting for something.

His breath fans over my cheek, a quiet shift in the air. "There's something else a demon can do."

A slow, wicked pulse uncoils in my stomach. I arch a brow. "Oh?"

Julian doesn't answer immediately. Instead, his fingers pause at my ribs, pressing just enough to make me feel him.

I know this look. It's hesitation, he's giving me a choice. Letting me decide.

The moment stretches, anticipation crackling between us. My pulse hums, sharp and needy, but I hold his gaze steady, my breath shallow.

I don't look away. I don't overthink.

I smirk, my voice barely above a whisper. "Julian."

His pupils darken, red bleeding into gold, his fingers tightening against my waist. His grip flexes, control slipping just enough to make me wonder how much he's holding back.

I want to make it known this is something we're doing together. I urge his eyes to mine. "I want this."

Julian doesn't blink. Doesn't smirk. He just stares, memorizing me, before his lips part, and his voice drops into something purely wicked.

And just like that—our clothes are gone. No movement. No effort. Just gone.

The rush of cool air hits first, kissing every newly exposed inch of skin. But the real heat is him.

"That's..." My voice fails me for a second, my head spinning, my body already too aware of his. "That's... cheating."

Julian grins, his mouth hovering just close enough that I can feel the heat of it.

"No, little artist." His lips ghost along my ear, his voice nothing but sin, slow and deliberate, silk over steel. "That's demonic efficiency."

He settles over me, his body a furnace, heat rolling through every inch of my skin. He's taking his time.

The bastard.

His lips barely graze mine, hovering, teasing, waiting. Like he's daring me to take what I want.

I don't wait.

I surge forward, crushing my mouth against his, swallowing the smirk before it can fully form. His responding growl vibrates against my lips—a dark, pleased sound that sends a sharp pulse through me, tightening my stomach, making my thighs press together.

His hands slide down my sides, fingers pressing into my ribs, firm and possessive, like he's reminding me exactly who he is. His mouth moves to my jaw, my throat, my collarbone—biting, soothing, worshipping—leaving heat in his wake. My head tilts instinctively, giving him more.

He feels it. He always does.

"You're so responsive," he murmurs, his voice velvet and smoke. "I wonder..."

I shudder. He hums—pleased, amused, starving.

"Julian," I whisper, but it's not a protest. It's a plea. A command. A surrender. I should tell him to hurry up. I should tell him I want more. But I don't—because I do want this. Every second of it.

His mouth travels lower, lips skimming down my stomach, his hands parting my thighs with ease. His breath is warm against my skin. Too warm. I feel his smirk before I see it.

"You're already trembling," he murmurs, fingers ghosting up my thigh, teasing, never quite touching where I need him.

I make a sound—frustration, need, something dangerously close to begging.

His eyes flick up, molten red-gold, utterly enthralled. "Tell me what you want, little artist."

I don't answer.

So he presses a single, devastating kiss between my thighs.

I jolt, sucking in a sharp breath, my fingers twisting in his hair, tugging, demanding.

He groans, deep and wrecked, entirely too satisfied. "That desperate for me already?"

I want to snap something back, something sharp, something that will wipe the smugness from his face.

His tongue flicks against me.

I forget how to think.

My back arches off the bed, a moan breaking free before I can stop it.

"That's it," he rasps against my skin, his grip tightening, holding me in place. "Take what I give you."

And I do.

I unravel beneath him, the world narrowing to his mouth, his hands, the merciless pace that sends me spiraling higher, faster, too much, not enough.

I shatter. Hard. But Julian doesn't stop. Not yet. He takes everything. Devours it.

I gasp, clawing at his shoulders as he moves up, kissing me again—deep, thorough, letting me taste myself on his tongue.

My legs wrap around his waist, pulling him closer, needing more. Needing him.

"Oh, love," he chuckles against my lips. "I'm not done with you yet."

Julian's lips crash against mine, his hands gripping my hips, my waist, my thighs, like he wants to touch every part of me at once. Like he can't get enough.

He pulls back just enough to look at me.

"You look wrecked already, little artist," he murmurs, his thumb brushing over my kiss-swollen lips, his eyes burning. "And I haven't even started yet."

I should say something sharp, something to wipe that arrogance off his face.

He rolls his hips against mine, pressing exactly where I need him. I forget how to breathe. My fingers dig into his shoulders, nails scraping over muscle. Julian groans, his control slipping—just slightly.

Good.

"I need you," I breathe, the words slipping out before I can stop them.

His expression darkens, something feral flickering behind his gaze. "Say it again."

"I need you." I pull him down, arching into him, aching.

His hands tighten, grip turning bruising.

"Say my name."

I meet his gaze, heat pooling low, drunk on the way he's looking at me. "Julian."

And he snaps. He kisses me like he's drowning—and I'm the only thing that can kill or save him. There's no hesitation. No air. Just fire and teeth and surrender.

I feel every inch of him, the tension in his muscles, the way he's barely holding back. Not for his sake. For mine. But I don't want restraint. Not tonight.

"Don't hold back," I whisper, tilting my chin, baring my throat to him. An invitation. A dare. A challenge.

Julian growls, the sound vibrating against my skin, his lips trailing down my neck, my collarbone, lower, lower—his tongue flicking against sensitive skin, his teeth teasing, threatening, never quite biting.

I am burning. I am desperate. I am losing my mind.

He shifts, one hand bracing my thigh to spread me wider, and thrusts into me.

One slow, merciless stroke.

He fills me completely, stretching me open, branding himself into my bones.

I cry out, my head falling back, my body arching, my fingers clenching around his arms.

Julian shudders, curses, his grip bruising, his control snapping completely.

"You feel—" He cuts off, his jaw clenching, his forehead pressing against mine, his breath ragged. "Fuck."

I can't think. Can't breathe. Can't do anything except feel.

And he's not done.

Julian pulls back—just enough to make me whimper, just enough to make me desperate—and slams back in, harder, deeper, perfect.

The pleasure is instant, blinding, a white-hot spark exploding inside me.

"Julian—" My voice breaks on a moan.

"I know, love." His lips graze mine, his hands pinning me exactly where he wants me. "I feel it too."

His pace builds, every movement deliberate, controlled, hitting exactly where I need, exactly how I need.

Too much. Not enough. Too perfect.

I am unraveling.

He knows it.

"Let go for me," he murmurs, his voice all heat and sin and command.

My body tightens around him, pleasure ripping through me in waves, white-hot and searing.

Julian groans, curses, driving into me faster, chasing his own release, pushing me even higher, not letting me come down.

"Again," he demands. "Give me another."

I do. Because I belong to him.

And now, he belongs to me.

Thirteen

JULIAN

I wake up before Ophelia, but I can feel her in my arms. I don't sleep in Hell. I never need to, but when I'm away for too long, I start to have more human needs. Yeah, I'm still immortal, but weakness and exhaustion are the first mortal things that hit.

I look down at Ophelia. She's a goddess. And she is all mine. She shifts, and her eyes open—those beautiful crystal-blue eyes staring into my very soul. She's bathed in the soft morning light, tangled in her sheets, looking at me like I am something worth staying for.

"Good morning," she says, smiling right at me.

A real smile. The kind she hasn't been able to give since it was taken from her.

"Good morning, darling," I respond, my voice low, still rough with sleep.

I let my fingers drift over her back, tracing slow, lazy patterns against her bare skin. She sighs, content, shifting just enough to press herself closer, her warmth seeping into me.

"I could get used to this," she murmurs, voice drowsy, soft, honest.

I smirk. "Waking up next to me?"

"Mmm." She hums, her fingers trailing over my chest, absentminded, thoughtful. "The peace. The warmth. The way you look at me."

My smirk fades, replaced by something quieter, something deeper.

"How do I look at you?" I ask.

She hesitates. Not because she doesn't know—but because she does.

"Like you see me," she finally says, voice barely above a whisper.

I brush a strand of hair from her face, tucking it behind her ear. "That's because I do."

Her throat moves as she swallow. "I've never really had that before."

I tip her chin up, forcing her gaze to hold mine. "You have it now."

I'm used to the occasional fling. More like daily, but that's beside the point. A one-night stand. But this is more. I know it. Immediately. I'm in love with her.

She leans in first, kissing me slow, lingering. Like she's learning me, choosing me.

I cup her cheek, deepening it just enough to let her know I'm choosing her too.

"Okay. I need to know," she says, her tone deadly serious.

"Know what?" I ask, tucking her hair behind her ear.

"What is it that you actually do?"

"I'm a demon. You know that," I say, already confused.

"Yeah, yeah, I get that," she waves a hand dismissively. "But like... do demons have jobs? Or are you just some kind of supernatural trust fund kid?"

I blink. "First of all, rude. Second, yes, I have a job. I torment souls, broker shady contracts, and generally make life—well, afterlife—more difficult. You know, customer service."

She squints at me. "So you're basically a demonic corporate middle manager?"

I nod solemnly. "With occasional smiting privileges."

She looks at me, genuinely distraught. "That's so depressing. You're literally immortal, and you still have a nine-to-five?"

"More like an always-on-call, morally questionable startup," I say, deadpan. "Our CEO is the Devil, and the employee benefits are... well, fire."

She groans, rubbing her temples. "Julian, I was hoping for mysterious and powerful villain, not overworked tech bro from Hell."

I smirk. "Not mutually exclusive."

She huffs but doesn't drop it. "Okay, fine. So what exactly do you do? Like, do you just go around making deals? Taking souls?"

Her tone is lighter, teasing—but there's something thoughtful in her eyes.

I lean back against the couch. "Yeah. I make deals. When the time comes, I collect," I respond, cryptically.

She doesn't like that answer.

"And if they can't?" she presses, tilting her head.

I exhale, stretching my legs out in front of me. "They can. They do. That's how deals work, Ophelia."

She studies me, unconvinced. "And what exactly are they paying with?"

I hesitate—just for a fraction of a second. But it's enough.

Her eyes narrow. "It's not their own soul, is it?"

Smart girl.

I tilt my head slightly. "Depends on the deal."

She frowns. "But if it was their own, you'd just say that."

I shrug. "People assume they're the ones paying. I don't correct them."

She goes quiet for a moment, tapping her fingers against her knee like she's working through a problem.

"So... someone else pays," she murmurs, more to herself than to me. "That's messed up."

I smile. "That's business."

She shakes her head, still thinking. But she doesn't push further. Not yet. And I let her sit with it. Because I know this isn't the last time she'll ask.

We are in a good spot when I hear his voice.

Evander: *Julian. We need to speak. Now.*

It isn't a request. The air around me tightens, a pull deep in my chest—unseen, but unmistakable. His voice cuts through the space between realms, dragging me toward something I already know won't be pleasant.

He does not sound happy.

I inhale slowly, exhaling through my nose, steeling myself before I stand.

Ophelia watches me, brow furrowing. "What?"

I shake my head, forcing a smirk that doesn't quite reach my eyes. "I have something to take care of."

She tilts her head, suspicion flickering across her face. "That sounded serious. Work emergency?"

"Something like that." I roll my shoulders, forcing the tension out of them before she can notice. "Nothing you need to worry about."

I give her one last kiss and get out of bed.

I feel her eyes on me before I even turn.

I smirk. "Like what you see?"

She blinks, then rolls her eyes. "I was just—never mind."

"No need to be shy," I say, stretching deliberately. "Appreciation is welcome. Encouraged, even."

She throws a pillow at me.

I laugh, catching it effortlessly. "Adorable."

Her glare sharpens. "Shouldn't you be off doing... whatever mysterious and totally-not-suspicious thing you need to do?"

I chuck the pillow back onto the bed, finally reaching for my clothes. "Much as I'd love to stay here and be objectified, duty calls."

I take one last look at Ophelia before closing my eyes.

When I open them, I'm standing in my parents' living room—and of course, they're not alone.

My father and mother sit near the fireplace, calm and composed. Across from them, sprawled on the opposite sofa like they live here, are my aunt and uncle. Naturally. Looking far too entertained for my liking.

This is going to be fun.

"You called?" I say, already bracing for it.

"We're worried," my mother says, tone even but laced with something heavier. "You haven't been home in days."

"Yeah, sorry, I was just—"

"Busy?" My uncle drawls, raising an eyebrow. "Swept up in the throes of passion? Entangled in fate? Possibly doing something catastrophically stupid?"

My aunt hums. "I vote for the last one."

"She's not wrong," my father mutters.

"Wow," I say dryly. "Nice to know I was missed."

"You were," my mother says, actually serious, which makes me feel like an asshole. "We just don't like what you're walking into."

"Owen said you've been with the girl," my father says.

"She's not just 'the girl,'" I snap. "She's my soulmate."

My aunt tilts her head at me, studying me. "You don't seem worried," she murmurs.

"Because I'm not."

"That's... interesting," my uncle muses. "Because everyone else is."

"I don't see the issue," I say.

"You're not looking hard enough," my father replies, voice level but sharp.

My aunt reaches out, brushing her fingers over my forearm. I don't pull away, but I don't like the way she's looking at me now.

"It's solidifying," she murmurs.

My uncle whistles low. "Oof. That's going to be a mess later."

"Julian," my father says, pulling my attention back to him. "You know what happens when the bond grows too strong without full commitment. You know what it could do to her."

"She'll be fine."

My mother presses a hand to her forehead. "Julian, you're linking yourself to someone who doesn't know what that means. You haven't told her."

My father watches me for a long moment, unreadable. "I guess we'll see."

A voice cuts through the room before I even see him. "So, you haven't told her yet."

I already know who it is before I turn. Owen. And, of course, he's not alone.

My brothers *and* cousins. They materialize out of thin air like a personal nightmare, all staring at me like I'm the idiot in the room.

I groan, dragging a hand down my face. "What, no grand entrance? No fanfare?"

Owen steps forward, arms crossed. "Figured I'd save you the embarrassment. You're doing a great job making yourself look like an ass all on your own."

"Fantastic. I so missed our heartfelt sibling moments."

Owen ignores me, eyes narrowing. "You haven't told her about the deal. The one you made with her father." Silence. "And," he continues, tone razor-sharp, "I'm guessing you also haven't told her about the process of claiming a mate."

My Aunt Selene decides to chime in now. "Wait. You haven't told her either of those things?"

"She's been through enough," I snap. "I was giving her time to cope. Remember how you all said I had to let her make the choice?"

"Yes," my father says, voice even. "But not while going into it blind, boy. She has to know what she's choosing."

"You need to tell her the truth," my mother, Liora, adds softly. "All of it. And she has to decide knowing that."

"Well, this is awkward," Adrian mutters, hands in his pockets.

I exhale sharply, already done with this. "Are you all just materializing for fun now?"

"More like showing up to watch you dig your own grave," Lucas says, smirking.

"Fantastic," I mutter. "Did you all schedule this intervention, or was it just a collective urge to piss me off?"

Owen steps forward, arms crossed. "No, just a collective urge to witness your downfall."

I shoot him a glare. "You're all so helpful."

Damian shrugs. "Look, man, we're just trying to figure out how much of a disaster this is going to be when she finally finds out."

"You know," Caleb cuts in, rubbing his chin. "The deal you made. The small, tiny detail where her entire existence was collateral."

"Yeah, Julian, when you put it like that—" Lucas whistles. "It actually sounds worse than I thought. And I already thought it was bad."

I pinch the bridge of my nose. "She's been through enough. I was giving her time to process—"

"Right. Because getting attached before she knows anything is definitely a solid plan," Owen drawls.

"She has to make the choice knowing everything," my father reminds me, his tone like steel.

"Right," Caleb chimes in. "So how much longer were you planning to let her think she has a normal life before it all burns down?"

"You don't understand—" I start.

Adrian claps me on the shoulder. "Oh, no, Julian. We understand perfectly. You're screwed."

It begins as a whisper beneath the surface. A low, bone-deep hum vibrating through the estate, rattling the foundation as if something ancient is stirring in the depths. The temperature plummets—not like a mere draft slipping through cracks, but as though warmth itself has been ripped from existence. The air turns thick, pressing against my skin, curling around my throat, leaving behind an unnatural stillness that doesn't just fill the space—it strangles it.

The ground lurches. Not a tremor. Not a warning.

A Hellquake.

The first impact slams through the floor like a shockwave, jagged fractures splitting across the obsidian marble, crawling up the walls in chaotic veins of destruction. The entire estate groans in protest, the ceiling trembling, the air itself vibrating as though it's trying to pull away from whatever is coming.

The world tilts.

Gravity wavers. The very laws that bind Hell together tremble beneath an unseen force, the space within the estate twisting—not just the physical structure, but something deeper, something more fundamental. A pulse of power surges upward from the core of Hell itself, warping reality like a tidal wave breaking against the fragile dam of existence.

The lights die.

Screens flicker once. Every automated system glitches, surges, and collapses into an unnatural, suffocating dark.

Not just the absence of light.

Something worse.

A void. A presence so vast it doesn't just erase light—it consumes it. The silence that follows is not empty. It is waiting.

With no warning, the shadows ignite. Not with fire. Not with light. With something else.

Darkness bleeds from the floor, twisting, writhing, coiling up from the marble in shifting tendrils of living void. It stretches upward, spiraling into towering columns that breathe, pulsing with an energy that does not belong to this world—or any world.

And from that abyss, they manifest.

The Infernal Council.

They do not arrive—they are simply here, as if they were never absent to begin with. Their presence does not fill the room—it consumes it.

They are not men. Not demons.

They are something else.

Their robes are woven from a darkness so deep it refuses to reflect light, shifting like liquid shadow, like something that has never been bound to a single form. The hems never touch the ground. They leave no trace of their passing—because they are not bound by the laws of movement as we know them.

And beneath their hoods—

Nothing. Not absence. Something worse.

A bottomless abyss where faces should be, a void so vast it feels like it could swallow the very concept of sight itself. Shapes coil and twist in the darkness—sometimes eyes, too many, blinking in and out of existence like flickers of dying stars. Other times, just an endless black, consuming everything it touches.

But the worst part?

I know they are looking at me.

Not just watching. Measuring. Judging. Deciding.

Even my father—Evander Duvain, whose name alone bends lesser demons to their knees—does not speak. My mother does not move. My aunt and uncle, so rarely disturbed, so rarely impressed, do nothing. No one breathes.

Not because they can't. But because they do not dare.

One of them steps forward. The space around them distorts, warping inward, the fabric of the room twisting to accommodate something that should not exist. Reality itself bends to make room for them, or risk breaking entirely.

"Julian Duvain."

Not a greeting.

A sentence.

I roll my shoulders back, crossing my arms over my chest, forcing a casual stance I do not feel. "Wasn't expecting guests."

"You were not given a choice." Their voices do not echo. They do not need to. They exist everywhere at once—woven into the very fabric of reality, a sound that does not vibrate through the air, but through existence itself.

The leader of the Infernal Council steps forward, and the very air tightens. Space itself warps around them, undecided—caught between making room for their presence or collapsing beneath it.

Their voice, layered and ancient, fills the room.

"Do you understand fate, Julian Duvain?"

The question lands like a hammer, but I don't flinch. I roll my shoulders back, keeping my expression neutral.

"Fate?" I echo, tone edged. "Destiny. The thing mortals blame when they fuck up?"

A ripple moves through them—not quite a reaction, but an acknowledgment of my ignorance.

"No." The answer comes in unison, voices woven into something too vast to be singular. "Not destiny. Not choice. Not control."

One of them lifts a hand. And something appears, a single, thin threat. It does not sway with the breeze of movement, it does not bend. It hums, not audibly nor visibly, but at a level of awareness that was never meant to be perceivable.

"Fate is not just a concept," they continue, turning the thread in their grip. "It is the fabric of existence itself, woven in a Loom beyond gods, beyond demons, beyond time."

The thread pulses—so faint, I almost miss it. The room presses inward, thick with something older than eternity.

"No one interferes with it."

Their fingers tighten around the thread, stilling it completely.

"Not angels."

"Not gods."

"Not the damned."

No hesitation. No doubt. This is truth.

And yet—

"Ophelia Arden was born to."

Born to what?

"What the hell does that mean?" My voice comes out sharper than I intend.

A long, unnatural silence follows.

Selene, normally unreadable, stills.

Theron exhales a slow, disbelieving breath. "No way."

Selene doesn't blink. When she speaks, it's not with sarcasm, not with her usual amusement—it's breathless. Stunned.

"Holy shit... she's the Weaver, isn't she?"

The leader inclines their head. "She was. Like her mother before her, she was chosen to maintain the Loom of Fate, to guide the threads that determine the course of existence."

The air thickens, heavy with something suffocating.

"Until it was taken."

A slow, creeping cold slides down my spine.

Theron lets out a short, humorless laugh, shaking his head. "That actually makes a terrifying amount of sense."

I shake my head once. "Taken?" My voice is razor-edged now. "Taken by who?"

I already know.

The Council does not move. They do not need to.

Because the answer is already here, sitting inside my ribs like a death sentence.

It was me.

And my father realizes it first.

Evander's voice cuts through the thick silence. "Why is everything changing?"

The answer doesn't come from the Council.

It comes from my mother.

"Because when you made the deal, Julian..." She pauses, just for a breath. "You transferred the gift to Melanie."

The words settle like a death knell.

A slow ripple of understanding moves through the room.

Owen, sharp as ever, lets out a dry laugh, shaking his head. "Yeah. But here's the problem." His eyes meet mine, his expression unreadable. "Melanie only cares about herself."

I exhale, something bitter curling in my chest. My voice, when it comes, is low and venomous.

"So I put the Weaver's gift—the hands of fate—" I let out a slow, humorless laugh. "In a self-indulgent bitch."

"You said her mother had the gift before," Adrian says, his voice sharper than usual. "Explain."

The Infernal Council does not turn, does not shift, but something in the air coils tighter, as if the very fabric of reality is bracing itself.

"She did," the leader confirms, their voice stretched thin, ancient, absolute.

Adrian doesn't react outwardly, but I see the slight flex of his jaw, the way his arms fold tighter across his chest. None of us rattle easily. But something about this unsettles me.

"Like all Weavers before her, Calliope Arden was meant to oversee the Loom, to guide the threads of fate, to preserve the balance of existence itself."

Calliope Arden.

Ophelia's mother.

A woman who, until now, had been nothing more than a name. But suddenly—she is everything.

"When she died," the leader continues, their voice layered, woven with something beyond time, "the gift should have passed to her daughter."

A slow, creeping sense of wrongness twists in my gut.

"Should have?" I say, voice low.

Damian clears his throat, sharply. "But it didn't."

"No," the Council confirms.

Nothing more. Nothing needed.

"Calliope Arden's gift was passed to her daughter, but fate was intercepted. A hand reached where it should not have."

They don't move. They don't need to, because the accusation is already here, they're looking at me. And I know what they're going to say, but knowing it's coming and hearing it are two different things.

"When you made your deal, Julian," the leader says, "you did not only take Ophelia's emotions. You severed her connection to fate itself. You stripped the Weaver of her thread, and in doing so, you unbalanced the Loom."

I don't move. I don't breathe.

Owen drags a hand down his face, exhaling slowly. "So let me get this straight—she was supposed to control fate. Her mother dies, and she inherits the gift. But Julian swoops in, makes a deal, and—" He snaps his fingers. "Oops. It goes to Melanie instead."

Theron lets out a low whistle. "That actually explains way too much."

Selene murmurs, half to herself, "And explains why everything has felt... wrong. Why Hell itself is shifting."

I clench my jaw. "That still doesn't explain why it's happening now."

The Council regards me for a long, heavy moment before they speak.

"Because the Loom is trying to correct itself."

The temperature drops further, the fabric of reality pulls tight, an unseen force pressing against my chest. The lights flicker—not like a power surge. Not like a failure.

Something else. A pull.

A shift.

The air hums, crackling with something neither living nor dead. The cold isn't just physical—it's hollow, absent, like warmth itself has been stripped from the room.

The next flicker comes harder, brighter—blinding.

Shadows stretch unnaturally across the walls, curling toward something unseen—

A voice. Soft. Steady. Unshakable. "I was murdered."

The light vanishes, sucked inward, and in its place—

She stands.

Just beyond the reach of the flickering glow, golden hair cascading in wild waves, as if even fate itself could never keep hold of her. Her eyes—Ophelia's eyes—lock onto mine. Bright and endless, filled with something that has already seen too much.

She is not quite here, yet not quite elsewhere. She's lingering in that space between existence and memory.

Her dress flows as if caught in an unseen current, shifting around her like she's never been bound to something as small as a body, as limited as time.

The Infernal Council does not move.

No one breathes.

Because Calliope Arden has returned to tell her story.

She is not angry. She is not afraid.

She just looks at me.

And in that expression—I see it.

She knows.

And I have no idea what I'm supposed to say.

"Every Weaver before me carried the name Lysandra." Her voice is steady, unshaken. "Every daughter. Every generation. We have always shaped the Loom, guided the threads. Until now."

The room holds its breath.

I feel the shift in the air—not just from her words, but from the stillness of the Council, from the way my mother and father are no longer just listening, but understanding.

I grit my teeth, forcing myself to keep my voice level. "You knew?" The edge in my tone is sharp, but Calliope doesn't flinch.

"I learned at sixteen, just as Ophelia should have." Her expression doesn't change. "But I never got the chance to tell her. I never got the chance to prepare her."

My grip tightens. "Because someone made sure you didn't."

A beat.

Calliope doesn't look away. "Because he made sure I didn't."

I study her carefully. The way she says it—he—it lands like a stone in my gut.

"You know who killed you." My voice is measured, cold. "You know who took the gift from you."

Calliope meets my eyes.

And for the first time, I see Ophelia in her.

The same cutting clarity. The same unwavering resolve.

"Yes."

My stomach twists.

"It was Cassius." The words hit like a blade to the ribs.

A sharp inhale—Evander. A flicker of something unreadable—Liora.

But I don't move. I don't breathe. Because this isn't possible.

Calliope tilts her head slightly, studying me the way one might examine a fraying thread. "You didn't know," she realizes, voice softer now. "You thought you were making a deal with a desperate man."

I force myself to blink. To exhale. To think.

"How?" The question is sharp, low, dangerous.

Calliope doesn't hesitate.

"Poison." Quiet. Absolute. "Slow. Painless, at first. It wasn't meant to be cruel—it was meant to be clean. Efficient. A cup of wine, laced with something ancient, something meant to sever my ties to the Loom before death could pass it on."

She pauses, gaze distant. "I felt it the moment it touched my lips. Not the pain—the loss. Like something had been ripped from my soul before my body ever failed."

She shakes her head once. "By the time I collapsed, he was already gone. He didn't even stay to watch me die."

Something inside me snaps. My fists curl, my teeth clench, something hot and venomous climbing up my throat.

"That son of a bitch—he used me." The words are a growl, sharp and dangerous. "He knew I would take the deal if I thought I was relieving a burden. That's why he framed it that way. He never meant to free her—he meant to strip her of everything."

Owen drags a hand down his face. "Jesus. So let me get this straight—when you made the deal, Julian, you unknowingly handed the hands of fate to Melanie instead of Ophelia."

The realization rolls through the room like an unspoken curse.

Liora, silent until now, lifts her gaze to me. "Because that's how fate works. When a Weaver dies, their gift does not vanish—it transfers. And when you made your deal, the Loom did not disappear."

She lets the words settle before delivering the final blow.

"You gave it to Melanie."

The room stills.

Owen barks out a sharp, humorless laugh. "Yeah. And here's the problem—Melanie only cares about herself."

I exhale slowly.

My laugh is quiet. Cold. Dangerous.

"So I put the Weaver's gift—the hands of fate—" I shake my head, a smirk curling at the edge of my mouth. "In a self-indulgent, power-hungry narcissist."

Theron lets out a slow breath. "That actually explains why everything's gone to shit."

Selene, usually the last to be rattled, runs a hand through her hair, looking up at the ceiling like she's asking the universe for patience.

"Holy fuck. No wonder the Loom is unraveling."

I take another breath, pushing down the urge to rip Cassius apart limb by limb.

Because this?

This isn't just a mistake.

This is a fucking catastrophe.

Fourteen
Ophelia

J ulian and I had an incredible night. I notice the mark is changing—becoming more solidified, the gold burning brighter.

I press my palm to it, and it starts pulsing.

I miss him. I never thought this would happen to me. I've always
been someone who enjoys solitude, someone who *needs* it. But now,
for the first time, I don't want to be alone.

I want to be with someone. With *him*. Not because of a stupid
mark. Because of who he is.

He said I could reach out—just think of him and speak.

Ophelia: *Julian?*

Crickets. Nothing. A big fat zero. I try again, because I'm not a
quitter.

Ophelia: *Julian?*

It's like a black cloud rolls in, and when I reach for him, I slam
straight into a mental brick wall. Is this asshole telepathically ghosting

me? Rude. Guess even soulmates come with call screening. What a dick move.

Seriously, *fucked up.*

I'm done. Why do I keep trying? What if I'm the only one feeling this while he's perfectly fine? My chest tightens. I can't breathe right. Maybe he doesn't care like I do. Maybe I'm just... *alone* in this. Wanting him. Needing him. And he's slipping away.

I don't know how to stop it. I don't even know who I am anymore.

I think of him one last time. Take a shuddering breath and close my eyes.

A single tear slides down my cheek.

Before I can even scream, I feel a yank—and we drop. I know this feeling. It's the same one from before, when we teleported.

"Oh shi—" I blurt, but I'm cut off.

I land in a living room. Not mine.

"Well fucking *shit.* Look who showed up," Owen says.

Wait. Owen?

"What—Owen? I—" I blink, totally disoriented.

That's when I see the others. Strangers. All of them.

A woman with sharp eyes and quiet grace, like she's holding secrets in the stillness between breaths. Another with a flowing, dreamlike presence—her gaze soft but piercing, like she sees right through me. A man stands nearby, broad and composed, with a kind of quiet control that hums in the air. Then another—taller, colder, the room dimming just from his presence.

They're all watching me.

Like *I'm* the one who doesn't belong.

"Where the hell am I?" I mutter, heart pounding. None of this makes sense. Did Julian do this? Am I losing my mind?

A voice drips sarcasm. "Hell, huh? Nailed it on the first guess," Seth says, slouched like he's been waiting just to piss me off. "Welcome to the shitshow, newbie."

And now I want to punch him.

Julian is across the room. Staring at me.

Fuming.

He looks *furious*, though I don't know why. He's the one who brought me here.

"Julian?" The man seated speaks with quiet authority. "Who is this?"

Julian doesn't hesitate. "Dad... this is Ophelia. My soulmate."

The woman cuts in. "What is she doing here?"

"I don't know," Julian says.

"You *don't* know?" I ask, eyebrows raised. "But I—" He cuts me off, guiding me aside with a firm, steady hand.

"What are you doing here, Ophelia?" His voice is low. Measured. Controlled.

"I have no idea," I say. "One second I was calling you—*being ignored*, by the way—and next, I'm in this living room."

"I was occupied," he replies flatly, eyes unreadable.

"Clearly," I mutter, arms crossed.

He gestures toward the group. "Come."

His stride is calm, almost too calm, as he leads me forward.

"This is Ophelia," he says. "Mother, Father, Aunt, Uncle—Liora, Evander, Selene, Theron."

"We've been expecting something like this to happen," Selene says, voice smooth, inscrutable.

"Something like *what*?" I ask.

"Your power is getting stronger," she replies.

"Power?" I frown. "You mean the bond?"

"No," Evander says, his tone final. "*You.*"

Julian steps in before I can question further. "That's enough. Lia, I think it's time we talk."

Owen chuckles darkly. "Whole damn tapestry's shifting—hope she's ready to stitch it back."

Before I can say a word, the room disappears.

One blink—and I'm somewhere else.

A living room, but his this time. I can tell.

Dim blue light flickers from torches mounted on sleek, black stone walls. Velvet drapes choke a massive window, and a fireplace burns low with flames that don't crackle—just glow. Strange, dark, and silent. The seats are deep and cushioned but not exactly *welcoming*—more like they're daring you to sit.

I turn to him slowly. The words come out low, tight with too many things to name. "Tell me everything."

He doesn't pretend not to understand.

Julian leans against the bookshelf, arms crossed, gaze steady but distant.

"Your father made a deal. A cruel one. He traded your power—the way you pour emotion and empathy into your paintings—and gave it to Melanie. To fuel her career."

I blink. "What?"

He keeps going. "Every stroke of your brush, every raw piece of you—he siphoned it. Melanie's tears on screen? Her 'gut-wrenching' performances? That's *you*. Stripped and repackaged."

I stumble back, hands shaking. "How could he—why would he do that? My paintings were *mine*."

"For power," Julian says, voice sharp. "His pride. Her fame. And there's more. He threw in your soul as the final stake. When Melanie hits her peak—when he's basking in the glow of her success—your soul becomes mine to take. 'The most successful,' he said. That was the trigger."

"My soul?" I whisper. "No. I don't believe you. He wouldn't... Cassius is cold, but this? You're lying."

Julian doesn't flinch. "It's the truth. Check the mark if you doubt me. It's pulsing brighter because the contract's closing in."

I glance down. The gold glows hot against my skin. My breath catches.

"He ruined my life," I whisper, tears burning. "He took my art. My *heart.* Everything I was. Dominic loved me for that—for my soul. And when it faded, he left. Fell for her. For Melanie. Because of what Cassius stole."

I spin toward Julian, rage burning through my grief. "And you! You took the deal! You let him rip me apart—my soul, my *everything*—for some contract? How could you?"

Julian straightens, his voice cool but not cruel. "It's what I do, Lia. I collect souls. I make deals. It's my nature. But I didn't know you were mine. I didn't feel the mark burn until it was too late. Cassius played us both."

I sink into the nearest chair. I don't even know where to start. He's telling the truth—I know it. I always knew what he was. But it's different now. It's me.

"There's more," Julian says quietly.

"More?" I ask. "I don't know if I can take more."

He exhales, gaze distant. "Cassius knew you're the Weaver of the Loom of Fate."

I blink. "The Greek myth? With the three women spinning destiny?"

"No myth," he says. "It's real. And it's you."

My knees wobble, and I grip the armrest to keep upright. "That's insane. I'm not—I don't control fate. I'm just *me.*"

Julian's gaze sharpens. "It's not insane. It's power. Ancient and rare. You *are* the Weaver. Every thread, every choice—they bend to you. Cassius knew. And he exploited it."

"Exploited it how?" I ask, dread curling in my stomach.

"To put Melanie in control," he says. "He didn't care about you. He used your power to fuel her rise. Your empathy. Your essence. All siphoned through the Loom."

I shake my head. "So I was just... a tool? He didn't even care if I survived?"

"You were never his goal," Julian replies, stepping forward. "You were the key. But he didn't expect you to wake up—to start pulling the threads yourself."

I stare at him, but the blows keep coming.

"Your mother was the Weaver before you," he says. "Calliope. The gift passes through the Lysandra line. Her maternal line. She was meant to prepare you. But she was killed before she could."

My throat tightens. "She was *killed*? How do you know?"

Julian's expression softens. Just a fraction. "She came to me. To my family. Warned the Infernal Council someone would come for the Loom. Someone like Cassius. She didn't have long."

My voice cracks. "The Infernal Council?"

"They oversee Hell's order. Old, powerful. They only intervene when it suits them. Calliope begged for protection, but... they stayed out of it."

"Who killed my mother?" I ask, though deep down, I already know the answer.

"Your father," he replies.

I stare at him, my breath catching in my throat. "So... do you have it?" I ask, quieter than I mean to. "My soul?"

His eyes lock on mine, steady and careful.

"I thought you did," I say, the words rushing out. "With the bond. With all of this. I thought it already belonged to you."

Julian shakes his head. "It doesn't," he says gently. "Not unless you give it to me."

I blink, trying to wrap my head around it. "But... my father sold it."

"He did," Julian says, the muscle in his jaw tightening. "But claiming it isn't automatic. Not with a soul like yours."

I pause. "What happens now?"

His expression shifts—something unreadable flickering in his eyes. "Now... you decide."

I search his face. "Decide what?"

"To willingly become mine," he says. His voice is calm, but there's weight behind every word.

My stomach twists. "Aren't I already?"

"You're marked. We're bound. But that's not the same. I can't take what you haven't offered."

"What?" I ask. "Does Melanie suddenly lose her success? Do I magically become the Weaver? What is my power?"

"If you take it back, she'll feel it. Whether she loses everything? That's not up to me. You already are the Weaver. You were just too numb to feel it. And your power?" He meets my eyes. "It's not something you use. It's something you survive."

"And if I decide to give my soul to you," I ask slowly, "what happens next?"

"The Infernal Claim," he says, voice low.

"The infernal what?" I raise an eyebrow.

He doesn't smile. His expression shifts—darker, weightier, like he's speaking something sacred and dangerous.

"It's not a spell," he says, his voice like a prayer sealed with ash. "Not a ritual. It's a progression. A descent. It begins the moment your soul reaches for mine—not with words, but with need. And yours already has."

My breath catches. "What does that mean?"

"It means," he says, dragging a hand through his hair, "the first call happens when you think of me. Not casually. Not in passing. It has to be real. Intimate. Vulnerable. When you feel something deep enough to break you open... the bond answers." His throat works. "That first time—you invoked it. You didn't know. But I felt it. In my blood. In every part of me."

I look away, heat blooming beneath my skin. "You mean—"

"Yes." His voice tightens. "That was the spark. That's what woke it up."

He continues before I can speak. "After that comes the kiss. The real one. That's when I give you a piece of my essence. It latches into you—carves itself under your skin. That's why you saw what you did. That's why it felt like something ancient waking up."

I nod slowly. "I remember." The fire. The visions. The way it wasn't just mine.

"Next comes the corruption touch," he says. "Your body starts to respond. You'll feel heat. Pain. Need. Even when I'm not there. The bond tightens. It feeds on proximity, on want, on denial. The more you resist, the more it takes."

"It already is," I murmur.

"I know." He watches me. There's a flicker of guilt there. Or maybe reverence.

"And the final step?" I ask.

He exhales, slow and deliberate. "Consummation." He meets my eyes. "But not the way you think. It's not sex that seals it. Not entirely. It's what happens after. What you give."

"What I give?"

"Yourself," he says. "Your mortality. Your softness. The part of you that isn't ready to become something else." A beat passes. "It hurts. Only you can do it. I can't help you. I can only hold you through it."

Something cold and electric dances down my spine. "And after?"

"If you survive it," he says, voice almost reverent, "you're rewritten. The Mark completes. The bond finalizes. But not with a bite—not anymore. Not with blood. With will. With sacrifice. With something you can't take back."

I go quiet.

"Then," he says, softer now, "if you want... you speak my true name. That's the knot. The end. If you say it, you bind us. Forever. If I die, you suffer. If you die, so do I. If we're apart too long..."

"It hurts," I finish for him.

He nods once. "More than anything."

The silence stretches between us, dense and trembling.

"What if I don't want to?"

His voice doesn't waver. "I won't take you. This isn't about power. This is about choice. Yours."

I think about Julian. The bond. I don't know how to hold all of this. It doesn't fit inside me.

My father didn't just ignore me. He didn't just favor her. He *sold* me. Carved out my soul and handed it to Melanie like a gift, wrapped in applause and red carpet lighting.

And I didn't even feel it go. I just knew something inside me had broken, and no one ever told me why.

I thought it was me. That I was too much. Too sensitive. Too intense. I thought maybe the world had just moved on and forgotten to take me with it.

But it wasn't me.

It was him.

It was them.

And Julian... he's not blameless. But he didn't lie. He didn't run from the truth. He looked me in the eye and gave it to me straight, even when he knew I'd hate him for it.

And I did. For a moment, I wanted to. I wanted to scream that he was just another monster trying to own me.

But I saw his face. He didn't know I was the one. He didn't expect this either.

And now... now he's offering something no one ever has.

Choice.

He could've claimed me. Could've used the bond, the rules, the loopholes. But he didn't. He gave it back to me—my agency. My soul. My say.

And somehow, that means more than anything I've ever been given.

I don't know who I am now—with the Loom of Fate coiled in my blood and a legacy I never asked for hanging heavy on my shoulders.

But I know if I give myself to Julian, it won't be because I was stolen. It won't be because I was tricked or bound or broken.

For the first time, I *want* something.

And it's something I'm willing to do anything to take.

"I want to do it," I say, barely audible.

Julian's eyes flick to mine. "Do what?"

"I want to claim you," I say, the words steady and deliberate, as if I've always known them—and only now found the strength to speak them.

Julian doesn't move, but something shifts in his expression—subtle, stunned, like the ground beneath him has tilted.

I step closer. My voice softens, but I don't hesitate. "I need your soul. Your love. The fire and fury you try to hide."

He doesn't speak. His silence feels like gravity, heavy and expectant.

I reach for his hand and guide it to rest over my heart. "I'm ready to give you everything," I say. "Not because of the mark. Not because fate demands it. But because you are the only thing in this world that has ever felt real."

I look up at him, my words weaving between us like a vow.

"I love you," I whisper. "Not in spite of who you are—but because of it. Because even when everything else was taken from me, *you* saw me. And now, I want to be yours. Completely. Willingly. Because I know *exactly* what it means."

Julian doesn't speak at first. He just watches me, eyes unreadable, hand still over my heart.

Finally, his voice breaks the silence. "You already are," he says. "You always were."

Fifteen
JULIAN

S he spoke it. She told me she claims me.

I never thought it would happen. Not in my wildest dreams. When my Mark burned into her skin and flared back onto mine, I figured it was inevitable.

But I wasn't expecting this.

Wasn't expecting to fall. Wasn't expecting *her* to become everything.

And now I have what my parents have. What my aunt and uncle have. A connection that won't fade.

I can't wait for the Infernal Union. But first—we seal the Claim.

Ophelia leans in, eyes locked on mine, no flicker of hesitation. Her lips part, and when she kisses me, it's not tender—it's pure will. Like she's not just choosing me. She's igniting something neither of us can contain.

The Mark flares beneath my skin, responding to her mouth like it's been waiting for this moment to awaken. And I know—this isn't surrender. It's her claiming me. Setting the bond ablaze. Stepping into the dark with her eyes wide open.

She jerks back with a sound I'll never forget. Bone? Muscle? I don't know. She hits the floor—*hard*. Not like she tripped. Like something inside her threw her down. Her back arches violently. Her hands claw at her chest, digging into the Mark, nails tearing skin as if she can rip it out.

The scream that rips through her isn't human.

It starts as a sound and ends as a weapon—echoing off the stone, rattling dust from the ceiling. Blood pours from her nose, her mouth, the corners of her eyes. She convulses. Muscles locking, spasming. Her spine bows like it's going to snap.

The Mark pulses. Gold spreads in sharp, jagged lines across her skin like veins—or roots. Like something inside her is trying to grow out of her body, and she's fighting it.

But it's winning.

I move, knowing I can't help her, and the bond punishes me. Heat lashes across my arm—hot enough to leave smoke in the air. I stop. Fists clenched. Useless. All I can do is watch her thrash, bleed, break.

Her jaw locks. Her teeth grind. Her eyes roll back. Her entire body is trembling like she's being electrocuted from the inside. Like the Claim is feeding on her.

I feel it all. Her fear. Her fury. Her agony. It crashes into me through the bond like a flood I can't outrun.

And I still can't take it from her.

The Claim was never meant to be shared. This is her crucible. I am only the shadow cast by her fire.

I've seen gods fall. Watched souls beg for mercy. But nothing—not war, not death—has ever hit like this. Standing here. Watching her be devoured.

And knowing she chose it.

"I'm here, baby," I say, low and raw. A vow. I drop to my knees just outside the circle of burning heat where the Mark keeps me back. I can't touch her. I can't stop it.

But I can stay.

And I do.

"I know it hurts," I murmur, the words cracking in my throat. "I feel it. Every scream. Every pulse. You're unraveling in front of me and I can't do a fucking thing."

She cries out again—guttural, broken—and I flinch like it hit me in the ribs.

"Come back to me," I whisper, steadier now. "Ophelia. Look at me."

She doesn't. Her eyes are rolled back. Her body still locked in the storm. But I keep talking. Because if I stop—I'll shatter.

"You're not alone," I say. "You never were. I love you. In ways I don't have words for. And I know this is yours. I know you chose it. But you don't have to carry it alone."

I reach out. Close enough to feel the air sear my skin. It hurts. I don't care.

The screaming pulls back like a tide. Her body goes limp. Her chest heaves. Blood streaks her skin. The Mark still glows—dim now, like embers dying in ash.

Her eyes open.

For a second—just one—I see blue.

Her blue.

She looks at me like she doesn't know where she is. Doesn't know *who* she is. And that's when I move.

I catch her before she falls. Wrap my arms around her and pull her into me. She collapses like gravity remembered her.

I hold her. Hands in her hair, on her back, grounding her to the world she just burned through.

"You're safe," I whisper, over and over. "You're here. With me. You did it."

She's shaking, her fingers twitching against my chest. But she's here.

And I don't let go. I hold her like she's the only thing that's ever been real—because right now, she is.

I don't care that my arm is scorched. That I'm bleeding. That I'm burned where the bond kept me away. None of it matters.

She came back to me.

And now, I'll be the reason she never falls again.

Her voice is barely there. "Why is everything blurry?"

I brush damp hair from her face, hand trembling. "It's the pain," I murmur. "Your body's still catching up. I'm sorry, little artist. I promise it'll pass."

She lets out a weak, raspy chuckle. "Well... that sucked."

I laugh—broken, grateful, ruined. Only my mate could survive hell and meet me with a smirk. Only she could bleed like this and still crack a joke.

And gods, I love her for it.

I press my forehead to hers. "You're back. And you're mine."

"I feel it," she says, "but also like... something's missing." Her eyes search mine. "I don't know what I am now."

I cup her cheek, thumb stroking gently over skin still flushed from the burn. "You lost your mortality. That's what you're feeling. You became something else. Something stronger." I pause, watching her face as the truth settles. "That's why it hurt. You were dying."

She flinches, barely, but I see it. She hates that word.

So I drop my voice, just for her. "Sweetheart... feel it."

"Feel what?" she whispers.

My hand glides down to her sternum, to the Mark—still glowing faintly beneath the blood and sweat. I press my palm to it.

"How alive you are now." My voice doesn't waver. "You didn't just lose something tonight. You gained something too."

She takes a shaky breath. My touch doesn't hurt her anymore. The bond pulses steady. Inviting.

"Let me show you," I say, voice low and rough. "Let me show you what you've become."

The world blurs around us as I lift her into my arms and take us to the bedroom, the bond carrying us in a pulse of heat and shadow. Her breath hitches as I lay her down on the silk sheets, but the moment my hands leave her, she moves—graceful, fluid, sure.

She shifts on her knees, eyes locked on mine, and begins to undress me—not with impatience, but with intent. Her fingers move to my shirt first, dragging it up inch by inch, knuckles grazing my skin like she's memorizing me all over again. When she leans in to pull it over my head, her mouth brushes the curve of my neck—deliberate. I groan, low in my throat, but she only smirks.

"You know I can just will these off, right?" I murmur, trying and failing to sound unaffected.

"Where's the fun in that?" she quips, fingers already working on the button of my pants. "Don't you demons believe in suffering?"

"Not like this." My voice is gravel now.

She laughs and slides the fabric down with a slow, sinful drag of her palms, like she knows she's unmaking me with every motion.

She drags the last of my clothes down my legs, slow like it's an indulgence, not a necessity. When I'm finally bare beneath her, she straddles me again, her fingers grazing my stomach and my chest, taking her time—like she's toying with her favorite possession.

"Now it's my turn to play," she says, her voice honeyed and wicked, tinged with that gleam in her eye that means trouble. The kind that ruins a man gladly.

I start to reach for her, already half-gone, but she swats my hand away with a smirk. "Ah-ah. You had your moment. Let me have mine."

She leans in, her lips barely brushing mine, her body hovering just enough to keep me aching.

"Lie back, demon," she murmurs against my mouth. "And let me show you what being newly immortal feels like."

I do as she says. No hesitation. No fight. Just the thrum of the bond pulsing under my skin as I lower myself into the sheets and let her climb over me—confident, commanding, goddamn glorious.

Her fingers trail down the line of my stomach, slow, deliberate, nails scraping just enough to make my jaw tighten. I'm already hard and aching, but she doesn't touch me. Not yet.

Instead, she shifts lower, kissing my lower abdomen, her breath ghosting over the place I need her most. My hips jerk, helpless. She smiles against my skin like she's in control and she knows it.

"Still pretending you're patient?" she purrs.

I try to laugh, but it catches in my throat when she drags her tongue from the base of my cock up the shaft in one slow, wet stroke. My entire body goes tight.

"Fuck, Ophelia."

She hums in approval and wraps her lips around the tip, sucking lightly before taking me deeper—slow and controlled. Her hand wraps around the base, stroking in time with the way her tongue flicks and swirls. I brace one hand against the headboard, the other still fisted in the sheets, knuckles white.

She's not rushing. She's not teasing anymore either. She's working me. Studying every twitch, every gasp, every curse that slips past my lips as she drags her mouth up and down my cock like she was made for it.

She lets go with a wet sound that leaves me wrecked. My chest heaves. I look down at her and I know I'm gone.

She wipes the corner of her mouth with her thumb and licks it clean without breaking eye contact.

"You gonna cum already?" she teases. "Or do I get to play a little longer?"

I want to flip her beneath me. I want to wreck her. But I don't. I won't. Not yet.

"You take what you want," I growl. "Just know when I get my turn, I'm not holding back."

Her smile could tear kingdoms down. She straddles me again, slick and ready, but she doesn't sink onto me just yet. She rolls her hips, guiding me through her slick folds—torturous, unhurried, like she's savoring the anticipation. My hands hover at her hips, desperate to touch her, to guide her, but still I don't move.

She leans down, lips brushing mine, her voice a whisper laced in heat.

"Don't break yet, demon," she says. "We're just getting started."

Her eyes stay locked on mine as she shifts her hips just enough to position me at her entrance. The heat of her folds wraps around the tip of my cock and I suck in a breath through my teeth—every muscle in my body tightening like a held breath.

And she sinks down.

Fuck.

The sound that rips out of me is raw—half groan, half growl. She takes me inch by inch, slow and steady, her eyes fluttering shut, lips parted as her breath catches. She's tight, warm, slick—like she was made for this. For me.

She braces her hands against my chest, grounding herself as she seats me fully inside her, her thighs trembling slightly from the stretch, from the feeling of being filled. I can feel the pulse of the bond between us now—demanding, molten, alive—like the Claim itself is watching, waiting to burn through us all over again.

"Gods," I rasp, barely holding it together. "You feel..."

"I know," she breathes, hips rolling once, slow and deep. "I feel it too."

Her rhythm starts slow, torturous, deliberate—rocking her hips in long, fluid movements that have me gritting my teeth and clinging to the last of my control. Her hands slide up my chest to my shoulders, her nails biting in just enough to keep me tethered, and she starts riding me with real purpose now—each thrust a little deeper, a little harder, chasing something that we both know is coming.

She falls apart above me again, body arching, voice cracked open on a gasp that sounds like my name.

And I need more.

I don't ask. I flip her over in one smooth motion, one hand on her hip, the other braced beside her head as I press her down into the sheets. She moans when I thrust back into her from behind—deep, full, perfect—and I feel her stretch around me like she was meant to take this.

The sound she makes goes straight to my spine. I snap my hips forward again—hard, rhythmic, claiming. The bed jolts beneath us, the headboard knocking against the wall in time with every thrust. She cries out, gripping the sheets, her body trembling but pushing back into me, hungry for it.

The slap of skin, the creak of the bed, the soft, wrecked sounds she makes—it's all for me.

"Fuck, Lia," I growl, my hand sliding up her back to tangle in her hair. "You feel like heaven and hell and everything I was promised and never got."

She turns her face to the side, breathless, dazed, wrecked. "Don't stop."

I won't.

My pace pounds into her a deliberate, punishing rhythm. I want her to feel this in her bones, in the way her legs won't hold her tomorrow, in the way the Mark will pulse long after the last wave fades. I want her to remember this—not just as sex, but as mine. Ours.

Her hand reaches back blindly, searching for me, and I catch it, lacing our fingers tight as I drive into her deeper, harder.

The bed bounces beneath us, the room echoing with every sound of it, and I don't care who hears. I want Hell itself to know what's happening here.

This is the aftershock of her transformation. This is what it means to be bound.

And when she comes again, screaming into the mattress, I lose myself right behind her—thrusting deep, spilling into her with a groan that shakes something loose inside me.

We collapse together, breathless, tangled in each other's skin and sweat.

She's draped over me, skin flushed, lips kiss-bitten, her hair sticking to my chest like she's melted into me—and maybe she has. Her breath is still a little uneven, but her grin is unmistakable.

I run a hand down her back, slow and lazy, and kiss the top of her head. "So," I murmur. "That was subtle."

She laughs against my chest. "You say that like you didn't beg."

"I grunted artistically," I say, deadpan.

She hums. "Oh, is that what that was?"

The bond hums low between us—satisfied, quiet. Finally still. But my pulse is not. And neither is hers.

She shifts slightly, brushing her thigh against me again—deliberate.

I arch a brow. "You planning something?"

She glances up at me, eyes gleaming with post-orgasm mischief. "Thinking about a second round."

I blink at the ceiling. "Of course you are."

"I'm newly immortal," she says, already sliding over me again. "You can't expect me to not test my stamina."

I sigh, dramatic. "This is how I die. Again."

She grins. "Don't worry, demon. I'll go slow. This time."

Sixteen
Ophelia

We were up all night—and I'm not tired. Not even a little.

Which... is unsettling.

I stretch, blink at the ceiling, and glance at Julian, who's just lying there next to me like a damn statue. Watching me.

"You're staring," I say.

He doesn't blink. "I'm appreciating."

"You're being creepy."

He smirks. "And yet, you still let me inside you. Twice."

I groan and hurl a pillow at his face. "Why do I even talk to you?"

He catches it midair. "Because you like when I ruin you *and* the conversation."

I sit up, still not even a little sore or foggy. "Okay, but seriously—I should be tired. We didn't sleep."

Julian props himself on one elbow, eyes raking over me like he hasn't decided whether to answer or drag me back under. "You're immortal now, love. You won't tire like before. And here in Hell? You're powerful. Your body knows it. It's adjusting."

I blink at him. "But you slept when you stayed at my apartment."

His mouth quirks. "Because I'd been on Earth too long. The longer we're away from our realm, the more the body bends. It dulls the edges."

"And exhaustion's the first thing to hit?"

He shrugs. "That, or irrational emotional outbursts."

I snort. "So basically, you get... human."

He grins. "Don't tell anyone."

"Wait... we didn't use protection."

"Nope," Julian says, maddeningly calm.

My stomach flips. "But... you're a demon. I can't—right?"

He doesn't laugh. Doesn't even blink. "Lia. How do you think I exist?"

My blood runs cold. "Shit. I can get pregnant."

He leans on his elbow, still watching me like this is the most obvious thing in the world.

"But... how?" I shake my head, hoping it'll clear the fog. "I mean, I know how, but also—how?"

Julian smirks. "Do you need a repeat of last night? I'm happy to provide a demonstration."

I throw the blanket at him. "Not helping, demon."

"You started it, little mortal."

"Immortal," I snap. "And you're a demon. A thousands-of-years-old, slept-with-legions kind of demon."

"Hey! That's an exaggeration." He opens his mouth. Shuts it. "Okay. Maybe not legions. But like... a battalion."

"A whole cursed infantry," I mutter.

"That's because," he says, brushing hair from my face, "children only happen with a fated mate."

I still. "So I could be pregnant."

He nods. "It's possible."

My breath catches.

"Would that be so bad?" he asks softly.

I don't answer right away. Because it wouldn't be bad. Not exactly. Not with him. But it's not about bad. It's about everything I don't know. "I don't know if I'd be good at it," I say finally, barely more than a whisper. "Being a mother."

Julian doesn't rush to answer. He just watches me, quiet.

"I had no role model. No one to show me how. My mom died. My father is a fuck. I can't even share this with Bella. The ache hits fast and sharp—like a shadow I didn't realize was still clinging to me.

Julian doesn't rush to answer. He just watches me, quiet.

Finally, he asks softly, "Why can't you share this with Bella? Or Rosalind?"

The words catch me off balance. He's not pushing—just opening a door I didn't expect.

"You don't have to cut them out completely," he adds. "And... you think love and softness are the only traits that make a good parent?"

I rest my head against his shoulder, eyes burning. His voice lowers to that quiet, careful place he only uses when he's trying to steady me. "That's not the only kind of strength a child needs."

I exhale slowly, the words catching at the edges of my breath. And even though I don't have an answer yet, I understand what he's trying to say. What he's giving me permission to feel.

Maybe this is just something I'll have to face—if I'm pregnant. When I'm ready.

His face changes—subtle, but I catch it. That faraway, hyper-focused look he gets right before something stupid happens.

"What's up with your face?" I ask, squinting at him.

He sighs like this is the greatest burden ever bestowed on a demon. "Someone's calling me."

"Calling you? Like mentally?"

"Yes, Lia. With their brain."

"Who?"

He gives me a flat look. "My dad."

Julian tilts his head, clearly trying to soften the blow. "He wants to... talk to us."

"Us?" My voice spikes. "Like together? Like some sort of post-claim check-in?"

Julian shrugs, but there's amusement tugging at the corner of his mouth. "Apparently word got around."

"Word got around? What the hell does that mean?" I fling my arms out. "Who told? Who was watching? Are there demon paparazzi? Is there some Hell-wide newsletter?"

He doesn't answer. He's too busy laughing.

"This isn't funny, Julian!" I start pacing, grabbing a throw pillow just to squeeze the life out of it. "I haven't even figured out if I'm pregnant and now I'm supposed to meet the head of the Duvain line like we're doing some demonic dinner party? What do I wear? Do I bow? Do I address him as Your Infernal Majesty? What if I mess it up and he incinerates me?"

Julian's shoulders shake with quiet laughter, which just fuels my spiral.

"I'm serious! What if he hates me? What if I say something offensive and he banishes me to a subrealm filled with lava and guilt? What if I—"

Julian grabs my wrist and pulls me back to him with an infuriatingly calm smile. "Ophelia. Breathe."

I glare at him. "Don't you dare demon-meditate me right now."

Julian just grins. The kind of grin that should come with a warning label. "You know what I think?"

"No," I reply, voice flat enough to iron linen. "But you've got that 'speech incoming' look, so go ahead."

He pulls me into his lap in one smooth motion, hands landing on my hips like they belong there—and, annoyingly, they do. "I think you're looking for reasons to stress because you're too afraid to admit you might actually be handling all of this just fine."

I shoot him a look. "That is... not entirely wrong. But also, rude."

"You're panicking because you're brilliant," he murmurs, lips brushing the shell of my ear. "But you forget one thing."

"What?"

"I know exactly how to shut your brain up."

My breath catches. "Julian."

"Mm?" His hand slides lower, fingers tracing along my inner thigh. "You were saying?"

"I was saying you are absolutely not seducing me out of a stress spiral right now. That's not how mental health works."

He nips at my neck, just enough to make me gasp. "Maybe not for humans. But for demons?"

I swallow. "This is emotional manipulation."

"Correction," he says, dragging his mouth back to mine. "This is effective multi-tasking."

I shove him off with both palms to his bare chest—he lets me, but he's smirking like he won anyway.

"No," I say, standing up and realizing—shit. "I have no clothes. I'm naked."

Julian reclines against the headboard like a smug demon prince. "Just will something on."

My brain short-circuits. "Excuse me?"

"You're immortal now. Your energy responds to intent. Just focus on what you want to wear."

I stare at him. "So you're telling me I can just... manifest outfits?"

He shrugs. "It's Hell, love. We have standards."

"Oh my god," I say, eyes wide. "I'm about to have a power-induced identity crisis. This is dangerous."

"I'm begging you," Julian says, already grinning. "Please make it dangerous."

I close my eyes and focus, envisioning something simple, classy, timeless.

There's a flash of heat—and I look down to find myself in a black silk slip dress with thigh slits that make it feel like a threat.

Julian whistles. "Not subtle."

"This is me trying to be respectable," I snap.

"Try again," he says, clearly having the time of his afterlife.

I throw a hand up. "Fine."

Flash—now I'm in red leather pants, a sheer corset, and platform boots that could double as weapons.

Julian sits up straighter. "Okay, that one's disrespectful—in the best way."

"Ugh!" Another wave—now it's a blazer with nothing underneath, tailored to filth.

Julian groans. "You're trying to kill me."

"You said I had to meet your dad," I hiss. "I'm trying to look dignified."

"Pretty sure he'll just be impressed you didn't show up in a dress made of flame."

"I mean... that does sound kinda iconic," I murmur.

"Stop," Julian says, laughing now. "No. Don't put that idea in your own head."

But it's too late. There's a flicker of heat, and now I'm standing in a molten flame gown that crackles when I move.

Julian's jaw drops. "Okay, I take it back. You're going to own Hell."

I look down at myself. The flame gown is iconic—but it's too much. I don't want to look like a threat. I want to look like I belong.

I take a breath and close my eyes again, focusing this time—not on drama, or distraction, but on clarity. On me.

When I open my eyes, I'm wearing a deep charcoal tailored suit—fitted, sleek, and sharp at the edges. The blazer cinches at the waist like armor. Underneath, just a sheer black lace bralette that hints without giving anything away. The pants fall clean to the floor, flared slightly over pointed boots. My Mark glows faintly at my collarbone, framed perfectly by the low V.

I lift my chin. "This."

Julian stares, slower this time. Like he's cataloging every inch.

"That's it," he says. No teasing now. Just quiet awe. "You look like sin dressed in order."

"Is that a compliment?"

"It's worship," he says. "And also a warning to everyone else in that room."

I smirk. "Good. Let them be warned."

"Ready, little artist?"

I nod, spine straight.

"Good," he murmurs. "Let's go show Hell who you are."

He wraps his arms around me, and off we go.

Honestly, I'm used to it now. I don't get sick anymore.

We land back in the living room I accidentally dropped myself into last night. This time, only Liora and Evander are here.

Which somehow feels worse.

Julian's hand rests at the small of my back, steadying me—but I swear they can see straight through me. Not just reading my body language. Reading *me*. Like they already know what I'm afraid of before I do.

"I see she figured out how to conjure a wardrobe," Liora says, eyes flicking over me like I'm a painting she's already critiqued. "One of the best perks of immortality. That, and manipulating wine temperature with a thought."

"Oh, you know what the best perk is," Evander adds without missing a beat.

Liora smirks. "You're inappropriate."

Evander shrugs. "You married me."

I give Julian a wide-eyed look. "Are they always like this?"

Julian leans in slightly. "As long as I've known them," he says, tone so dry it could ignite.

Liora gestures toward the velvet sofas. "Sit. Unless the Claim completely obliterated your spine."

"Almost," I say, dropping onto the couch. "But Julian has fast hands."

Evander chuckles, clearly approving. Liora sips her wine like she didn't hear that—though the glint in her eye says otherwise.

"So," she says, studying me. "You're still glowing."

"Is that normal?"

"For someone who just died and came back in fire? Yes. You're stabilizing. It'll pass."

"You say that like it's casual," I mutter.

"It becomes casual," Evander says. "Eventually."

I hesitate. "Can I ask something?"

Evander lifts a brow. "You can try."

"You're... bonded, right?"

Liora brushes her hair off her shoulder and unclasps her blazer and pulls it aside—just enough to reveal what lies beneath.

The Mark. Just above her heart, carved into the same place mine lives.

Same shape. Same golden curl spiraled around the black. Only hers looks older—etched deeper, like it's lived through war.

My breath catches. "It's just like mine."

Liora nods, calm and certain. "It should be," she says softly. There's something in her eyes—recognition, maybe. Or memory.

"You weren't born with it?"

"No. I was mortal," she says, folding her blazer closed with easy grace. "But the moment Evander saw me, it burned across my skin. Just like yours did."

Evander's expression hardens. "The bond always works that way. It sears itself into the soul. No questions. No mercy. Just truth."

Julian brushes his fingers against mine, grounding me. "It's how you know it's real," he murmurs, glancing down at my collar where my Mark glows faintly beneath the fabric. "There's no going back."

I stare at them, throat tight. "I thought it was because I'm the Weaver. Or the Claim. Something special."

Liora tilts her head, voice gentler now. "It is special. But not unprecedented. This bond is ancient. The Mark chooses—but it's only the beginning."

"The bond doesn't seal just because it appears," Evander adds, leaning forward. "It takes time. Pain. Will."

Julian nods. "Ours burned long before the Claim. It doesn't all happen at once."

"You need the space between," Liora says. "Between the Mark and the Claim. That's where the soul shifts. Where you decide what you'll become."

I'm still trying to process all of it when Evander leans back with a wicked grin. "She screamed, by the way. When the Mark hit."

Liora lifts a brow, unbothered. "I broke a window. Punched a priest."

"What?" I say, my eyes fluttering like the words didn't land right.

"It was a dramatic time," she says, swirling her wine. "Bloodletting. Corsets. Powdered wigs. My soul combusted in the middle of a wedding."

Julian laughs. "You were getting married?"

"To a man my father selected," she says, lips twitching. "He thought quoting Virgil made him interesting."

Evander chuckles. "He wept when she vanished mid-ceremony."

"I didn't vanish. I was claimed. There's a difference."

"You tackled a priest and set the carpet on fire."

I stare at them. "Wait. How old are you?"

Liora lifts her glass. "I was born in 1701."

"You fell in love before electricity," I manage, my lashes fluttering like they're buffering for comprehension.

Julian leans in. "You okay?"

"I'm talking to a woman who predates plumbing and could still headline Paris Fashion Week."

Liora smiles, warm and wicked. "Immortality doesn't erase time. It just teaches you how to wear it."

A knock sounds at the door. Julian and Evander move instantly, stepping in front of me and Liora with predator-smooth reflexes.

"Enter," Evander calls.

The door creaks open. Theron steps in, calm and composed. Selene follows, her posture effortlessly royal.

"Did you just... knock?" Evander asks, visibly offended.

"Yeah," Theron says. "Selene told me to."

"I believe in manners," Selene replies, flicking lint off her sleeve like she's preparing for battle. Her gaze lands on me—sharp, curious, amused.

"So," she says, crossing her arms. "What are we talking about?"

"Our markings," Liora answers. "Tell them about the night you were marked."

"That night wasn't dramatic," she says. "No altar. No moon. Just a holding cell. Under a church. Salem."

"Wait—Salem, like the witch trials?"

"1692," Selene says, her voice all silk and barbed wire. "I was mortal. Educated. Unapologetic. A little too outspoken for men who preferred their women docile and afraid."

She meets my gaze, eyes cold and daring.

"I stood up for girls they called liars. For women they called witches. I questioned their authority. Challenged their narratives. Corrected their sermons."

She lets her lip curl, voice dripping with disdain. "They called me dangerous."

Her smile sharpens—a threat and a promise. "They weren't wrong."

"You were one of the accused?"

"I was a woman with opinions and no husband," she says dryly. "So yes. That was enough."

"I thought they burned witches."

"No," Selene says flatly. "That was Europe. In Massachusetts, they hanged them."

"Oh." I wince. "Sorry."

"It's fine," she says—but it isn't. "Most people think fire. But I remember the rope. The cold. The silence. I'd stopped screaming by then."

"You weren't dying," Liora says, glass clicking against the table. "You were surrendering."

Selene doesn't look at her. "Same thing when no one's coming."

"But someone did," I say, glancing at Theron.

"I felt it the second I entered the town," Theron says. "The bond was already awake."

"I didn't even see him," Selene says. "The Mark burned into me before the door opened. I thought I was hallucinating."

"She clawed her chest open," Theron adds, voice low. "Tried to rip it off her skin."

"He tore through the courthouse," Selene finishes, voice suddenly bright with bite. "Lit up the sky. Dragged me through the fire like a myth no one was ready for."

"They thought the Devil had come for her," Liora says.

"They weren't entirely wrong," Selene says, her smile thin. "Especially now that I'm the one who gets to hang the souls of the men who did the hanging."

The room stills.

"How old were you?" I ask quietly.

"Twenty."

"So you were born in..."

"Sixteen seventy-two," she says, grinning like she's been waiting for me to ask.

"You're older than Liora?"

"Don't sound so surprised," she says, throwing a look at Liora.

"She's older," Liora concedes. "Just less refined."

"I survived a Puritan noose," Selene says. "You survived corsets and powdered wigs. We all have our struggles."

"I wore the wigs beautifully."

Julian leans in again. "Feeling normal yet?"

"She dodged the noose and wound up immortal," I mutter. "I trip on a cobblestones and spiral."

Theron chuckles. Liora sips her wine. Selene smirks.

"Welcome to the family," Theron says.

"Now we must discuss the Infernal Union," Selene says, as casually as if she were suggesting afternoon tea.

"The first of my boys to have one. How exciting!" Liora claps her hands, already radiating the energy of someone planning florals that breathe fire.

Julian groans and drags a hand down his face. "Gods, here we go."

"You didn't tell me about this," I say, rounding on him. "You gave me the soul-claim breakdown, the burning, the cravings—but you left out the part where we have a wedding?"

"It's not really a wedding," he mutters.

"Oh, it's *basically* a wedding, dear," Liora cuts in, waving a perfectly manicured hand like the matter is settled. "Men never understand the ceremonial gravity of these things. That's why we don't let them plan them."

Evander raises a brow, entirely unbothered. "She's not wrong."

"You're lucky," Theron adds, smirking. "Mine started a fire. Literally."

Selene rolls her eyes, but her mouth twitches. "It was symbolic."

"Of what? Chaos?" he mutters, with the kind of tone that says he already knows the answer and isn't impressed.

She shrugs. "Love."

"Okay," I say, tipping my head. "But what is this ceremony, exactly?"

Evander's voice drops low, the humor fading from his face. "It begins with fire. You each walk the Procession—through columns of living flame. Alone."

"If the fire burns you," Julian adds, quieter now, "you're not ready. The flame doesn't lie."

"No veils. No softness," Liora says, her smile all teeth and memory. "You wear black, crimson, obsidian—colors of legacy. Power walks beside you."

I can't help it. "Do I get a script for all this, or am I just supposed to vibe with the infernal energy?"

Selene answers, dry as dust. "You'll feel it. Trust me."

"And after the fire?"

"The Circle of Witnesses," she says. "Chosen souls—family, friends, rivals. Anyone with something to lose or protect. They don't just stand there. They come armed."

I frown. "Why the weapons?"

"Tradition," Theron says. "A reminder that nothing sacred stays unchallenged."

"Lovely," I mutter. "Please continue."

"At the center of the circle," Liora picks up, "you meet at the Binding Flame. A brazier filled with black-gold oil. You offer something of yourself—blood, a weapon, a name you're willing to lose forever."

I stare. "A name?"

Selene nods. "Some truths are more binding than blood."

"After that?" I ask, voice softer now.

"The Vows," Julian says, his thumb brushing along my hand. "Not vows of love. Of bond. Of choice. Of will."

"You are not my weakness," Liora begins, her voice like silk wrapped around steel. "You are my edge."

"If the world falls, I fall beside you," Selene says without looking away.

"You are my shield," Evander murmurs. "I am your blade."

"I chose this," Theron finishes. "I choose you still."

A hush settles—those ancient words humming in the air like magic already begun.

"And when it's done?" I whisper.

"Your Marks flare again," Selene says. "They change. A sigil appears—crown, flame, serpent devouring its tail. Whatever the bond has become."

"Lastly," Evander says, gaze locking with mine, "you take the Throne of Ash. Side by side. Not as rulers. But as dominions—souls who survived the fire and earned each other in it."

Julian squeezes my hand under the table, his eyes never leaving my face.

But something shifts. Not in the air—*beneath* it.

The fireplace roars to life behind us, the flames climbing high and sharp, burning black-gold. Heat pulses like a heartbeat, and from the fire's core, something emerges—not thrown, not placed.

Born.

A blackened scroll, etched in molten gold, floats down onto the hearth like a verdict.

I stand before Julian can stop me.

It's hot in my hand. Heavy, humming. No seal. No ink. Just the carved symbols—his Mark and mine, intertwined.

Beneath them, a message that doesn't read so much as *declare itself* into my mind.

Julian reads over my shoulder, but I'm already there.

The bond has been witnessed. The flame has answered. You are summoned. The Council awaits.

The words don't threaten. They don't ask.

They expect.

I stare at them, pulse steady, blood thick with something no longer fear.

The Council has spoken. But so have the flames.

And whatever comes next will have to burn through me first.

Seventeen
JULIAN

The Infernal Council doesn't frighten me—not in the way it used to. I've stood before them more times than I care to count. I know the weight of their gaze, the way silence folds under their authority like ash under pressure.

But Ophelia? She's another story entirely.

It isn't fear for her that tightens my chest—it's fear of her reaction. Not because she's fragile. She far from it. It's that she doesn't filter herself when she should. She'll speak when silence is safer. Push when stillness is survival. And she doesn't yet understand that down here, boldness isn't admired. It's tested.

She has a way of challenging power that makes the ground shift. And in this room, the ground is already alive.

The Council's chamber is not what mortals would imagine. There's no judge perched above two tables. No gavel. No script of polite arguments exchanged in hushed tones. That kind of structure can't exist in Hell. It wouldn't last a second.

This place is older than that. Older than order.

The hall is vast, carved from what feels like the ribcage of the underworld itself—vaulted high above, the ceiling lost to shadow. No benches. No jurors. No comfort. Only jagged crescents of cold flame floating overhead, casting flickering light onto obsidian walls that drink sound whole. The floor beneath us doesn't just exist—it breathes. Slow and deep.

At the far end of the chamber, the thrones await.

Seven in total. None of them the same. None of them empty.

One is forged from bone, yellowed and cracked. Another from molten gold that still bubbles at the edges like it remembers fire. There's one woven from petrified roots and cinders, another etched with screaming faces frozen mid-agony. One throne flickers with shifting shadows, its form changing by the moment. The rest are carved from materials I wouldn't name even if I could.

They don't simply sit. They loom.

Figures cloaked in darkness—no faces, only hints of glowing orbs where eyes should be. The light from their forms pulses faintly, like stars hidden behind storm clouds. Ancient. Watching. Waiting.

Ophelia's voice is quiet but steady. "Julian... is this the Infernal Council?"

I expect panic. Instead it's the curiosity in her voice that unnerves me.

Before I can answer, the violet flames above shift—colder, more focused. One of the seven speaks, voice like iron dragged across cathedral stone. "Julian Duvain. Blood of the Old Line. Son of War."

Another follows, slower, deeper. "And the soulmatch."

The thrones remain still, but something glows beneath their hoods—no eyes, only pulsing light. Like stars flickering behind storm clouds.

"She who bears the mark. Chosen."

"Formerly Arden... now Duvain." The words land heavy. She doesn't flinch. Their voices wrap around us like a closing door. "You were summoned for a purpose."

Ophelia tilts her head. "What purpose?"

The silence isn't quiet. It's watching. Judging. The flames twitch. The floor tightens beneath our feet.

"You stand before the Concord. You will not question. You will answer."

"You are no longer mortal."

"The bond has chosen. The bond has sealed."

"You belong to this realm now."

"To linger too long in the mortal world is to unravel."

"You are Duvain. Claimed. Changed."

One last question hangs between them, weighted like a blade.

"Do you accept what you are?"

"I accept." She lifts her chin, not in defiance, but in pride.

The flames stir again. Violet curls rise from the floor, licking the air between us.

"Step forward," one says. "Let the fire show you why."

The Concord falls silent. They don't need to speak.

The flames rise, not from torches or wood, they build from the space itself. Breathing through cracks in the obsidian floor, coiling upward into a wall of flame. Towering. Alive.

It doesn't burn like mortal fire. It pulses—violet and gold, white at the center—like lightning caught mid-breath.

The flames twist, curling inward as if aware of her presence.

Ophelia steps forward. She pauses, not because she doubts but because she recognizes it.

The Concord speaks again, voices layered like pressure through stone. "This is the Truthfire. It answers only to fate. To truth. To what is."

I've stood before it. I've seen warriors fall apart in its light. I've seen kings weep at what it revealed. It doesn't show what you want to see. It shows what you've buried.

Ophelia steps into the center. The heat doesn't burn her—it welcomes her. The flames part, curling around her like a memory. And they begin to show her everything.

One of the figures leans forward, the molten gold of their throne glowing gently beneath them. "You have crossed the threshold. Now you must understand how to live beyond it."

Another voice joins, steady and calm. "There are laws that govern soulmatches. Not punishment. Protection."

"The bond must not stretch more than seven days apart. Distance weakens it. Weakness breaks it."

"You are to reside in this realm with him. This is not exile. It is realignment."

"You may reach across realms—speak, feel, listen—but only when allowed."

"You are not ornamental. You are instrumental."

"You will be summoned when the Loom calls for you. You will answer without resistance."

"And above all," the final voice softens, "you will not pretend to be what you were. You are Duvain. You are immortal. You are not returning. You are becoming."

The flames ripple, curl inward and show her the truth.

Melanie stands beneath studio lights too bright for comfort. Her makeup is flawless, her hair styled to perfection. But none of it matters—her eyes are wrong. Distant. Empty.

It's a memory, but we're watching it unfold like it's happening now.

A scene begins.She faces her co-star, voice trembling just enough to suggest emotion. "No one else ever mattered. Just you," she says, delivering the line like it's been drilled into her spine.

It lands with a thud.

"Cut," someone barks from behind the camera.

Harrison Drake stands, tight-lipped and frowning. He exhales through his nose. "Let's go again."

Another take. Same line. Same emptiness. "Cut."

Melanie's brows furrow as she steps forward, tension tightening her shoulders. "I don't know what else you want from me."

"I want you to feel it," Harrison replies, stepping into the light. "Not recite it."

She stares back at him insulted, but she doesn't argue. However, the silence that follows says enough.

The fire flickers.

Melanie walks down a pristine hallway, her heels clicking like a clock winding down. A studio rep waits for her. Cool. Distant. Not offering a seat.

"We're recasting," he says flatly.

Melanie stiffens. "You're joking."

"You're not right for the role."

"You said I was the lead," Melanie snaps, voice brittle.

The rep doesn't flinch, doesn't pause. "You were. Until you weren't."

The fire shifts.

She storms into her agent's office, the smile she perfected years ago faltering. Her headshot is gone from the wall. The space where it hung now just empty drywall.

"You're not serious," she says, eyes narrowing.

He shrugs, stepping around the desk to collect a few loose folders. "You're not marketable anymore."

"I'm Melanie Arden."

"That used to mean something," he replies, not unkindly. He extends a hand to shake.

She doesn't take it, instead she turns and slams the door as she leaves.

The fire coils again. Heat rising.

A red carpet premiere. Not her film, not her night. Still, she poses.

The photographers barely glance at her. Their attention flits past—onto newer faces, younger names. She adjusts her posture anyway. Puts on the smile.

By morning, the reviews flood in, each one more brutal than the last.

Cardboard couture
A mannequin in mascara
She emotes like a haunted mirror. Something's there, but it isn't human

Ophelia shifts beside me, the echo of those words hitting like a slow bruise. She watches as Melanie stares at her own reflection, glassy-eyed.

The flames tense, hardening to a point.

Melanie's apartment. Pristine marble counters and white, emotionless walls. A phone buzzes across the table.

Her breath catches when she picks it up, eyes wide. Photos flood the screen. Her and Harrison Drake. A shadowed hallway. His lips on her throat. Her hand tangled in his shirt.

The phone slips from her grip. Her expression doesn't change. She already knows what's coming.

The fire swells again.

Dominic. He's sitting on the couch, dress shirt still tucked, sleeves rolled, the knot of his tie loosened like he couldn't decide whether to breathe or fight.

He stares at the phone in his hand. The headlines glare back, merciless.

On-Set Chemistry Becomes Off-Set Scandal
Melanie Arden Caught in Affair With Director
Dominic Forsythe Betrayed by His Leading Lady

He doesn't say a word. Just sets the phone down on the table like it's suddenly too heavy.

Melanie steps into the room, still in heels, still wearing the perfect dress. She freezes when she sees him.

He stands slowly. "You slept with him."

She opens her mouth. "It wasn't—" she starts, but he cuts her off with a look that could silence fire, it holds no anger, but something far colder.

"You lied."

"It meant nothing," she says, crossing her arms, but her voice breaks at the edges.

He lets out a breathless laugh, there's no humor in it. "You mean nothing too," he says—and walks out.

Behind him, a glass shatters.

The fire twists.

Dominic stands in the hallway of a legal office, one hand holding his coat, the other clenched into a fist.

The door behind him opens. His lawyer steps out, eyes already tired. "She won't settle privately. She's pushing for court."

Dominic closes his eyes like he expected this. Like he hoped he'd be wrong. "I wanted to make it easy," he mutters. "No spectacle. No mess."

"She doesn't want clean," the lawyer replies. "She wants the spotlight back."

The fire tightens.

The courtroom. Dominic sits on one side, composed and worn.

Melanie sits across from him, draped in black silk like it's a funeral. Her expression is half-grief, half-performance. She watches the cameras more than she watches him.

Dominic doesn't look at her once.

The judge reviews documents. Pages shuffle.

Dominic's voice cuts through the stillness. "This marriage is over. I asked for nothing. Just space. I want it done."

Melanie leans into her lawyer. Her whisper is sharp enough to sting.

She doesn't look like someone fighting for love. She looks like someone who can't bear to lose—even if she already has.

Later that night, her social media floods with carefully curated grief.

There are betrayals deeper than infidelity. There are silences louder than screams.

Truth will come out. Until it does, I'll heal in private.

The comments are split. There are some that pity her, but most don't.

Dominic never responds. But a photo goes viral the next day. It's him, leaving the courthouse. His sunglasses are on, his suit is pristine clean, and he's carrying a new script under one arm.

The caption below the photo spreads like wildfire.

Dominic Forsythe Signs Onto New Project Days After Divorce Filing

Beneath it, more headlines pile up, bitter as ash.

Not Even Forsythe Wanted to Keep Her

Melanie Arden Alone and Out of Time

Affair, Abandonment, and the End of the Arden Reign

The last flame holds longer.

Melanie, alone in her apartment. The white marble gleams too bright. Her makeup, usually so perfect, is smudged. Her dress is wrinkled like she hasn't changed in days.

She stares at her phone, waiting for it to ring. It won't.

The city hums outside her window, oblivious. And she is surrounded by silence. The kind that is louder than applause ever was.

The fire pulls back.

Leaving only the echo.

The flames dim but don't die. They linger, flickering low like they're catching their breath.

Ophelia stands still, her arms at her sides, fists loose. Hollowed out in a different way. "She didn't fall," she says, her voice low. "She just got everything she asked for." There's no pity in it. "She never took from me. It was given to her," she adds, quieter now. "Cassius made sure of that."

She turns her head slightly toward the Concord. Her tone shifts—no longer dazed, but direct. "Is this what happens when the balance resets?"

The Concord answers in unison, their voices like distant bells tolling through stone. "This is not punishment. It is a correction."

"She fed on what was never hers to hold."

"And without you," another says, "her cup runs dry."

Ophelia exhales slowly, lifts her chin. "Show me him."

The fire ripples—colder this time.

The vision blurs, reforms.

Cassius.

Not in court, nor at some high-powered gala. In his house. The Arden house.

He paces the study floor, barefoot, dressed in a tailored shirt unbuttoned at the throat, sleeves rolled up, like he's been fighting his own skin. The once-pristine space is fractured—papers everywhere, books pulled from shelves, contracts torn at the corners. His desk is a ruin of ink and shattered glass.

He mutters to himself, sharp and fast, eyes flicking like they're chasing shadows.

"They said she'd rise. They said—" His voice breaks off, twisting into a growl. "She was chosen. She was promised."

He slams a fist against the desk. The frame of one of Melanie's old awards clatters to the floor, the glass splintering.

In the reflection of the window, he looks older. More withered than powerful. Like the mask of legacy has started to crack.

The house groans.

He storms toward a stack of legal files—some old, some fresh. Names scrawled in red ink. Melanie. Arden Holdings. Film options. Lawsuits pending.

On the floor beside the fireplace lies a scorched contract. The original deal. The infernal markings barely visible now, the blood-written seal faded.

He picks it up like it still might burn.

"You said she'd be eternal," he whispers. "You said she'd carry the line. That we'd rule."

The fire doesn't answer.

Phones ring in the distance. He doesn't pick them up.

Later, he's in a boardroom. Cassius sits at the end of a long black table, suit immaculate again—but his hands won't stop shaking. The executives around him glance at one another, nervous, careful.

"We can't protect your name anymore," one of them says, voice thin. "The investments—"

"I built this industry," Cassius snaps, slamming both palms on the table. "You owe me your careers!"

A pause. "No, Mr. Arden," another replies, folding her hands. "We owe you nothing. And frankly... you scare people now."

The room empties. Not one of them looks back.

He's back in his house again, alone. The rooms are too quiet. The halls are too long.

Cassius stands at the fireplace, fingers grazing the frame of an old family photo.

Melanie, young and beaming, front and center. Ophelia stands beside her. Arabella too. But they're out of focus—blurry, unimportant.

Only Melanie is clear. Only Melanie ever mattered.

He doesn't speak this time. Just stares into the embers.

And the fire closes.

"He chose her," she says. "He made his deal. Let him live with it."

No anger, no sadness. Just a quiet dismissal. She's done carrying that weight.

She turns to the thrones, her voice steady. "Can I see Rosalind? And Bella?"

A figure shifts. The one cloaked in ash and root leans forward, voice low.

"You must ask the flame."

Ophelia steps forward, like she knows exactly what to do, like she was born for this. The fire responds, curling inward, brighter, sharper.

"Show me Rosalind," she says. "Show me Bella."

The flames shift.

A kitchen appears, cast in gray morning light. Rain pecks gently at the windows. Rosalind sits at the table, shoulders tense, one hand wrapped around a chipped mug, the other pressed against her forehead. Bella paces the floor in wide circles, hair tied back in a messy knot, her voice strained.

"She wouldn't just disappear," Bella says. "She always checks in. Even when she's spiraling."

"She didn't disappear," Rosalind replies. Her tone is calm, but her eyes are raw. "She was taken. Or something worse."

"No one's seen her since Melanie's premiere of *The Sun Will Forget Us*," Bella murmurs. "No new posts. No calls. Nothing."

Rosalind looks down at the phone in front of her—Ophelia's. Cracked. Cold. Still locked.

"She didn't run," she says. "I don't care what they think."

The fire shifts again.

A bulletin board covered in flyers and maps. A timeline drawn in color-coded markers. Photos of Ophelia tacked between newspaper clippings and missing person posters.

Rosalind stands before it all, arms crossed, lips tight. A detective beside her flips through his notes.

"With all due respect," the officer says, "the public fallout with her sister, the premiere—it fits a certain emotional profile."

"She's not hiding," Rosalind snaps. "She's missing."

"She's humiliated—"

"She's stronger than that."

The detective doesn't press further.

The image shifts again.

Bella curled up on the couch, wrapped in one of Ophelia's old sweaters. Rosalind watches from the window, her reflection pale in the glass. She holds the phone like it might still ring.

But it doesn't.

The room is quiet.

And Ophelia just watches.

She doesn't cry. She doesn't speak. But I can feel it—how still she becomes. How much she feels. She watches them try to find her like someone peering into a version of the world she can't quite touch anymore.

Someone learning how to grieve what she hasn't even lost.

She turns toward me, eyes wide, shimmering with something between guilt and disbelief. "I thought I still had time."

"You do," one of the Concord says, voice quiet, but not unkind. "Not to undo the past. But to close what remains."

Another speaks, the molten gold of their throne glowing faintly beneath them. "You may return—for a short time."

"Not to stay," a different voice clarifies, older, clipped. "But to say what must be said."

"You are no longer mortal," comes the next, calm and precise. "But the ones who knew you deserve the truth. And you deserve peace."

Ophelia lifts her head, steadier now. "You want me to tell them."

"To say goodbye," the Concord confirms. "To leave the world as you found it—with clarity, not shadows."

"To speak your truth," says another, "before you begin weaving others."

The fire flickers again, but it doesn't show visions now. Only soft light, curling like smoke around her feet.

"You will not return to live among them," the voices continue, layered like wind through a hollow. "But you may return to remind them of who you were—and who you have become."

"And after?" she asks. "What happens next?"

"That's when you begin again," says the Concord. "As a Duvain. As soulmatch. As Weaver."

Her hand moves instinctively to her chest, fingers brushing the place the bond first took root.

No flames rise this time. Only stillness. But I feel it. The shift, the weight of fate settling into her shoulders—not as a burden, but as something real. Something hers.

And she nods, not for them, but for herself.

She presses a hand to her chest like she can feel time there, ticking differently beneath her skin. The threads. The bond. The world she used to know pulling tight against the one she stands in now.

"I'll go," she says, voice quiet. "But... does this mean I never see them again?"

One of the figures leans forward, the glow beneath their hood softening—just barely. Still cloaked in shadow, but not in cruelty.

"No," they say, and the word settles like a balm. "This bond is not exile. It is expansion."

Another speaks, voice like polished stone. "You are not lost to them. Only changed."

"They may still call to you," says a third, older than the others. "And when they do—you will hear them."

Ophelia turns to me, eyes wide, searching. "How?"

"I'll show you," I tell her. "The hallways. The paths that thread between worlds. If they reach for you with truth, you'll feel it. You'll know."

She exhales shakily. It's not relief, it's something deeper. Permission.

"So I won't have to cut them off?" she asks. "Bella. Rosalind. I can still—"

"If you choose," one of the Concord interrupts gently, "you may answer."

"The bond was never meant to sever," another adds. "It was meant to bind. To bring you to where you're most needed. To who you truly are."

"And to those who truly see you."

I watch her shoulders ease—not drop, not collapse—just settle. Like for the first time, she understands that becoming something new doesn't mean losing everything old.

She turns to me. The fire behind her fades, but the glow hasn't left her eyes.

There's no fear there. No doubt. Only resolve, she's whole.

"I need to do this," she says, not asking for permission—just making it known.

"I know," I say. And I do. Because this part—closing the door on the life that hurt her, choosing the one that's hers now—it has to be her choice. Her path. Her hands tying the last threads.

I step back, just enough to show her I trust her to go alone. But not alone forever.

"When you come back," I murmur, "we start everything."

A small smile ghosts across her face. It's soft, real.

"I'll be back," she promises.

One second she's there, the next, she's gone.

No sound, no spectacle. Just a shimmer in the air where she stood. The weight of her still lingering in the space between.

I close my eyes and hold it. Not her absence. Who she is becoming.
And if anyone dares to touch her—*I'll burn them out of every realm they try to hide in.*

Eighteen
Ophelia

I open my eyes to my apartment. It looks like it's been torn apart. Probably the police or Bella looking for me.

I've never realized how loved I am until I saw the way Bella and Rosalind were looking for me. They are heartbroken.

Although it may get worse for them, I know I need to see them, to explain as best as I can.

I look around the room for my phone and that's when I realizeBella has it. Figures. Because of course, on the one night I actually need it, I'm phoneless.

My gaze lands on the dusty old landline mounted on the wall. I've kept it for years—never turned it off, never really used it either. Just emergencies.

Well. This feels like one.

I grab the receiver and dial Bella's number from memory. She answers before the first ring even finishes.

"Hello? Who is this and why are you calling from Ophelia's landline?" Bella spurts out all at once.

I hear Rosalind in the background yelling, "Who is it? Is it Ophelia?"

"I don't know, mom, but I'm going to find out," Bella responds.

"Who is this?" Bella says, back in the receiver.

"It's me, Bella," I say.

"You're sick. Whoever you are, this isn't funny," she says.

"I know how it sounds," I say, trying to keep my voice steady. "But please, just listen—"

"You're calling from her apartment. Do you think that's *clever*? You think you're helping?" She's shaking. I can hear it. "We've been searching for *months*—"

"Bella." I cut in softly. "The last time we talked, you were crying on your bathroom floor. You'd just come home from work. A case with a kid named Marcus—you said his bruises looked like shadows someone was trying to hide."

The line goes silent.

"You said if you filed the wrong report, you'd lose him forever. That if you did nothing, you'd lose yourself."

Bella doesn't speak.

"I made you tea," I continue. "Chamomile with too much honey. You hate chamomile, but drank it anyway."

A broken sound leaves her throat.

"Ophelia?" she whispers.

"I'm here."

In the background, I hear Rosalind say, "Put it on speaker."

A click.

Rosalind's voice comes through next—low, clipped. "If this is really you, what did you give me for your first Christmas living with us?"

"My birth mother's music box," I say without missing a beat. "You said I didn't have to. That it was too much. I told you that's why I gave it to you."

Her breath catches audibly.

"I thought you were dead," she says. "Everyone did."

"I know."

Bella's voice jumps in, thick with disbelief. "Where the hell have you *been*?"

"I can't explain everything. Not yet. But I didn't choose to disappear. And I'm okay now. I'm safe."

"That's not enough," she snaps. "You don't get to vanish for months and call us from your apartment like nothing happened."

Months.

I know that. I was told that. But hearing it from Bella makes it feel real in a way the Infernal Council never did.

Because for me, it wasn't months. It felt like days. Maybe a week, if I stretch it. But not months.

"I'm not asking you to be okay with it. I just need you to understand that I didn't leave you. I had to go somewhere. And now I have to go back."

"What does that even mean?" Rosalind asks. "Back where?"

There's a beat of silence on my end. One that stretches long.

"To the place I belong," I say. "To who I'm supposed to be now."

"You're scaring me," Bella says. "Just come home."

"I *am* home," I whisper. "It's just... not where it used to be."

Neither of them speaks.

"Dominic's still looking for you," Bella says quietly, like she's trying to gauge my reaction.

I close my eyes.

"He filed missing person reports. Flew to cities you never even stepped foot in. Talked to your coworkers. Went to that field outside town every week. Just sat there and waited. Thought maybe you'd show up like a ghost."

My throat tightens.

"I want you to go to the field," I start. "All of you."

"I'm bringing Rhys," Bella says suddenly.

I freeze. My fingers curl tight around the base of the landline. The name lands like a slap across memory.

"Wait—what?" I breathe.

"Rhys. Rhys Westwood."

I blink. Like maybe that'll change the name she just said. "The investigative reporter?"

"Yes," she replies, softer now. "He's the reason the search for you never stopped. He kept digging when everyone else gave up. And... he and I are together now."

"You and Rhys," I echo. My voice is hollow. "Wow."

I close my eyes. It doesn't matter. Not right now.

"Okay. Bring him," I say. "Leave now."

She responds, low but certain. "We're on our way."

Before I leave, I need to start packing up my stuff and quick. I don't want to be away from Julian for even a night.

Ophelia: *Julian?*

Julian: *Yes, love? Are you ok?*

I sigh in relief, I know he's trying to give me this, but I also know how hard it is for him to be out of the loop.

Ophelia: *I'm fine, but I need your help. I want to clear out my apartment today. We can figure out what we're going to do with it later, but I want to get this part over with. I have to meet everyone soon.*

Julian: *Say no more. We're on it.*

Ophelia: *We?*

He doesn't answer because he doesn't need to. He pops in along with his brothers and cousins.

"Go do what you have to do, little artist," Julian murmurs, pulling me into his arms like he's memorizing the feel of me.

I press my face against his chest, breathing him in—ink and fire and something softer that only exists when he touches me.

He tips my chin up. His eyes are molten gold in the light.

"We'll handle things here," he says. "Just come back to me."

He kisses me—not rushed, not desperate. A promise sealed in fire and tenderness.

I close my eyes and slip through, landing behind a tall tree near the edge of the field. The grass is cool beneath my feet, the air still and charged with something I can't name.

I don't want to scare them, not after everything. But I need to see who's here first. Who believed me enough to come.

Bella stands at the center, arms crossed, eyes scanning the trees. Rosalind is beside her, tense but hopeful. Rhys hovers close, his hand brushing Bella's back. And Dominic... he's here too. His posture is tight, like he's bracing for impact.

Relief mixes with something sharper.

Something moves in the corner of my eye.

Two more figures storm across the field with the kind of fury that turns the air electric. Melanie and Cassius. And just like that, the moment shifts. What the hell are they doing here?

Cassius lifts his chin, like he's delivering a final, brilliant twist in some grand speech.

"You think that's the whole story?" he says, smugness curling through his tone. "You don't understand the magnitude of what I did." No one speaks. The silence crackles with unease. "I didn't just trade a feeling," he continues. "I corrected a mistake. A flaw in the bloodline."

Bella stares at him. "What are you even talking about?"

He glances her way, but his gaze slides past her. Fixed on something no one else can see.

"Calliope Arden was never meant to hold power like that," he says, voice almost reverent. "She wasn't obedient. She was erratic. Dangerous. And when I learned what she was—what she carried—"

He smiles. Too wide. Too pleased.

"I ended it."

The reaction is instant.

Rosalind lets out a tiny gasp, a hand flying to her mouth. Bella's breath catches. Melanie stiffens.

"You... killed her?" Rosalind asks, barely able to form the words.

"She was the Weaver," Cassius says flatly. "And she refused to give it to me. So I made sure it passed somewhere else."

"Passed what?" Bella snaps. "What are you even talking about?"

"The Loom," he says, like it should be obvious. "Fate. It needed guidance. And I found someone worthy. Someone who could use it with me."

He nods toward Melanie.

"Together, we could've shaped everything. Power. Legacy. Destiny."

Melanie's voice trembles. "You said it was just about building my career. About control over... image."

He doesn't even look at her.

"She was interfering," he says. "Ophelia was never supposed to be part of it. She threw off the balance. So I corrected that, too."

A long beat.

Rhys speaks. Calm. Cold. "You sound insane."

Cassius turns, but Rhys doesn't flinch.

Dominic shakes his head slowly. "You expect us to believe all this?" he says. "A Loom of fate? Magic threads? That you... what—rewrote the universe because your wife didn't listen to you?"

"You don't get it," Cassius says, louder now. "This was never about magic. It was about order. We had a chance to—"

"To what?" Dominic cuts in. "Destroy anyone who didn't fall in line?"

Melanie's expression is unreadable. But she moves again. Just one step further away from him.

Even Rosalind's voice hardens. "You sound delusional."

Cassius laughs. But it's brittle. Cracked.

Enough is enough.

I step through the veil and land in front of them—right in the clearing, where the air cracks like it's been holding its breath too long.

One second, I'm hidden. Next, I'm there.

Magic coils off me in waves, heat shimmering through the grass as the bond settles. Bella gasps. Rosalind lets out a cry, stumbling backward as her hand flies to her chest. Melanie screams like she's seen a ghost.

Cassius freezes, lips parting—but no sound comes.

I don't wait.

"He's not entirely wrong," I say, my voice cutting through the air like a blade.

Dominic spins to face me. His eyes are wide. Rhys lowers his camera, stunned.

"But he didn't know the kind of demon he made a deal with," I go on, stepping closer. "Or who I really am."

Cassius finds his voice, and it shakes. "You—You shouldn't even be here. You're not supposed to—"

I cut him off with a slow, deliberate motion, fingers curling around the collar of my shirt. I tug it down.

The mark glows faintly at my collarbone—elegant and brutal, the seal of the Duvain bloodline.

Julian's mark. My mark. Cassius staggers back like it burned him.

"I'm not yours," I say, voice steel-wrapped velvet. "Not your pawn. Not your sacrifice. And definitely not your redemption arc."

I step forward again. "I'm his soulmate. And that makes your deal null."

The air goes still. Cassius's mouth opens, but it takes him a moment to speak. When he does, it's not triumphant. It's unhinged.

"No. No, that's not how this works," he says, laughing suddenly—dry and sharp, a man grasping at pieces that no longer fit. "That's not the deal I made. That wasn't what was promised."

"You were promised power," I say coldly. "Not me."

He shakes his head, wild now. "She was mine. My blood. My legacy. You were just—"

"Wrong," I say flatly. "You were just wrong."

Melanie decides to speak. Her glare whips toward Cassius, her voice rising, brittle with frustration. "This wasn't how it was supposed to go. You promised she'd feel nothing. You said she already felt nothing! That it wouldn't even matter—"

She freezes. Everyone stares at her. My heart stops. "What did you say?" I ask, my voice low. Dangerous.

Melanie opens her mouth. Closes it again. Her lips press tight, but the damage is done.

"You said she already felt nothing." My breath shakes. "That's what he said. That's what he told Julian when he made the deal."

Panic tightens her face, her eyes wide with the sudden weight of what she's revealed.

"You were there," I whisper. "You knew."

"I didn't—"

"Don't," I snap. "Don't lie. You knew exactly what he was doing. You just stood there. Let him do it. Took what wasn't yours and played innocent."

"I thought it would help me," she blurts, voice cracking. "He said you didn't even want it! That you locked yourself away, that you didn't create anything—"

"And you believed him?" I laugh, but it's hollow. Bitter. "You believed the man who called his own daughter poison?"

There's a beat of silence.

Bella whistles, slow and stunned. "Well, shit," she mutters. "You really are a good actress, Mel."

Melanie doesn't respond. Can't. Her mouth twitches like she wants to argue, but nothing comes out. She looks away, ashamed. Cornered.

Dominic's voice is quiet, cutting through the tension. "She's not the better actress. She's just been given a better script."

And I finally see her for what she is. She's not a lost fool, she's just selfish enough to pretend that she was.

"You don't get to rewrite fate. You just became a footnote in it," I say, letting the words land.

Melanie doesn't answer. Her hands curl into fists at her sides. Her breath stutters like she's trying not to scream.

"I'm taking my place," I add. "As the Weaver. And at Julian's side."

She jerks like she's been slapped.

"No," she snaps. "No—it was supposed to be me. That power... my power. He promised it to me."

Her voice is raw now, cracking at the edges. Something in her finally breaking.

"You were never meant to have it," I say, my tone quiet but firm. "You didn't earn it. You stole it."

"You don't know what I gave up for this," she hisses. "What I sacrificed—"

"You sacrificed me," I whisper.

The silence afterward is deafening.

Dominic steps forward, voice strained. "Ophelia, please. Don't leave."

I look at him, and everything in me twists. His face is all the things he never got to say. But it's too late for that now.

"I have to," I say, softer this time.

"No," Bella says, shaking her head. "No, you don't. There's got to be a way to stop this."

"She's right," Rosalind says, her voice breaking. "You don't have to go."

"I'm not walking away," I say. "I'm walking toward who I really am."

The air rips open. Heat pulses through the clearing, a seam of pressure splitting the world in half. Julian steps through it, his coat trailing smoke, a scroll clenched in one hand.

He doesn't speak. Not right away. Just looks at me. At them. Down at the paper like it might bite.

Cassius smiles slowly, like rot blooming in the dark. "Right on time," he says.

Melanie narrows her eyes. "What is that?"

"The contract," Julian says.

His voice sounds like it's coming from somewhere far away. Like it hurts to say.

"The last clause is active," Julian says, looking at me like it might break him.

I don't breathe.

"Who?"

The scroll in Julian's hand blackens at the edges. The ink bleeds with a name that sears through the page like fate can't bear to hold it.

I look up, and my voice is barely heard. "Julian..."

His eyes meet mine.

And in them, I see it—grief. Grief like he's already lost me.

"I tried to stop it," he says, barely louder than a breath. "But the contract has to be fulfilled."

His gaze drops. His grip tightens. "It's not your soul I'm here for. It's hers."

Nineteen

JULIAN

My brothers and cousins are helping me empty Ophelia's apartment.

Which, in practice, means sorting her life into boxes while mercilessly roasting mine.

"She owns three different tea steepers," Seth says from the kitchen, holding one like it's a cursed artifact. "Are we dealing with a hot beverage cultist?"

"Who alphabetizes their spices?" Owen mutters, peering into the cabinet. "Is that cute or deeply concerning?"

"Depends," Adrian chimes in, rifling through a bathroom drawer. "If she has color-coded cotton balls, I'm calling a priest."

"That's rich coming from a guy who labels his sock drawer," Lucas throws back as he passes with a box.

Every drawer they open is just another excuse to dissect the woman I'm bonded to, like judgment is part of the packing process.

"Found some journals," Caleb calls, flipping one open like he's unveiling ancient secrets. "Passive-aggressive poems, a paper to-do list titled *End the Bloodline*, and a lot of scratched-out groceries. I think she was either writing a spell or hexing someone named Carol."

"Poor Carol," Damian mutters. "Never stood a chance."

The teasing is familiar—easy. The kind only brothers and cousins can pull off while packing up your life like it's both a comedy show and sacred rite. Damian opens the hall closet.

"Uh... guys?" His voice shifts—no sarcasm, just quiet urgency. "You need to see this."

We gather around. He pulls out a few canvases. Each one wrapped and tucked carefully behind coats and storage bins, like secrets sealed in linen.

Seth's the first to say it. "These are hers?"

We unwrap one slowly. The room stills. Color explodes across the them in sweeping strokes—riotous, delicate, deliberate. Emotion breathes beneath every layer of paint. Grief wrapped in shadow. Joy barely veiled in gold. It's the kind of beauty that looks like it bled to exist.

"Holy shit," Owen murmurs.

No one laughs or teases. They just... stare.

We keep unwrapping. Portraits. Dreams. Worlds she built inside herself and had nowhere to send. Each one more impossible than the last. They don't just depict feeling—they *are* feeling.

"She's not just talented," Lucas says.

"She's..." Adrian starts. "Unreal."

I crouch in front of a self-portrait. Her expression isn't posed. She looks straight out—unguarded, unafraid. Like she didn't paint it for anyone else. Just to remember who she was.

"She painted these before the deal," I say. "Before everything was taken."

They don't answer. They don't need to. The room already knows what she lost. And now—what she's about to take back.

Owen straightens with a grunt, stretching his back like he carried the emotional weight of every canvas. "So," he says. "Do we bubble-wrap her soul, or is that, like, a deluxe upgrade?"

Lucas runs a thumb along the edge of a box. "We're gonna need a new system. These can't go in a portal with your leftover mugs."

Adrian snaps his fingers. "Art gets its own stack. And if anyone lets a painting touch their protein powder box, I swear by all ten hells—"

"Nine," Seth interjects.

"Whatever. If it happens, I'll smite your ass with a rolled-up canvas."

Caleb reappears holding duct tape like it's a threat. "Who needs labels when you have fear?"

"We'll stack them by category," Damian says, already moving. "Books. Paintings. Weirdly aggressive tea accessories."

"And teleport each stack one at a time," Lucas adds. "Safer. Less chaos. Less chance of turning the Van Gogh of the underworld into a pile of abstract firewood."

I nod, still beside the self-portrait. "She'd hate that. We do it right."

"Also," Seth says, hefting a heavy box, "remind me to apologize when she realizes we've read her journal entries about 'severing the mortal coil through bad spaghetti.'"

"She's definitely cursing Carol," Caleb mutters.

"And the pasta."

We start stacking again—but it's not the same kind of silence as before. This one hums with meaning. It's filled with effort, with care. The occasional grunt of lifting, the low thrum of teleportation runes—little sounds that say, *we're bringing her home.*

This isn't just about moving her things. It's about carrying the pieces of her she lost—and making sure she gets every single one back.

Once everything is in place, we start sorting out who's taking what. I claim the paintings. There's a spare room in my house—empty, quiet and untouched. I could make it into something just for her. Maybe we'll finish it before she comes back.

It feels like a small promise.

Soft embers catch in the air—not a flame, not fire, but the familiar hiss of infernal magic slipping between realms.

A contract. My spine locks. I know that sound. I know what it means.

Someone's deal has come due.

But it can't be mine. I don't have any open contracts. Not anymore. And the only one I've been tracking closely is Cassius Arden's—but his isn't ready. Not yet.

I don't move. Not until the parchment folds out of nothing and drops directly into my hands.

The parchment is ice against my skin. The room stills as I look down.

Payment Due.

My heart doesn't just stop—it drops out of rhythm entirely. This isn't possible. It shouldn't exist.

This should've been voided. The second our bond was sealed, any previous claim should've unraveled. That's law. That's structure. That's the one constant in all this chaos.

I swallow and hold out the contract. No one speaks right away. They just read. One by one.

Seth is the first to break the silence. "That can't be real."

"It's not just real," Caleb mutters, eyes narrowing, "it's current. That flame mark means it's already in motion."

"But it shouldn't exist," Lucas says, sharper now. "You're bonded. That's a full override. Nothing's supposed to touch her now—not legally, not magically."

"There must be a mistake," Adrian says. "Or a manipulation. Something someone slipped past the system."

Damian folds his arms. "Unless this wasn't a normal deal. Or it was set so deep that even the bond didn't kill it."

"No," I say quietly. "Even Echo Cases dissolve once a soul is claimed. That's the whole point."

"But it didn't," Seth says, looking at me. "So what does that mean?"

It means I'm done standing here.

"I'm going to her," I say, already pulling my magic into my hands. "Now."

"You think she's in danger?" Owen asks.

"I don't know what this is," I answer, gaze still locked on the name seared into the parchment, "but I'm not waiting for a second notice."

The air tears open around me, heat pressing at my back as I step through the portal. Smoke trails behind my coat, the contract still gripped in my hand, burning faintly at the edges like it knows what it's about to do.

I glance down at the scroll, expecting confirmation of what I already feared.

Her name is slashed through in thick, final ink.

And beneath it—another. One that shouldn't be here. One that rewrites everything.

My chest goes tight. My heart sinks, hard and sudden, like it's dropped straight through me. This isn't possible. There are no names left in this bloodline. No terms active. No reason for the contract to shift. Except it has. And now it's binding.

I don't speak right away.

The others are already watching—Ophelia, her family, Cassius with that slow-spreading smirk like he's known something all along.

"Right on time," Cassius says, teeth flashing through the grin.

"What is that?" Melanie asks, folding her arms.

"The contract," I say, my voice low. Tired. "The last clause is active."

Ophelia's eyes are on me now. Searching. Already knowing.

"Who?" she asks, and it's not just a question—it's a prayer.

"Julian..." she says, soft—like she already knows.

Our eyes meet, and it hits me all over again. The contract has chosen. And no matter how hard I tried, no matter how many loopholes I chased or seals I reinforced, it was never going to let go. Not without blood.

"I tried to stop it," I say, and the words barely make it past my throat. "But the contract has to be fulfilled."

I can't look at her anymore. My gaze drops, my grip tightening around the scroll as if I could crush the outcome just by willing it.

"It's not your soul I'm here for," I say, and my voice barely holds. "It's hers."

Ophelia steps forward before anyone else moves. She takes the scroll from my hand, too calm at first—like denial still shields her from what she's about to see. But the moment her fingers touch the parchment, it pulses with heat. Magic recognizes her, even as the contract tries to resist her grip.

She tears it open anyway.

The scroll unfurls in her hands with a crackle, ink bleeding across the page like it's trying to rewrite itself. Cassius's name burns first—sharp, bold, final. Next is hers. Written in blood.

She exhales once—too sharp, too fast.

ere it is. A single, brutal slash through her name.

And beneath it, glowing freshly, impossibly, irrevocably.

Arabella Arden.

Her breath catches. She doesn't speak at first, just stares. Her hands start to shake. Her throat works around words that won't come out. When she finally does speak, it's thin and cracking.

"No." She blinks, like the page might change if she just looks again. "No, that's wrong. That's not— That's not supposed to—"

She presses her palm to the bloodprint, trying to rub it away like it'll come off. Like it's just ink and not a signature carved into the bones of Hell.

"Julian," she says, her voice rising now, breaking apart. "This was mine. The deal was mine. How is this—how is this happening?"

I don't have an answer. Not one that would matter. The contract has chosen. It's binding.

And she knows it.

Her chest heaves. Panic spreads in her eyes like wildfire—fast, feral, uncontrollable.

"I was supposed to pay for it," she says, more to herself than to me. "Not her. Not her. I was the one who made the choice—"

The scroll curls in her grip as magic settles into place, final and absolute. Her hands drop. Her body doesn't collapse, but something in her expression does.

I reach out to Owen. Maybe he is able to get more information from the council.

Julian: *Do you know anything?*

Owen: *Yeah. She was added to the list. Aunt Selene says there's no such thing as loopholes. So she went to the archives and looked to see how Arabella was added to the contract.*

He sends me a telepathic link to what she found. All of this information. It's all coming to light.

"How could this happen?" Ophelia begs me for an answer. Unfortunately, now I have one to give her.

She looks at me like I'm the only one who can make this make sense. A telepathic surge hits me—raw and fast. It's the trail she found, the pieces she didn't know she was collecting until now. Headlines. Reports. Data. Rhys's article. The awards. The case. Bella. It's all there. And as I sift through it, the truth clicks into place with brutal precision.

I look around the circle—at the faces waiting for me to fix this, to lie maybe, to say there's still a way out.

"There was no loophole," I say quietly, my voice low but heavy. "There never was. The deal was simple," I continue, my eyes locking with Ophelia's. "The most famous would be taken. That was the clause. That was the price. At the time, it was you."

She stiffens.

"Even after you stopped painting for yourself—even doing the ghost commissions—you were still everywhere. Your name carried weight. Your work kept you at the top, whether you wanted it to or not. But you disappeared. You vanished from the scene. You stopped producing. You stayed in Hell for too long."

She swallows hard, but doesn't interrupt.

"In your absence," I say, turning slightly to the others now, "your name faded. You lost your clients. You dropped out of the public eye. And while all of that was happening..." I glance toward Bella, my chest tightening. "Arabella cracked the trafficking case."

Cassius's jaw ticks.

"She exposed something massive. Rhys wrote the article. It went viral. Her face—her name—was everywhere. She won awards. Gave speeches. Became internet famous overnight."

Ophelia's lips part in horror. "No..."

"She became the most famous Arden," I say. "And when Melanie fell, the deal didn't dissolve. It adjusted. It took the next in line."

I glance down at the scroll in her hands. The blood signature still burns there. A record, unchangeable and absolute.

"It had to be fulfilled. And since I spared you..." I force the words out. "Someone had to take your place."

The silence that follows isn't empty. It's thick. Devastating.

Ophelia turns to Bella—who hasn't spoken, hasn't moved, frozen in disbelief. And for a long moment, no one knows what to say.

Ophelia is already at Bella's side, her fingers digging into her sister's arms like she can anchor her to the world. "There has to be something we can do," she says. "Say there's something. Please."

I want to. I want to tear the sky open and rewrite the laws myself. But I've already read the contract. Already seen the ink shift. Already felt the pull of Hell binding itself around a new name.

And Bella knows.

She's not asking questions. She's just... still. Her expression isn't blank, it's resigned. A quiet kind of understanding that looks far too much like peace.

"I'll go," she says.

Ophelia recoils. "No. Don't say that."

Bella meets my gaze. "It's my name on the scroll. It's my signature in blood. It doesn't matter how it got here, or if I asked for it. It's me."

"No, it's not," Rosalind snaps. "It was never supposed to be."

"It's always someone," Bella says, voice soft. "And I'd rather it be me than—"

"No," Rhys says, stepping forward like the word costs him. "Don't you dare finish that sentence."

Bella turns to him, and her composure cracks, just a little.

"I was going to ask you to marry me," Rhys says. "I had the ring. I had the words. You don't get to just give yourself up."

Her eyes flood with tears, but she blinks them back. "Rhys, I love you. But this isn't a choice. It's already written."

Ophelia shakes her head, frantic. "We rewrite it."

"I'm going to fix this," I say, already feeling the beginning of a plan start to form in the back of my mind. "There's a way to break it. There has to be."

"Do it, demon," Rhys says, stomping towards me.

"Stop! This isn't his fault, Rhys," Ophelia says.

Rhys looks at Ophelia like he doesn't even recognize her.

"You left," he says. No rage yet—just the tremor in his voice. "You disappeared. No call. No note. Just gone."

"I didn't mean—"

"You didn't *mean*?" His voice spikes. "You didn't *mean* to vanish while Bella cried herself to sleep every night? While I had to lie to her, day after day, saying you'd come back? You didn't *mean* to shatter her entire world just so you could run off and play immortal soulmate with a demon?"

Ophelia flinches. "Rhys, that's not what happened—"

"Oh, isn't it?" he snaps, eyes flashing. "You always find a way to make yourself the victim. But this time, *this time*, someone else is paying the price for your absence."

He steps closer, and she doesn't back away. She just stands there, swallowing down whatever's clawing its way up her throat.

"You should've stayed gone," Rhys says, his voice quieter now, but shaking with fury. "At least she'd still have a future."

Ophelia's breath hitches. "I never wanted this."

"No," he says. "You just made it inevitable."

She stares at him, stunned silent, her pulse pounding in her ears. Her fingers twitch at her sides like she's searching for something to hold onto—anything to anchor herself.

Rhys's voice drops lower. "And for the record? I hope you look at that contract every single day. I hope you remember what it cost to keep your name off it." He pauses, breathes once. His next words are ice. "I wish it was his name on that scroll instead."

"I wish it was too," I say quietly—flat, without heat. "Because if it were, you wouldn't be talking right now." Rhys freezes. "You think you're angry?" my eyes narrow, just a sliver of the fury I keep buried leaking through. "You don't know what it means to lose someone piece by piece and not be allowed to fall apart."

I look at Ophelia—not at Rhys. My voice softens, but only for her. "You think pain gives you a license to destroy her? You don't get to break the people she loves just because you're hurting."

Rhys says nothing.

"She's already lost everything once. She doesn't owe you her grief just because it's more convenient than yours. But..." I say, almost to myself. "You just gave me an idea."

I lean in and kiss Ophelia.

She doesn't realize it, but I'm already letting go. This isn't a promise—it's a farewell dressed in silence. She kisses me like we still have time, unaware the moment is already slipping through my fingers.

The scroll burns hotter in my grip, the blood ink blistering the air around it.

"I refuse the contract!" I shout to Hell itself.

"What are you doing?" Ophelia's voice cuts through the haze, panicked, rising. She grabs my arm, eyes wide. "What's happening?"

I can't answer. The ground splits, heat surges beneath our feet, but it's not fire—it's pressure. Old magic. A summons that no one made, but someone answered.

From the scorched line in the earth, shadows begin to rise. The Infernal Council has come. And the world holds its breath.

Ophelia's eyes are wide, terrified as she repeats herself. "What are you doing? What's happening?"

I don't answer yet. Not until the Council speaks, voices fused into one that echoes in the marrow of my bones. "You reject the contract?"

I stare at the scroll in my hand—Bella's name carved into it like it was always meant to be there. My fist tightens around it until the paper begins to burn.

"I know the rules," I say, lifting my head.But I can take her place."

"No," Ophelia breathes. "No, don't do this. Don't you dare—"

"I have to." I look at her like it's the last time I'll ever get to. I need to memorize her while I still have the chance.

"Julian, please," she chokes, stumbling forward. "Don't go. We can find another way. There has to be something—"

"There isn't." My voice is raw now, but I keep it steady. "Deals have no loopholes. You know that."

The Council speaks, voices like stone grinding against fate. "Are you certain?"

I don't look away from her. Not even for them. "I am."

Cassius staggers back like he's seen death itself. Melanie doesn't move. Her expression is unreadable.

I glance at them only once. "You lose."

The air splits with a thundercrack as infernal arms—burning, skeletal, merciless—erupt from the earth. They wrap around me, binding tight, dragging me backward.

Ophelia screams. "Julian!"

She runs forward, reaching for me. But she can't touch me—her hands pass through ash and flame. I'm already being pulled under.

"Don't take him," she sobs. "Take me. Please—take me instead—"

I shake my head. "No. You survived for too long to be taken now."

"I love you," she cries.

"Across lifetimes. Through every version of you. In every form of me," I say, and I let it be the last thing she hears.

The heat swallows the light. The sky fractures above me, and the last thing I hear isn't the Council, or the tearing earth. It's her voice—shaking, shattering, screaming my name into the dark.

But I'm gone.

And this time, I don't get to come back.

Twenty
Ophelia

I don't even realize I'm shaking until I round on Rhys again.

"Are you happy now?!" My voice cracks as I shove the words in his face. "You got what you wanted. He's gone. So go ahead—celebrate."

His expression twists, but he doesn't speak.

"Say something!" I scream. "Say it was worth it. Say you'd choose her again even knowing what it would cost—because you did."

I take a step closer, shaking, unhinged, breaking apart. "You hated Julian so much you couldn't even see what he was trying to save."

Bella steps between us, her eyes wide and glassy. "Ophelia, please," she says, voice gentle but urgent. "Don't do this. It's not Rhys' fault."

I laugh. It's hollow. "Isn't it? Because when I said it wasn't Julian's fault, he tore me apart. But for you? He stands there and says nothing."

I look between them, bitterness flooding every vein.

"Well, if being silent is enough to be spared, let me make this easy." I pull away from all of them. "I'll be good. I'll be quiet. I'll disappear again—just like before."

And before anyone can stop me, I close my eyes. If I still have anything left—if there's even a shred of power still mine—I use it.

I vanish. When I reappear in my apartment, the first thing I see are the boxes lined up in perfect rows, ready to be taken to Julian's. Ready to start a new life.

Except there's no one to bring them to now. No Julian. No bond. Just the echo of what should've been.

I stagger a step forward and stop cold. My mark is silent. Empty.

It used to thrum—quiet, constant, like a heartbeat beneath my skin. Now... nothing.

The pain hits so fast, so violently, I don't have time to scream.

It's not just gone. It's ripped out. Like something ancient and burning has been torn from the deepest part of me, taking every breath with it. My knees hit the ground. My hands clutch at my chest. I press my hand over it, like I can force it to come back. Like maybe if I just stand still, he'll come through the door and tell me it was all a mistake.

But he doesn't. He traded everything for me to have my family. And now he's gone.

The sob hits before I can stop it, sharp and shaking and loud in the quiet space. I sink to the floor between the boxes—neatly stacked memories of a future that never had a chance. I try to breathe, but my chest won't expand. My lungs won't work. Everything inside me feels like it's breaking.

I curl in on myself and cry.

Because I'm alone, I'm still here. Because the one person who saw me—really saw me—took my place in hell.

And left me behind.

I do the only thing I know how to do. I call Owen.

Ophelia: *Owen. Please... I need you.*

He appears in a blink, the scent of smoke and shadow trailing behind him. His eyes widen when he sees me, crumpled on the floor, surrounded by the boxes that were meant to be the start of my new life, my happy life.

He crosses the room quickly, kneeling beside me.

"I'm here," he says gently, wrapping his arms around me. "I've got you."

I press my face into his shoulder, barely holding together.

"Have you seen him? Is he okay?"

Owen hesitates. "I have. He's... alive."

"But?" I step closer. "There's something you're not saying. What is it?"

He looks away, his voice lower now. "No one's ever done what he did. Not like that. No loophole. No trick. Just... offered himself. Completely."

I feel my pulse stutter. "What does that mean?"

"It means he gave up more than his life." Owen's voice softens, like the truth might hurt less that way. "He gave up his soul. And when that happens, the connection—whatever bound you two—" He swallows. "It breaks. Or maybe... it burns out. You still feel it, because you loved him. Still do. But he—"

He shakes his head. "He's not yours anymore, Ophelia. Because he's not fully... him. Not in the way you knew."

"So I'm still his... but he's not mine."

"Not really," he says. "Not the way he was."

I stare at him, waiting—needing more than that.

"Julian gave up his demonhood when he gave up his soul. That's the cost," Owen continues. "He has a soul now—fully, painfully human. No magic. No power. No way to shift or command or defend himself."

My breath catches.

"He's stuck in Hell," Owen says, quieter now. "Powerless. And because he's no longer part of their system, the other demons see him as broken. Worse. They see him as prey."

I shake my head, barely able to speak. "But he still remembers me?"

"Yes," Owen says, quickly. "He still loves you. That didn't change. But he can't feel you through the bond anymore. He thinks of you constantly—he just doesn't know if you'll ever be able to reach each other again."

He pauses. "And he's alone, Ophelia. Really alone. Trapped in a place that was once his to control. And now... now he's something the rest of Hell would love to tear apart."

Owen doesn't wait for a response. He steps back, eyes shadowed with something that looks too much like mourning. He vanishes.

And I'm still here—sitting in the ruins of a life I barely got back.

The boxes Julian packed are still lined against the walls, untouched.

I walk to the one marked paintings, press my hand against it, and feel nothing. No spark. No echo. No warmth through the mark on my chest.

It's still there. But he isn't.

I sink to the floor, knees hitting wood, fingers curling into the edge of the box like it might hold me together.

I break. No noise. No screams. Just the quiet collapse of someone who loved too much and still lost everything.

I don't know how long it's been.

Days blur into nights, and nights stretch into something that doesn't feel like time at all. Maybe it's been a week. Maybe it's been a month. Or maybe I died the second he was dragged beneath the earth and no one bothered to tell me.

I don't care anymore. I've barely eaten. I don't sleep. I stare at the wall until the light changes. Sometimes I cry, sometimes I can't, sometimes I think the silence will finally swallow me whole. I wish it would.

He's gone.

And not just gone—not the kind where someone might come back. Not the kind that leaves a door open. He gave up everything, and the world just... moved on. Like he never existed. Like I imagined it all.

I tried to call Owen. The others, anyone. I begged—whispered their names through the bond, over and over like a prayer.

No one answered. They can't hear me anymore. And I can't feel him.

My mark is still there—barely. A faint shimmer under my skin, like a burn that never healed right. It used to pulse. It used to sing. Now it just... hums. Faint. Hollow. Like a memory trying not to fade.

I remember what the council said. Their voices echo every day. The longer you're apart, the weaker the bond becomes. Until one day, there is nothing left at all.

I wake up sometimes with my hand clutching my chest. Right over where the mark used to burn. Like I can hold onto it the same way I held onto him.

But it's slipping. So am I.

My apartment is still filled with boxes. Lined up just like he left them. Every time I look at them it feels like a joke. Like the universe gift-wrapped his absence just so I could open it again and again.

I talk to him sometimes. I tell him how sorry I am. How I would've taken the deal if I'd known. How this kind of loneliness doesn't feel like heartbreak—it feels like torture. Like something inside me is decaying one memory at a time.

And every day I wonder if he regrets it. If he remembers me at all. If the part of him that loved me is buried somewhere deep in Hell, screaming to come back.

Because I am. And no one is listening.

I don't hear the knock. Or maybe I do, and I just don't care. The door creaks open, soft and slow, and I brace for someone I don't want to see—someone here to tell me to eat, to sleep, to pull myself together.

But the voice is softer than I expected. Familiar in a way that disarms me. "Ophelia," Rosalind says gently. "It's just me."

I don't turn around. I'm still curled in the corner of my room, knees pulled to my chest.

I hear her walk in, her heels clicking once against the floor before she slips them off without a word. She doesn't hover, doesn't ask for permission. She just sits beside me, silent, until it becomes something I can breathe in.

"You weren't answering," she finally says. "And I figured... if there was ever a time you shouldn't be alone, it's now."

I want to speak, but my throat burns. I don't even know what I'd say. So I just whisper the only truth I have left. "I can't feel him anymore."

Rosalind doesn't flinch, she doesn't try to fix it. She lays her hand over mine, warm and solid. "I know."

It's those two words that undo me. "I talk to him," I admit, the words breaking apart in my mouth. "I tell him I'm sorry. That I would've done anything if I'd known. I don't even know if he'd want to hear it. I just—"

My voice catches. "I just want him back."

Rosalind nods, still so quiet. There's no pity in her face. Just grief. Real, quiet, maternal grief—for the daughter she chose, and the man who gave himself up so that daughter could live.

"I know what it's like to lose someone you love," she says softly. "And I wish I could say it gets easier. But it doesn't. It just... changes."

She squeezes my hand. "You're not selfish for hurting. You're not weak for breaking. And you're not alone."

I lean my head against her shoulder. My breath shakes, my body aches in places grief has taken root. "I don't know how to keep going."

"Don't try to yet," she whispers. "Just let yourself feel this. Let it hurt. Let it be messy. I'll sit with you through every second of it."

And I do.

I cry until I can't anymore. Until the pain becomes too heavy for tears and all that's left is the sound of breathing, hers and mine.

"Rosalind said it's been four months," he says gently. "That you haven't spoken. Or eaten."

Four months. So that's how long it's been. Time stopped mattering, days blended together and folded in on themselves until I forgot how to tell them apart.

I don't respond. I haven't in weeks. Maybe longer.

He steps inside, carefully. Like the air might shatter if he moves too fast.

I'm still in the same spot. The corner of the room. Back against the wall, knees hugged to my chest. The boxes around me are untouched, still lined up like soldiers waiting to be dismissed from a war that never ended.

Dominic lowers himself to a crouch. "You don't have to talk," he says. "I'll talk." And he does.

He talks about Melanie. About regret, guilt, how he's not sure what he's mourning anymore—his wife, his marriage, or the man he used to be.

I barely register the words. They drift past me like smoke. Until he says it. "He didn't trade his soul so you could disappear too."

That cuts through everything. I look up at him for the first time in months. Really look. And the moment our eyes meet, I know he sees it. What's left of me... isn't.

He stands slowly, and his voice drops. "I don't know how to fix this. But I want to try. For him. For you."

My voice is barely a whisper. "There's nothing left to fix."

He doesn't argue. He just leaves. And I don't stop him. Because he's right. Julian gave up everything so I could live. And all I've done is vanish.

Four months since I watched him vanish into the earth. Two since I stopped pretending I could survive it.

When the knock comes, I don't move. The door creaks open, followed by soft footsteps and a sharp gasp that barely registers.

"Ophelia?" Bella's voice wavers like it's already breaking.

I'm on the bathroom floor. The tub behind me is stained with blood from last night—maybe it was this morning. I've lost track. Of everything. The lights are off. Curtains closed.

I don't look human. I haven't in weeks. My skin is ash-gray. Lips cracked. There are deep bruises on my arms from where I've clawed at myself trying to feel something. My ribs show. My hair is matted. I smell like sweat and iron.

My collarbone—the mark—has been torn open more than once. I've tried everything to wake it up. Burned it. Carved around it. Bled for it. Nothing worked. It just sits there, cold and faded, like a tombstone etched into my skin.

"Dominic—get in here," Bella calls, and her voice breaks mid-word.

He enters with Rosalind and Rhys on his heels. The sound of Bella sobbing is the only thing louder than the silence I've lived in.

"Jesus fucking Christ," Dominic mutters, dropping to his knees. "What the hell did you do to yourself?"

I lift my gaze slowly. My eyes are hollow. My voice is a whisper. "Tried to make it stop."

"Stop what?" Rhys demands, but it's not anger—it's desperation.

I hold up my hands. My wrists. My thighs. My chest. The scabs. The burns. The empty bottles of pills scattered on the floor. "Everything."

"Ophelia, no." Rosalind drops beside me, cradling my face in her hands. "You didn't—please tell me you didn't—"

"I did," I breathe. "And I failed."

"Why?" Bella chokes out. "Why would you—"

"Because I don't want to be here without him," I snap, suddenly too loud, too sharp. "I don't want to breathe if he's not breathing. I don't want to wake up. I want the pain to end."

Rhys has tears in his eyes. Dominic turns away. Rosalind can't stop whispering "I'm here, I'm here," like maybe if she says it enough, I'll believe it.

Bella falls to her knees beside me. Her hands hover over mine like she's afraid to touch me—afraid I'll disappear.

Dominic pulls out his phone, voice low but urgent. "We're getting you help. Real help. I'm not losing you too."

"No." My voice is raw, but steady.

Bella steps forward, eyes shining. "Ophelia, please—"

"No help." I back away, hands trembling. "Nothing."

"You need—"

"I need him!" I scream, and the sound cracks the silence open like glass under pressure.

Rhys opens his mouth to speak, but I cut him off too. "You want to patch me up? Put me in some white room with humming lights and strangers who don't know his name? That's not healing. That's pretending. And I won't fucking do it."

Bella's crying again. Silent tears. Her hands are still hovering.

"I'm not sick. I'm grieving." My voice cracks, but I don't look away. "I lost my soulmate. I lost myself. I don't want to be fixed. I want to disappear."

Rosalind's eyes fill, but she doesn't speak. None of them do. Because now they see it—the depth of it. The void I've become. I'm not broken, I'm not sad, I'm not even depressed.

I'm gone. And I have no intention of coming back.

Find the summoning. The words echo again, but they're not spoken. Not really. Just a pulse in the back of my mind—louder now, as if the silence made room for it.

"I don't know where it is," I whisper, my voice more breath than sound. "I don't know how."

The journals. It's not a voice, not in the traditional sense. But it answers. Soft. Steady. Like something ancient and patient that's been watching me unravel, waiting for this exact moment.

My limbs scream when I move. Every part of me aches with the weight of nothing. But I push off the floor, staggering to my feet, half-hoping I collapse before I can go any farther.

But I don't.

I cross the room, dragging myself toward the stacks of boxes still lined up by the front door. I never unpacked them. Couldn't bear to.

Now, I tear them open like they're filled with oxygen.

Not this one.

Not that one.

I dig through old canvases, shattered frames, journals stained with tears and paint and grief.

My hands land on something strange. A book I don't recognize. It's old. Bound in something that isn't quite leather. It's not mine. It's in a language I know I can't read, but yet I can. The book isn't just old—it buzzes under my skin.

I flip through its pages, expecting nonsense. Gibberish. A metaphorical scream in ink. But it isn't that. It's a manual.

Summoning a Demon Without Knowing Their Name.

My heart skips. The letters feel alive on the page, like they're watching me as I read.

The summoner must still provide an offering – blood, a personal sacrifice, or a deep emotional cost.

Instead of calling a specific demon, they invoke any entity willing to answer.

The summoning phrase must be general yet binding: "I call to the ones who walk between shadow and flame. Let one who would bargain step forth."

My breath hitches.

No name. No control. Just... whoever hears me. And they will come. Something always comes.

The strongest, most interested demon will respond – but the summoner has no control over who appears.

A low-level demon may answer and demand a steep price.

A powerful demon may be insulted and punish the summoner for wasting their time.

Some demons will not bargain fairly and will take more than what was intended.

A chill spreads through my chest. Julian would never answer something like this. Not unless fate forced him to.

And it did.

He wasn't supposed to get that call. But he did. Because the bond tugged the thread. Because fate doesn't ask permission.

It brought us together when it shouldn't have. And tore us apart the same way.

I may hold the Loom now. But fate has always known how to pull its own strings.

Before I can turn the page, it flips on its own.

Summoning a Specific Demon.

The words below it aren't just instructions—they're obsession. Precision etched in ritual and consequence.

Know the Demon's True Name.

Provide a worthy offering—blood, memory, soul.

Speak the invocation with intent: "By oath and fire, by shadow and will, I call upon [Name]. Step forth and heed this summons."

Draw the circle. Blood, ash, chalk—whatever binds the edges of power.

My pulse roars in my ears.

I know I'm calling someone's name.

I've bled for him. I've died in pieces for him. And if I have to offer what's left of me to bring him back, I will.

I wipe my nose on the sleeve of the oversized sweater I haven't taken off in days—weeks, maybe. The journal lies open on the floor beside me, the pages warped and stained with something that might be blood, or just the echo of everything I've lost.

Summoning a demon isn't something you do casually. It's not lighting candles and whispering into the dark. It's sacrifice, precision, and intent. And I have all three.

I grab a piece of chalk from one of the old moving boxes, the kind I used to mark canvas edges. It feels wrong to use it like this—but everything about this feels wrong. That's the point.

I clear a space in the middle of the floor and begin to draw. The circle is messy at first, but my hand steadies with each stroke. Symbols, runes, the binding points—it all comes together like muscle memory I shouldn't have. Like something buried inside me finally waking up.

I light the candles—each one flickering with a life of its own.

The blade trembles in my grip as I drag it across my skin. Blood wells and drips onto the floor, slow and deliberate. And now the invocation. The book lies open beside me, the words ready.

"By oath and fire, by shadow and will, I call upon Owen Duvain. Step forth and heed this summons."

The air tightens. The blood begins to sizzle. And the summoning circle pulses, like a heartbeat not entirely my own.

Owen doesn't answer right away.

He just stares. Not at the circle, not at the blood smeared across the floor—but at me. And something in his expression fractures. "Gods, Ophelia," he says quietly. "What happened to you?"

I don't respond.

"You're... different. You look like you haven't slept in weeks. Your face, your body—there's no light in you anymore." His voice dips, low and raw. "You look like someone who already died and forgot to lie down."

I force myself to stay standing, even though every word cuts like glass. "I'm here to make a deal," I say, steadier than I feel.

"How did you even know how to summon me?" he asks, ignoring everything else.

"I found a journal," I say, hesitating just enough for it to matter.

"What journal?" he asks, brow furrowing.

"I don't know whose it was," I say. "It wasn't mine. It was in one of the boxes by the door."

"Who told you to look there?" he asks, stepping closer, tension drawing his shoulders tight.

My pulse stutters. "...A voice."

His gaze narrows. "What voice?"

"I don't know. I just heard it. It told me to check the journals." My arms tighten around my middle like I'm trying to hold something in. "It felt... familiar. Like someone I should trust."

Owen goes still. The kind of stillness that feels unnatural—like something is calculating behind his eyes. His jaw clenches. "Aunt Selene."

My mouth goes dry. My body sways, like the floor tilts beneath me. "What?"

"She's done this before," he mutters. "Shown up when she shouldn't be able to. Whispers in the cracks between things. She doesn't meddle unless she sees something the rest of us can't."

"So you believe me?"

He nods, wary now. "I believe something wanted you to find that book. And if Selene had a hand in it... this isn't just grief. It's fate. And that terrifies me."

"Good," I whisper. "Because I'm done being scared alone."

His expression hardens. "And what do you think happens next, Ophelia? You trade whatever's left of yourself and hope he comes back the same? You think he'd want that?"

"I don't care what he'd want," I snap, voice sharp with pain. "I want him. And I'll give whatever it takes."

Owen's jaw clenches. "And if what it takes is you? You think that's a fair trade? You think he would let you do that?"

"He did do that."

"That's not the same—"

"It is!" My voice cracks, rising. "He didn't ask. He didn't warn me. He just left. So now I'm making the same choice. The same sacrifice. I learned from the best."

Owen steps forward, anger sparking. "That's not learning. That's falling into the same damn pit. And you think I'm just going to stand here and let you?"

"You don't get to decide," I fire back. "You don't get to stop me."

"I'm his twin," Owen growls. "You think this doesn't kill me too? I saw him fall. I felt it when the bond broke. And now you're standing in blood summoning me like I'm your shortcut to self-destruction."

"I'm summoning you," I breathe, "because no one else would listen."

He falters for a second. His shoulders drop, but the fury in his eyes stays.

"I am listening," he says, softer now—but no less intense. "I see you, Ophelia. I see what this has done to you. But this... this is the part where someone's supposed to pull you back."

"You can't pull back someone who's already gone."

His silence is deafening. "What are you offering?" he asks, his voice low and edged like a blade barely sheathed.

"Whatever it takes." I meet his eyes, steady despite the tremor in my chest, even as my fingers dig crescent moons into my palms.

"No," he snaps, jaw tightening as he takes a step forward. "Be specific."

"My soul." The words leave my mouth like a blade pressed to my own throat, quiet but unwavering.

He flinches, just barely—like I struck something raw beneath the surface. His eyes darken, grief and fury flickering in the depths. "You want to trade your soul for his?"

"Yes." My voice is steady now, cold, certain. I straighten, refusing to look away.

"And what if I say no?" he growls, his arms crossed like a shield he doesn't know how to lower.

"I'll find someone else." My pulse pounds in my ears, but I don't back down. "In a heartbeat," I add, chin lifted, the tremble in my limbs no match for the fire in my voice.

Owen studies me for a long moment. There's no more arguing left in him—only a quiet, heavy understanding. He nods once, sharp and solemn, and pulls a scroll from the air.

It doesn't burn, doesn't sizzle with magic. It just exists, the parchment thicker than paper, smoother than flesh. A contract waiting for blood.

Owen holds it between us, and with a flick of his hand, the terms appear in ink that looks disturbingly like it was carved from shadow.

One soul. One return. Equal exchange.

"You sure?" he asks, voice quieter now.

"I've never been more sure of anything," I whisper.

He hands me a dagger. It's elegant.

I press the blade to my palm without flinching. Drag it down in one clean line. The blood spills freely and as it hits the contract, the ink glows, the letters sealing themselves with every drop.

The mark flares once on my collarbone—so bright it hurts. The contract vanishes in a single breath, smoke curling into nothing.

Owen doesn't say anything at first. But then... he smiles.

"Good choice," he says, almost gently. "We'll make sure your boxes make it to his house."

The floor beneath me splits. The room dissolves. And in the next heartbeat, I'm standing in the middle of Julian's bedroom.

Alive. Whole. And staring at the man who gave everything for me.

Twenty-One
JULIAN

I used to watch her.

Even after the bond began to unravel, when the mark on my forearm dimmed from gold to ash, I kept reaching. Every breath she took echoed inside me. Her grief throbbed like a phantom limb. I'd hear her whisper my name, so faint it felt like a dream. But the bond doesn't hum anymore. It doesn't burn. It flickers now, like the final breath of something sacred.

The mark remains. Faint and quiet—a memory carved into skin. My soulmate's mark. But it no longer connects us. She's gone.

And I'm left powerless. Disgraced. Still immortal, but nothing like the creature I once was.

My power is gone. My blood is silent. The shadows refuse me. Fire won't rise. Everything that once defined me—magic, rage, control—has gone still. Dormant. I can't shift. Can't conjure. Can't feel anything but the cold.

They locked me in this house for protection, they said. Truthfully, it was to protect the name. The Duvain legacy can't be seen bleeding. If anyone in Hell knew what I'd become, they'd circle like vultures.

So I rot here. Alone.

Some days I scream until my throat gives out. Her name is always first. Other days, I make no sound. I sit in the solarium, surrounded by the flowers she once touched. They wilt now, no matter how I tend them. Even the garden remembers.

I trace the mark like it still belongs to her. Even though it doesn't. Not anymore. But I can't let go.

They visit. The ones who used to define my world.

Owen arrives first. Always first. Quiet, like he knows words can't touch what I've lost. He stares at the mark like he's willing it back to life. But it stays cold.

Seth fills the silence with fury, politics, plans. Lucas leaves food. Damian watches me like he's waiting for a version of me that's long gone. Caleb reads poetry meant to stir something inside me, but it doesn't. Adrian screams, calls me a coward. My mother rages against the dust in the halls. My father nods once, stoic, like dignity will keep this house standing.

Selene stays the longest. She brings tea, her quiet presence, and a warmth I don't deserve. I never speak. She never asks.

They come because they have to. Because appearances matter in Hell. Because weakness isn't allowed. They visit the ghost of who I was, say words they no longer believe, and leave.

And I stay.

A prisoner in a house without fire. A shadow in a body that forgot how to burn. I lost her. And with her, I lost everything.

Hell was never the punishment. Losing her was.

I finish the last chug of whiskey. I'm officially out. The bottle is empty, the silence too loud, and my eternity stretches out like a punishment without end. But this isn't just my sentence. It's hers too. Ophelia is immortal now, bound to the deal I made and the cost I paid. None of us—not even the Infernal Council—know what to do with that. The loom of fate is unraveling. Threads slip loose one by one, everything falling apart before we can catch it.

I push off the couch, unsteady from too many nights of nothing. Suddenly, I see it.

A flicker. Smoke curling at the edges of the room. A shift in the air, like something remembered how to burn again.

And suddenly, she's there. Not an angel. Not a savior. A wound in the shape of a woman.

Ophelia. But not the one I remember. This isn't the woman I danced with in darkness and firelight. She looks like something death forgot to finish.

Her eyes are sunken, ringed in exhaustion. Her hair hangs limp, tangled and dull. Her skin is pale, bruised in places, stretched too tight across bones that barely hold her together. She's so thin it hurts to look at her.

Her arms are wrapped in haphazard bandages, but not enough to hide the damage. Deep cuts. Jagged scars. Burns. I catch a glimpse of her ribs—something carved there in desperation, in rage or sorrow or both. Above her heart, the mark. Mine. Still glowing faintly, barely clinging to her skin. The flesh around it is red and raw. Like she tried to rip it out.

She doesn't speak, just stands there, shaking, more ghost than girl. And for the first time in months, the silence doesn't feel like mine anymore. It feels like hers.

I get up and go straight to her.

I don't even think. My body moves before my mind can catch up—like she's gravity and I've been drifting too long without an anchor.

But when I stop in front of her, it hits me. The bruises. The scars. The way she's barely holding herself up. The mark on her chest that still glows, flickering like a dying star.

And I realize—I don't know what this is. A dream. A punishment. A reckoning.

She's here, but I don't know how. This isn't how this happens. The mark flares to life and I see her. More importantly, I feel her. I feel power flood within in me. I know what this is. My abilities are back. And there is only one way that could happen.

"What did you do?" I ask in complete disbelief.

She doesn't say anything, but she does raise a brow. Like I should know. Like I should have an idea. The worst part is I do know. Maybe too well. She made a deal.

"What were the terms?"

"A fair trade. My soul for yours," she responds. Finally I get her to say something, but it's not what I want to hear.

The silence that follows is brutal. I feel it crush down on my chest like stone.

"I gave my soul so you could live," I breathe, stepping forward. My hands are shaking now, fists clenched to keep from falling apart. "So you could breathe again. So you could stay."

She laughs—sharp and wrecked. The kind of sound that doesn't belong in her mouth.

"I couldn't breathe, Julian," she spits. "I couldn't fucking breathe without you."

Her hands fly to her chest, tearing at the fabric like she wants to rip the pain out physically. Her sleeves fall, and I see the damage. Deep, brutal, intentional. Not cries for help. Not hesitation. These were meant to end her.

My stomach twists.

"You call that living?" I ask, voice rising. "You call this surviving?"

"It was hell," she screams. "Every day. Every second. Waking up and not knowing how to keep going. Talking to the walls, Julian. Whispering your name into the dark like it was a prayer no one ever planned to answer."

She staggers back a step, like the weight of it all is finally too much. Her knees buckle, but she doesn't fall. She's trembling, breath ragged, eyes too wild. "You saved me," she snarls. "And I died anyway. Just slower."

She rips the bandage off her forearm—where the skin still bleeds—and holds it out like proof. "This is what I became without you. A ghost. A fucking corpse that kept waking up."

"You were supposed to live," I whisper, the words tearing out of me. "You were supposed to forget me. Move on. Heal."

"I don't want to heal!" she shrieks. "I want you. I wanted us. And if I couldn't have that, I didn't want anything."

Her chest heaves. Her mouth opens, but no words come. Just that broken, strangled sound of someone who's finally run out of grief to scream.

"You gave up your soul to save me," she breathes, her eyes burning like she's daring me to flinch from the truth. "And I gave up mine to bring you back."

"We're both fools," I say, closing the distance. "Because I'd do it again. Every time. Even knowing how it ends."

"I wouldn't change a thing," she whispers. "Except maybe how long it took us to say it."

My fingers find the mark on her chest and the second I touch her, it detonates.

The bond doesn't just reform. It erupts. It scorches. Crawling up my arm like wildfire through dry earth. Her spine arches with a choked sound as it tears across her chest, carving my soul back into her skin.

The air fractures. Like fate itself just snapped back into alignment.

She exhales and in the space between breath and regret, her fingers seize the front of my shirt. The fabric bunches under her grip as she yanks me forward, crashing her mouth into mine like she's trying to erase the distance in one violent pull.

Her teeth catch my bottom lip. Her nails dig into my shoulders. And when her lips part, it's on a broken sound that shatters between us. A sob. A gasp. A plea. I don't know which—but I take it. Swallow it like it's the only thing tethering me to the surface.

She tastes like salt and blood and something I haven't had in months—hope.

Her hands thread into my hair, tugging me closer, like she's afraid I'll vanish again if she lets go. And I kiss her like I'm anchoring her to this moment—my mouth bruising against hers, my fingers trembling where they clutch her waist.

She moves against me like someone drowning. Like touch is oxygen. Like if she presses close enough, we can undo every minute we spent apart.

And maybe we can. Because right now—I don't know where her pain ends and mine begins.

"I hate you," she gasps against my mouth.

"I know," I rasp. "I love you too."

I shove her back against the wall, hard enough to make her gasp, and claim her lips again. She kisses like she's punishing me. I kiss her like I'm owning what's always been mine.

"You're shaking," I growl into her throat, dragging my mouth along the fragile curve. Her pulse hammers under my tongue. "Still trying to pretend you're not mine?"

Her breath catches.

"You are," I say, slow and brutal. "Every fucking inch of you." I slide my hand beneath her shirt, fingers curling against her ribcage, and drag it upward until the fabric is gone, flung somewhere behind us. I don't rush. I watch her. Watch how her breath hitches when I trace my thumb under the swell of her breast, circling her nipple until she whimpers.

"You've been starving," I murmur, dragging my hand lower. "Haven't you?"

She nods, barely. "Julian—"

Her name feels like prayer on my tongue, but I don't say it. I drop to my knees instead.

I press my mouth to her stomach, her hips, her thighs. I taste her skin like it's the only tether to life I have left. I grip her legs and pull her to the edge of the bed, stripping her bare—slow, reverent, but with the kind of hunger that leaves no space for hesitation.

I spread her open and groan when I see her.

Wet. Swollen. Mine.

She jerks at the first touch of my tongue. My name breaks from her lips like she's choking on it. I grip her thighs tighter, holding her in place as I drag my mouth up her slit, circling her clit with deliberate, unrelenting pressure.

"Oh—god—Julian—"

Her hips buck. She tries to run. I don't let her. "You're going to cum on my mouth," I growl. "You're going to scream for me. Now."

And she does. And when I finally pull back, her entire body is trembling, wrecked and open, chest rising in shattered gasps. But I'm not done.

I strip off what's left between us and push her back on the mattress, sliding between her thighs with a snarl that's barely human. My cock presses against her entrance, thick and hard, and she arches up to meet me.

"Please," she whispers. "I need—"

I thrust into her in one long, brutal stroke. Her scream is my name. Tight. Hot. Perfect. I feel everything.

I take her like I'm staking a claim—every thrust hard enough to remind her who she belongs to. I grab her wrists and pin them above her head, hips slamming into hers again and again, skin on skin, sweat and moans and breathless curses.

"You're mine," I snarl into her mouth.

"Yours," she cries. "Only yours."

Her walls clench around me and I lose it. My rhythm shatters. My mouth finds hers in a final, desperate kiss as we fall apart together—louder, rougher, more broken than anything I've ever known.

I carry her to the couch. Her body melts into the cushions, one leg draped over mine, her head resting against my chest. The fire crackles beside us, casting low light across her skin. Her mark pulses steady now—bright and sure, like it never left.

She looks up at me. "I think I'm supposed to take my place at the Loom."

I nod slowly, brushing a hand down her hair. "It always belonged to you. Even before you knew."

Her fingers find the center of my palm, tracing slow circles like she's still grounding herself. "And you?"

"I go back to work," I say, voice low. "The Council can't hide me forever. I have debts to settle. Power to reclaim."

"You'll be different now," she murmurs, watching me carefully.

"I already am." I meet her eyes. "But I'll be stronger for it. And so will you."

She leans forward, mouth brushing my jaw. "We'll do it together?"

"Always you," I promise, my voice breaking just a little. "Always us. No more giving pieces of ourselves away."

We dress in silence—not heavy or awkward, but reverent. Like something sacred has been rewritten between us. Her movements are smooth now, deliberate. Gone is the fragility that once lived in her frame. Her eyes, when they meet mine, are bright with clarity and strength. Not the kind she had before—but something new. Something earned.

When I reach for her hand, she takes it without hesitation. No words pass between us as we leave. None are needed.

The Council doesn't summon us. They don't need to. The moment our bond reformed, the Loom stirred awake, sending a pulse through the old veins of Hell that only the ancient would understand. And they felt it. They knew.

We walk together through the deepest corridors of the underworld—past the Vaults, beyond the Throne Hall, through the roots of Hell where even shadows are afraid to linger. At the very end, the doors wait.

Obsidian. Towering. Carved with old runes too deep for translation. They do not open for me.

But for her they part like breath, slow and thunderous.

The room beyond is nothing but darkness to my eyes. I see walls carved in black stone. An altar of sorts. And in the center, what I know must be the Loom. I can't see it—not truly. Not without her eyes, without her power. Without what she was always meant to become.

But I feel it. Ophelia steps inside alone.

She doesn't hesitate. Doesn't flinch. She walks with the kind of certainty you don't learn—you remember. Like her feet already knew the way. I stay at the threshold, because this isn't my place. This part belongs to her.

She moves toward what I cannot see, guided by a pull older than memory. When she kneels, it is not submission—it is arrival. And I let her go, into the dark, into the silence, into what was always hers.

Twenty-Two
Ophelia

The room hums with power, alive in a way that presses against my skin. Light ripples across the obsidian walls, not from torches or fire, but from floating, endless screens. They shimmer with motion—fragments of lives unfolding like ghost stories. A child's first laugh. A mother's scream. A betrayal whispered under breath. Thousands of moments suspended in time, flickering across the surface of the dark like candlelight on water.

Blue fire coils in the center, rising without smoke, bending toward me as I step forward in recognition.

And there, suspended like a question in the dark, is the Loom.

It isn't made of anything I can name. Not string. Not metal. Not wood. It's built of something closer to nerve and light—threaded with strands that shimmer in impossible colors. Some glint like starlight on oil. Others twitch, barely tethered. Some are frayed so finely they could disappear if I blinked.

I lower to my knees. Not out of reverence, but inevitability.

The air tastes electric. The space hums with something sharp, like a held breath at the edge of a scream. A stool waits in the corner, simple and shadowed, as if carved from memory itself. I take it. It fits, just like it's been waiting for me to arrive.

I reach toward the threads. And they move.

Not all—just the ones that know me. A gold strand grazes my fingertips and flares, stuttering with a rhythm I know too well. Another twines with it, barely pulsing. Fading.

I don't question. I don't flinch. I don't think. I begin. The threads twist around my hands, guiding me—not like a teacher, but like a partner. Like the loom isn't just a tool, but a listener. A witness. A participant.

I find the thread that broke. The one that tore when he fell. And without apology, I start to weave.

I don't know how long I've been sitting here, threads humming through my hands, but something inside me has shifted. I can feel again. I want to create again. I want to live.

I turn on the stool and look over to Julian. He's still there, arms crossed, and smiling wide at me.

But he's not alone. His parents and brothers are standing to his right. His aunt and uncle along with his cousins to his left. Right beside him is a woman I almost forgot.

Not in truth—but in detail. Time softened her edges. I held on to fragments and prayed they were real.

But now she's here.

And I remember everything.

The way her curls fall in soft spirals, always scented with lavender and honey. The faint dimple in her cheek that only appears when she smiles—like a secret she never meant to share. Her eyes—blue, wide, and full of that look she only gave me, like I was the center of every story she ever wanted to tell.

"Mom?" I whisper, breath snagging in my throat.

She nods, and tears spill before her smile can reach me.

I run to her and throw myself into her arms. She still feels the same. Like lullabies and warm sweaters. Like the safest place I've ever known. She pulls me tighter, hands cradling the back of my head.

"My sweet girl," she whispers, voice trembling. "I've missed you every day."

I squeeze my eyes shut, burying my face against her shoulder. "I thought I'd forgotten you."

"You didn't." She leans back just enough to look at me, brushing hair from my face. "You remembered the parts that mattered."

I nod, unable to speak, afraid that if I try, I'll fall apart all over again.

She presses her forehead to mine, her thumb catching one of my tears. "You're here now," she says softly. "That's all that matters."

I can't even put into words how good I feel. It's like spring bursting through my chest— every flower blooming at once just to say, you made it.

"We need to talk about the Infernal Union," Selene says, practically vibrating with excitement.

"Really?" Julian groans. "Ophelia just came back to me and is reconnecting with her mother. Is this really the moment?"

I laugh, walking straight into his arms. He wraps me up without hesitation, his warmth sinking into me like sunlight through skin. I tip my head back, and he leans down—

But this kiss isn't light.

It's lingering. Deep. A promise pressed to my mouth like he's afraid to let go again. Like the only way to prove I'm real is to kiss me until I forget we were ever apart.

When we finally pull away, my heart is pounding—and his smile tells me he felt it too.

"Yes! Julian, this is our first Infernal Union!" Selene practically squeals, clapping like a schoolgirl at a blood ritual. "Do you even know how rare it is to plan a wedding where the vows might summon an elder god?"

Julian groans. "We just got back together. Can we wait, I don't know, five minutes before picking out hellflowers and soulbond fonts?"

"Son," Liora cuts in, her tone as regal as ever. "We just want what's best for you. Both of you." Her gaze sharpens. "And I will be reviewing your guest list."

"Noted," I mutter.

My mother grins, floating just an inch above the floor. "I get to walk my daughter down the aisle! Sure, I'm dead, and it'll probably be through a portal of fire, but hey—I'll be there."

"That's horrifyingly sweet," Julian mutters under his breath.

"Also, Selene," my mom adds, tilting her head. "If there's going to be fire, I refuse to wear polyester in the afterlife."

"Please, you'll both look fabulous in custom-stitched soul silk," Selene chirps.

Julian leans in, voice dry. "Do I need to sign a separate deal to survive this ceremony?"

"No," all three women say at once.

"...Terrifying," he mutters.

"We have some unfinished business first," I speak up. I approach the seven vacant thrones—massive, carved from obsidian, bone, and time itself. Each one pulses faintly with the echo of dominion. I stop before them, pressing my palm to the floor as I lower myself to my knees.

Eyes closed, I summon them. I don't speak aloud. I don't have to. My thoughts are threadbare but resolute.

Come.

The room changes. The air bends. One by one, they arrive. First, the scent of ash and roses. Cold follows. Flame comes last.

None speak, but I feel the weight of their eyes. Of eternity watching me. I rise. My voice doesn't tremble, though my bones ache with the pressure. "I have a request."

A pause. Permission to continue.

"I want to return to the living."

Gasps echo through the chamber. A sharp flicker of movement. Something hisses. They think I mean forever. That I want to forsake my station.

I raise my hand before they can protest. "Not to abandon my place. To fulfill a thread. I wove a fate for Cassius and Melanie that must be completed with my own hands. And I want to see the rest of my family—to let them know I survived. That I found my place. You said I could keep those I love close."

My voice softens. "I want to show them I didn't disappear."

A voice—not one, but many—speaks. One will. Seven powers. "Weaver of the Loom. Guardian of the thread. We grant your passage."

My breath stutters.

"You may return, with the mother who bore you and the soulmatch who bled for you." Their eyes blaze, each a different color of judgment and balance. "But remember, child of fire—fate does not forgive twice. What you take with you, you must honor."

I bow low, my heart thunderous in my chest. "I will."

And I rise—Ophelia Duvain, threadbender, soulbound, keeper of the Loom—ready to return.

We don't walk. We descend. From Loom to world, from thread to flesh. And when my feet touch the earth again, it's different. I'm different.

"We start with Cassius and Melanie." My voice is calm. The kind that comes when anger runs out and something colder takes its place.

Julian doesn't ask why. He just reaches for my hand. We disappear in smoke.

We reappear on a sidewalk that smells like stale desperation and overcooked microwave dinners.

The house in front of us looks like karma personally slapped it. Peeling paint, crooked shutters, a mailbox hanging by one screw, like it gave up halfway through delivering the bills. The porch sags like it knows this whole situation is beneath it. The grass? Dead. As if even the weeds were like, "No thanks."

Julian raises an eyebrow. "This the right place, or did we accidentally land in a cautionary tale?"

I shrug. "Both, probably."

He smirks. "Lovely. Shall we knock?"

I don't answer. I just walk straight up the steps, letting my power leak out in little pulses—just enough to short out the electricity and make every mirror crack from the inside.

Inside, I hear scrambling. Footsteps. Panic. Good.

Let the show begin.

The door doesn't open.

It *explodes*.

Splinters rain down like confetti at a funeral. Smoke curls through the gaping threshold like a storm trying to remember its name.

We step through. Julian appears beside me in a ripple of shadow and heat, calm and coiled like a blade sheathed in velvet. I'm flame. He's the match. Together? We're arson with a vendetta.

Inside, the house is exactly what I expected—cheap furniture, fake florals, the smell of microwave dinners and unresolved trauma. And right there in the middle of it, frozen like deer in demonic headlights—

Cassius.

Melanie.

Cassius is halfway out of a fraying recliner, mouth parted in what might be a scream or a stroke. Melanie stands at the kitchen island, a wine glass in one hand and terror in the other.

"Miss me?" I ask, voice sugar-sweet and full of venom.

Melanie drops the glass. It shatters against the floor, wine blooming like fresh blood. Cassius doesn't speak. Not yet.

Julian steps forward, slow and deliberate. "You really downgraded. The aesthetics are..." He glances around, lips twitching. "Unfortunate."

"Wh—what is this?" Cassius chokes. "You're supposed to be—she was supposed to be gone."

"Funny thing about fate," I murmur, stepping closer. "It doesn't like being rewritten. So I did what you never could."

Melanie's voice is barely a whisper. "What did you do?"

I smile. The lights flicker above us, every bulb pulsing with unnatural rhythm.

"I rewrote the Loom."

Cassius stumbles back like I slapped him. "That's impossible."

"No," I say, eyes locking with his, "what's impossible is thinking you could rip my life apart and not pay the price."

Julian crosses his arms, gaze deadly. "Go on. Tell them. What's their fate?"

I let the silence stretch, tasting their fear like dessert.

I don't whisper it. I declare it. "Oblivion."

Melanie gasps. Cassius swears under his breath.

"You don't get fire," I continue, voice rising. "You don't get glory. You don't even get remembered. Your threads are already unraveling, strand by strand. In every realm, every version of time—your names are fading. Your power? Gone. Your legacy? Forgotten."

They try to speak. I raise my hand—and the shadows hush them like a blade at the throat. "I was mercy," I hiss. "I was forgiveness. I was *done*. But you kept reaching. Kept hurting. Kept taking. So now?"

I turn to Julian, my voice dropping to a near whisper. "Now, I collect."

From the floorboards, from the smoke, from the corners of every forgotten shadow — Calliope rises.

Not like a ghost. Like vengeance incarnate.

Her curls are a wild halo of flame, golden hair ignited at the ends, eyes glowing with eldritch green light — not human, not heavenly. Something older. Something crueler. She floats, barefoot and graceful, wrapped in smoke.

Even the air recoils.

Melanie chokes on her own breath. "You—no. No, you're dead," she whimpers, eyes wild as she stumbles backward into the counter.

Calliope smiles like a knife dragged across glass. "Death was a nap, darling. You, however…" she says, voice like honey dripped over a blade, "are an offense to memory."

Cassius scrambles, arms raised like that could help. "What do you want?" he pants, his voice already breaking.

Julian doesn't move. Doesn't blink. "She wants what was stolen," he says, voice low and sharp. "And she came to collect."

Calliope's feet never touch the ground. She glides across the floor like a painting come to life — too vivid, too powerful. Her hands glow faintly as she raises one finger, and the moment it points to Cassius — his body locks.

Every tendon, every joint — frozen.

"You took my daughter. You erased her future. And you ran like a coward," Calliope says softly, almost lovingly. "But no one outruns me."

Cracks spiderweb under his feet, glowing orange and red.

The floor splits. Not with grace—with violence. Like Hell biting through its leash.

Flames shoot up, runes, burning words, written in the language of the damned. They sear into Cassius's skin as the chains rise—black, barbed, and alive, wrapping around his wrists, ankles, ribs, throat.

He tries to scream. The chains cinch tighter.

"Your soul never belonged to you," Ophelia says, stepping into the glow of the fire. "You bartered with blood that wasn't yours. So now?"

She lifts her hand. He starts to burn. Not fast. Not mercy. Slow. Peeling. Ripping. Screaming.

His mouth opens wide, teeth cracking from the heat, skin blistering down to muscle, not one part of him dies clean. The chains jerk downward, dragging him inch by inch toward the maw in the floor. His fingernails rip from his hands as he claws at the edge.

Julian doesn't flinch. I doesn't blink.

Calliope tilts her head, watching him like one might observe a fly drowning in syrup.

The floor yawns wide—

And Cassius vanishes in a final, blood-curdling scream.

Gone.

Melanie doesn't scream. She begs. "No—no no no—" she says, crawling backward, sobs choking her words. Her skin begins to gray. Veins collapse under her skin, turning her translucent. Her fingers scratch at her chest like she can hold her identity in place.

"What's happening to me?" she gasps, her mouth shaking, eyes wild and unseeing. "I—who—"

Calliope kneels beside her, speaking softly, as though she's talking to a child. "You'll be nothing. That's your punishment. No fire. No eternity. Just absence."

"Not one person will remember you," Ophelia adds, stepping closer. "Not your family. Not your lovers. Not even yourself."

Melanie screams — but it's not even sound anymore. It's static. A void bleeding out of her mouth.

Her hair fades next. Her eyes follow. Her name peels off her soul like paint stripped from rotting wood.

And with a final, shuddering breath—she turns to dust. Not ash. Not smoke. Just dust.

Calliope stands, brushing invisible dirt from her hands.

"That was for her," she says, not even looking back at what's left. There's nothing to look at.

"So," Julian murmurs, his hand tightening around mine, "are you ready to see the rest of your family, my love?"

"I hope they understand," I whisper, eyes fixed on the place where Cassius and Melanie ceased to exist.

"They will," my mom says gently, brushing a curl behind my ear. "You're stronger than when you left. And they'll see that." She smirks — full of mischief and maternal menace.

"I do look forward to meeting Rosalind," she adds. "Maybe I'll bring a flaming pie."

Julian chokes on a laugh, half-wincing. "Please don't traumatize the humans who actually likes us."

"They'll be fine," I say, grinning despite myself. "They're tougher than they look."

It doesn't take long to find them. I follow the pulse of memory and magic straight to the doorstep of the only home I'd still call safe. No warning. No knock. Just the crackle of heat and shadow curling into air as we land.

Bella's car is here. So is Dominic's. And knowing him, Rhys is somewhere nearby, probably pacing like the storm he always is.

I freeze for a moment—long enough for Julian to reach for my hand. His fingers thread through mine, warm and grounding.

He doesn't say *Are you ready?* He already knows I'm not. And I love him for not asking.

"They helped me," I murmur. "Even when I was breaking. And I disappeared. Again."

"You were surviving," he says softly.

I look at the front door. The laughter I hear through the walls. The life that kept moving while I tried to stop mine.

"Okay," I breathe. "How do you want to play this?"

Julian's mouth curves just a little. "This is your moment, not mine." He raises a brow. "We could knock... or we could just walk in like the immortal power couple we are."

I snort, half-nervous, half-relieved. "Subtlety is dead, huh?"

He leans in. "We are literally from Hell, my love."

And with that, I step forward, twist the doorknob and open the door.

They are all on the couches in the living room. Dominic and Rhys have their backs to the door, but when they come in, the two guys pull Rosalind and Bella behind them. That is, until they realize it's me.

"Ophelia!" Bella gasps. She's across the room in a heartbeat, barreling into me like gravity doesn't exist. Her arms wrap tight around my shoulders, crushing, desperate.

"You're okay," she breathes into my neck, her voice thick with tears. I feel them—hot and real—soaking into my skin. "You really came back."

I nod against her shoulder, letting myself sink into the hug for a second longer. "I missed you," I whisper.

"Don't ever do that again," she says, pulling back just enough to cup my face. Her mascara's smudged, her lip quivers. "Promise me."

"I'll try," I manage, blinking fast.

"Holy shit," Dominic mutters from the doorway. His voice is low, reverent, like he's trying to convince himself this isn't some cruel hallucination. "You look... like yourself again."

I offer him a soft smile. "I feel like myself again."

He walks forward slowly, gaze flicking to Julian before resting on me. "I didn't think I'd get to see this day. I'm glad I was wrong." His smile is small, but real. "And if this ends in wedding cake and chaos? Count me in."

Behind him, Rosalind steps forward. Her hands hover near her heart, like she's holding something fragile and afraid to let go.

"You look like your mother," she says quietly.

I turn—my mom is already stepping into the light behind me, golden curls loose around her shoulders, eyes shimmering with memory and recognition.

Rosalind exhales sharply. "Calliope."

"Rosalind." There's history in that name. And when they move toward each other, there's no hesitation—only understanding. They embrace like old friends who lost too much, and finally got something back.

"Thank you," Calliope whispers. "For loving her like she was your own."

Rosalind swallows. "She is mine." She turns to me, her voice softer. "But she was always yours first."

"I don't mean to cut in..." Julian starts, his voice quiet but pointed, "but I think you should tell them about Cassius, Lia."

I nod, heart thudding like thunder against bone. "I'm sorry," I say, voice steady even as my chest tightens, "but Cassius' soul was taken. Melanie's time too."

"Lia..." Julian murmurs, his gaze steady on mine, but there's warning in his tone. He knows what's coming.

"Who's Melanie?" Rosalind asks, her head tilting slightly, eyes narrowing in quiet confusion.

My breath stutters. "What do you mean, who's Melanie?" I say, staring at her like I can force the memory back into place.

"That's what I'm trying to tell you," Julian says, folding his arms as his voice drops. "They don't remember her."

I glance at Bella, searching her face for recognition. "Your sister."

"You're my only sister," Bella replies, shaking her head, her brow furrowing.

I shift to Dominic, hope flickering in my chest. "Your ex-wife."

"I was never married, Lia. I haven't been with anyone since we broke up," he says, blinking slowly, a frown tugging at his mouth.

My pulse spikes. I turn to Rhys, desperate now. "You investigated her. With my father. The corruption case. We met at a coffee house to talk about it. "

"I investigated a lot of corruption," Rhys says, lifting his shoulders in a small shrug. "But… I don't remember anyone named Melanie."

He's not lying. None of them are.

"She's been erased," Julian says quietly, his jaw tight. "Not just gone. Unwritten."

"Who are you talking about, sweetheart?" Rosalind asks, her voice gentle, but wary.

"No one, I guess," I say, forcing a tight smile. "Doesn't matter now."

My mom clears her throat. "Well," she says brightly, like she's throwing open a window, "this took a turn. How about something more celebratory?"

Julian tilts his head. "Such as?"

"The Infernal Union," she says, already grinning. "There's a ceremony to plan. Fire. Magic. Matching cloaks if I get my way."

Bella leans forward. "Wait—Infernal what?"

"We're getting married," I say, resting my hand on Julian's chest. "And I want you all there."

Julian meets their eyes, voice low but certain. "You're our family. You belong."

My mom nods, proud and radiant. "And I get to walk my daughter down the aisle. I might be dead, but I've still got style."

Rhys exhales, rubbing the back of his neck. "Well… guess we're going to Hell."

Julian chuckles, low and real. "You'll fit right in."

They all laugh—uneasy, but genuine. The kind of laugh that feels like release.

I step back slightly, letting the moment settle, watching the people I once thought I'd lost forever. Bella is clinging to my arm again, asking about wardrobe requirements. Rhys is already trying to convince Dominic to wear something other than black. And in the corner, my mom and Rosalind are talking like old friends who were always meant to meet—two halves of the same strange fate finally aligned.

Julian moves beside me, brushing his knuckles against mine. I don't have to look at him to feel the calm he carries now—not the sharp-edged power he used to wear, but something steadier. Something real.

"This is what you fought for," he says softly. "Not vengeance. Not the Loom. This."

And he's right. I look around at the people I love—Bella's laughter filling the room, Rosalind's hand resting over my mother's, Dominic pretending he's not tearing up, Rhys shaking his head like he's not half the chaos himself.

This.

This is what I never thought I'd get back.

And now?

It's mine.

I take a breath. Not shaky. Not afraid.

"Let's go home," I whisper—meant for all of them, but mostly for the girl I used to be.

The one who finally made it.

Epilogue
Owen

The Infernal Union.

I missed the ceremony. Summoned mid-ritual by some fool with shaky hands and a death wish. The ink wasn't even dry on the sigil before I ended the deal and sent him screaming. Idiots like that don't deserve to call demons.

I would've stayed longer—made him bleed, maybe—but my brother was getting married. And even I have priorities.

I return just in time for the celebration. The afterglow.

Julian's house has been transformed. Runes etched in gold light shimmer above the archways. Enchanted candles float midair, their flames shifting between colors like they can't decide whether to burn holy or infernal. Laughter fills the halls. Music curls through the air like silk. For once, Hell doesn't feel like punishment.

I stand near the entrance, drink in hand, watching the crowd shift and glitter. Souls and demons, fae and mortals, all tangled together in something dangerously close to joy.

Julian and Ophelia, moving through the space like they were born from it. His hands on her waist. Her smile like a secret she finally gets to keep.

She wears obsidian silk—sleek, backless, lined with fine silver thread that catches every flicker of light like spun stars. Her hair is half-pinned, wild curls falling like flame around her shoulders. No crown. No jewels. Just bare feet and the mark glowing faintly at her collarbone, where his soul lives inside her skin.

She is the embodiment of power reclaimed. Of survival worn like armor.

Julian leans in and murmurs something against her ear. She laughs—light, full. And he looks at her like he's still not convinced she's real.

It's almost enough to make me believe in happy endings.

"They look smitten," Seth says, appearing beside me like smoke with a grin, and handing me a glass of something that probably costs more than most souls.

I take it without looking. "They look disgusting."

He snorts. "That's demon-speak for happy."

"Whatever it is," I murmur, swirling the drink, "it's loud."

Julian's got that look on his face—like he found the last piece of a puzzle he didn't know was missing. And Ophelia... Ophelia looks like she finally remembers who she is.

"Honestly?" I add, glancing at Seth, "I'm happy for them. Even if the PDA is aggressively excessive."

Seth raises his glass. "You're going soft."

"I'm adapting," I reply, dry. "Big difference."

He laughs, eyes flicking to the dancefloor. "Weird, right? Seeing him like this?"

"I thought the world would end before he smiled like that," I admit, sipping slowly. "And meant it."

"And yet... here we are. Happy endings and all."

"Don't push it."

He laughs and walks away. I just stay there. Something inside me feels broken. A piece missing.

I turn to get another drink when I hear a squeal—sharp, sudden, too full of joy for a room of demons.

Ophelia.

She's running toward someone in the far corner, arms wide.

I glance over. Expecting a cousin. A friend. Another dead soul back from the ashes.

But it isn't just another woman.

It's her.

The moment I see her, something in me stills. Not freezes. Not startles. *Stills*—like the world paused to breathe around her.

She's dressed in emerald, the color catching the light like fire trapped in silk. Her hair spills in loose waves, dark and glossy, framing a face I shouldn't remember but somehow do. Lips parted in surprise. Eyes that haven't met mine yet—but I already feel them. Like the moment before a storm cracks open the sky.

She glows.

"My sister got married!" she announces with a squeal, her joy cutting through the music as she races across the room.

She throws her arms around the man beside her and another woman, looping them both into a breathless, spinning embrace. They're laughing, all of them, caught in the kind of happiness that only happens in moments like this—when pain feels distant and the future feels like sunlight.

The woman lifts her eyes to meet his.

I feel it the same moment she does.

A sudden heat blooms beneath my skin, not soft or subtle, but violent—alive. It coils up my arm like a brand being pressed into flesh, ancient and unforgiving. I glance down, already knowing what I'll see.

The mark.

Seared into my forearm. Shining.

Undeniable.

The moment I register it, I hear the scream.

Not a cry. Not a gasp.

A scream that tears the air in half, guttural and strangled—like her soul is being torn open.

She stumbles back, clutching her chest, her fingers clawing at the fabric of her dress, at her skin, like she can rip the pain free if she digs deep enough. Her knees give out. Her body twists, wracked with agony she doesn't understand, and she lets out another raw, broken wail.

Ophelia is already beside her, catching her before she hits the floor, arms wrapping tight around her trembling frame. She's saying something, voice low and urgent, but I can't hear it over the pulse roaring in my ears.

The mark is still glowing. Right over the woman's heart.

I don't respond.

Because across the room, her sister—Arabella, apparently—is still collapsed in Ophelia's arms, gasping like the air was just knocked out of her lungs. She's clawing at her collarbone, nails dragging over skin that now glows with the same sickly-gold pulse I know too well. Like the bond just carved itself into her flesh with fire and didn't ask for permission.

"Fuck," I mutter.

Julian appears beside me like a curse I forgot to dodge. He lifts his glass, sips like this is just another Tuesday in Hell.

"I know that look," he says, casual as sin. "That's the 'oh-shit-I-just-got-soulmarked' face."

I don't bother denying it.

Because across the room, the girl who just branded herself into my eternity is still screaming.

And somehow, I already know— this is going to be my fucking problem. Soulmark burning. Eyes locked. Of all the people in all the realms... it had to be her.

Of course it did.

Bonus
Content

Epilogue
Arabella

Ophelia's wedding is objectively unhinged—in the most gorgeous, gothic, terrifyingly-on-brand way possible.

The entire estate looks like it was dressed by power itself. Runes shimmer above the archways. Candles float in midair like they've been enchanted by fire gods. The floor is polished obsidian, and the air tastes like magic.

Honestly? It's kind of perfect.

I sip my champagne, watching the chaos swirl around me, when Rhys wraps his arm around my waist.

"I want a party," he murmurs, voice low and smug. "A real one. Big. Loud. Immortal-level drama. Fire in the cake. Maybe an animal-shaped ice sculpture that breathes smoke," he adds with a grin that makes me snort.

"That sounds like a hazard," I say, arching a brow.

"Exactly," he replies, pleased with himself. "Come on, we deserve it. After what we just did."

My heart flutters a little. "You mean eloping in secret and not telling anyone yet?" I tease, nudging his side.

"That's the one," he says, bumping his hip against mine.

I roll my eyes. "You are way too excited about this," I say, trying not to smile.

"I married you. Of course I'm excited," he murmurs, brushing a kiss against my temple.

That's when I feel her before I see her—Ophelia, sweeping toward us in a dress that looks like it could command storms. Her smile is bright, but knowing. She stops in front of us, hands on her hips.

"You two look suspicious," she says, narrowing her eyes.

Rhys raises both hands like he's about to be frisked. "No idea what you're talking about," he says, deadpan.

I grin and step closer to my sister. "We got married," I tell her.

Her jaw drops. "What?" she gasps, eyes wide.

"Surprise," I say, barely able to contain the grin threatening to split my face. "We eloped. Just us. Quiet. Quick. Perfect."

Ophelia stares for one more beat—then gasps, full volume, like her soul just lit up.

She throws her hands in the air and yells across the room, grinning like a maniac.

"My sister got married!" she shouts, pure joy slicing through the music like a spell.

Ophelia hugs me so hard I nearly drop my glass. Rhys is practically vibrating with joy. For one wild second, I actually think this might be my happy ending.

I lean into her, into Rhys, letting the warmth of it all settle over me like gold. For a second, it's perfect. Bright and loud and full of everything I thought I'd lost.

It hits like a blade to the chest—no warning, no build. Just *pain*. Blistering, immediate, all-consuming. Like fire poured straight into my veins, like something inside me is being dragged out through my skin with claws and teeth.

I can't breathe. Can't move. My spine locks, my lungs seize. The burn tunnels into bone, into marrow, into the deepest parts of me I didn't even know could feel. It's not heat. It's not magic. It's *violation*. Like something ancient and angry is carving its name into my soul.

My mouth opens on a scream I can't control—raw and jagged, ripped from the center of my chest. It doesn't even sound human. My body arches, back bowing hard, legs buckling as my knees slam the floor. The agony doesn't fade. It intensifies—pulse after pulse, wave after wave, like the fire is trying to hollow me out.

I claw at my collarbone, nails raking down my skin, trying to *get it out*. Whatever's inside me. Whatever's crawling beneath the surface, branding me from the inside. My vision blurs. My blood howls. I don't know what's happening—but something in me is *changing*. And whatever it is, it's not asking permission.

Hands—Ophelia's—grip my shoulders, grounding me just enough to stop the spiral. My vision's still swimming, my chest still searing, but her voice cuts through the haze like a blade.

"Bella," she says, voice sharp and urgent. "You have to breathe. Just breathe."

Rhys is at my side in seconds, eyes wild. "What the fuck just happened? What is this?"

"She's been marked," Ophelia says tightly, her gaze flicking to the glow now pulsing across my collarbone.

She scans the crowd, and her breath catches. Her eyes land across the room—on someone I haven't seen before.

"The only one missing from the ceremony," she says slowly, "was Owen."

I turn to look. And there he is.

A stranger in every sense, except my bones already know him.
Our eyes meet, and something inside me screams—run.

Ophelia's Painting Playlist

*T*he art doesn't speak. But the music did.

Some people keep journals. Ophelia kept soundtracks. These are the songs that bled under her brush—back when she felt everything, when she felt nothing, and when Julian Duvain made her feel too much again.

Era One: Before She Stopped Feeling

(Back when color still mattered.)

– **"Fast Car" – Tracy Chapman**
She didn't just want to escape—she wanted to outrun herself.

– **"Crush" – Ethel Cain**
Sweet, raw, and a little dangerous. Like wanting someone you're not supposed to.

– **"Doo Wop (That Thing)" – Lauryn Hill**

Played on loop every time she painted with her windows open and thought she was invincible.

– **"Good Days" – SZA**

The kind of soft that wrapped around her shoulders and said, *you'll be okay*.

– **"Strange Mercy" – St. Vincent**

For the nights she painted past midnight and didn't feel crazy for it.

– **"Vienna" – Billy Joel**

Gentle permission to stop running. Not that she listened.

– **"Borderline" – Tame Impala**

That slightly-off, dreamy feeling of drifting and caring too much.

– **"Don't Start Now" – Dua Lipa**

Peak confidence era. She painted something in neon pink. It was obnoxious. She loved it.

– **"Cranes in the Sky" – Solange**

She didn't know what she was running from yet—but this felt like running.

Era Two: After She Went Emotionally Offline

(The brush still moved. She just didn't.)

– **"Riot" – Summer Walker**

When she remembered how much she used to love and hated herself for it.

– **"Creep" – Radiohead**

She didn't cry. But her hands shook a little.

– **"Tears Dry on Their Own" – Amy Winehouse**

Too upbeat. Too real. Played while pretending to feel nothing.

– **"Fingers Crossed" – Lauren Spencer Smith**

Painted with it playing once. Accidentally cracked the canvas.

– **"Love Galore" – SZA feat. Travis Scott**

Sex. Regret. Power. Which, ironically, describes several Julian encounters.

– "I Found" – Amber Run

She didn't. But this song made her want to pretend.

– "i hate u" – SZA

Not a phase. A lifestyle.

– "Elastic Heart" – Sia

The closest she ever got to crying after her mother died.

– "Wasted Times" – The Weeknd

Painted something violent. Claimed it wasn't about him. Lied.

– "Smells Like Teen Spirit" – Nirvana

Too loud. Too much. Perfect.

Era Three: When She Fell for Julian

(She didn't mean to. Then the mark burned. And nothing was safe anymore.)

– "Love in the Dark" – Adele

She wanted to believe this was love. She didn't.

– "Like Real People Do" – Hozier

A quiet ache in the dark. She never painted to it. She just listened.

– "My Little Love" – Adele

Too raw. Too intimate. Like someone had peeled her open.

– "Another Lifetime" – Nao

He felt like a memory. One she hadn't earned.

– "Middle of Love" – Synae

It didn't feel like falling—it felt like drowning in velvet.

– "Wicked Game" – Chris Isaak

This was the one that made her realize she wanted him.

– "Moon River" – Frank Ocean

A moment of peace. It didn't last.

– "Gravity" – Sara Bareilles

He kept pulling her back in. She kept letting him.

– "Stargirl Interlude" – The Weeknd feat. Lana Del Rey

She painted her thighs red after this one. Didn't explain why.

– "Young and Beautiful" – Lana Del Rey

This played once while he watched her paint. She didn't speak for hours.

JULIAN

She stands in the center of the room like a flame that learned how to walk.

The Infernal Claim dress clings to her like sin—obsidian silk, slit high, open back, hugging every curve like it was tailored to be destroyed. Her throat is bare. Her feet are bare. Her eyes? Anything but.

She doesn't look innocent.

She looks like a fucking temptation.

And I'm done pretending I can resist her.

I stalk toward her—slow, deliberate. Every muscle in my body pulled tight like a bow. The bond thrums under my skin, a golden burn in my chest, in my cock, in my fucking teeth.

"You wore that for me," I say, voice low and dangerous.

She lifts her chin. "Obviously."

I don't kiss her.

I don't ask.

I grab the silk at her hip and tear it. A vicious rip, loud and satisfying, the fabric splitting like paper in my hands. She gasps—sharp, startled—but she doesn't stop me. She never stops me.

The dress falls in shreds around her feet.

And she's bare.

Holy fucking hell.

No panties. No bra. Just flawless skin glowing gold in the low light, the mark above her heart pulsing like it's alive. Her nipples are already tight, flushed and begging for my mouth. Her stomach dips with each breath. Her thighs part, just barely.

She's already glistening. Already swollen. Already mine.

I step back and drink her in, my chest heaving like I've just come through battle. I drag my gaze over every inch of her: the soft curve of her belly, the way her hips flare, the muscles in her legs from all that running she used to do—before I made her crawl.

"Do you know what you look like right now?" I rasp.

She swallows. "Tell me."

"A feast. A sacrifice. A goddamn masterpiece."

I step in close, fingers skimming the dip of her waist, the swell of her ass, the heat of her between my fingers.

"And I'm going to ruin every inch of it."

I step in close, eyes dragging down the line of her throat, her tits, her belly, the soft swell between her thighs. Every inch of her is flushed, glowing, trembling like she knows exactly what I'm about to do to her.

And still—she doesn't move.

I run my hand over her bare ass, and grip it—tight, hard enough to bruise.

"You were meant to be seen like this," I mutter, voice rough with hunger. "But only by me."

Fuck, I want to paint her in cum and claw marks.

I drag my fingers between her thighs again—she's soaked, dripping, pulsing around nothing. Her body's already begging and I haven't even given her cock yet.

She whimpers.

That sound—desperate, filthy, mine—shreds what's left of my control.

"Beg."

"Please," she gasps. "Julian—please, I need you—"

That's all it takes.

I move fast—too fast for her to breathe, too fast for her to question. I grab her by the hips, lift her clean off the ground, and slam her back against the nearest wall.

She gasps, legs instinctively wrapping around my waist, hands flying to my shoulders to anchor herself—but I'm already there. Already between her thighs. Already rubbing the thick head of my cock against her dripping slit.

Her back hits the wall with a thud, and she moans—loud.

"Julian—"

I grab her hips and lift her onto my cock with a snarl, slamming her against the wall as I thrust deep until I'm fully buried. Her walls squeeze me like a vice—slick, hot, trembling around every inch of me. It's perfect—she's perfect—and I want to fucking ruin her.

"Fuck, Ophelia," I growl through clenched teeth. "You're so tight. So fucking wet for me."

She lets out a choked moan, head falling back against the stone, fingers digging into my shoulders as I pound into her. Her legs tighten around my waist with every thrust, her pussy clenching like it's trying to keep me buried inside her forever.

"That's it," I breathe. "Take all of me. You can do that, can't you, sweetheart?"

"Y-yes," she gasps, voice breaking. "More. Please, Julian—more—"

I shift my grip—one hand under her thigh, the other cupping the back of her neck as I fuck into her like she's made for it. She's not running. She's not hiding. She's taking it. Every brutal thrust. Every filthy word.

"You like being filled like this?" I hiss against her ear. "You like me fucking this tight little pussy until you can't think?"

She tries to nod, but she's already too far gone—just breathless, wrecked, begging.

I slam into her again—harder, deeper—until she shudders and cries out, nails biting into my skin.

"Cum on me," I command, voice low and lethal. "Right now. Let me feel you break."

And when she does?

Fuck.

She cums screaming, body locked around me, soaking my cock as her orgasm tears through her—and I follow, thrusting once, twice, before spilling inside her, deep, holding her up as she trembles and shakes, her back pressed against the wall, her body full of mine.

She sags against me, boneless, her cheek pressed to mine as she gasps for air like I stole it from her.

I don't move.

I stay buried inside her, one hand still gripping her thigh, the other pressed to the wall beside her head. My forehead rests against hers, our skin slick with sweat and something deeper.

She's trembling.

So am I.

"That's what you feel like when you're mine," I murmur, voice low, hoarse, wrecked. "Every fucking inch of you."

She doesn't speak. Doesn't need to. Her pulse is racing under my lips as I kiss the side of her throat—slow, reverent. My mark still glows faintly at her collarbone, pulsing like it's satisfied.

But I'm not.

I shift my hips just slightly, and she moans—broken, overstimulated.

"Every time you feel me leaking out of you," I murmur against her neck, voice low and ragged, "remember—I put it there. And I'm not done."

She whimpers, barely standing, her body trembling in my arms.

I lower her, just enough for her legs to give out. She sways, boneless and bliss-drunk, and I catch her before she falls.

Her glare is ruined. Flushed. Gorgeous. "You're the worst."

"You love it." I press a kiss to her temple, smirking against her skin. "Now run."

Her brows lift. "Excuse me?"

"To the bedroom," I growl. "Thirty seconds. Or I carry you."

She snorts—actually *snorts*—and takes off with a shaky laugh, nearly tripping over her own feet as she runs.

Her laughter echoes down the hall.

And gods, I swear it's the most beautiful sound I've ever heard.

I give her a two-second head start.

I follow—already hard again, already planning exactly how I'll ruin her next.

How This World Burned Into Existence

I have a weird fascination with the seven deadly sins. This isn't a new obsession. I've been into them since I was a little girl. Yes, I've always been this strange. Let's not talk about it.

To me, sins and demons go hand in hand—classic, right? But I didn't want to stop at the obvious. I didn't want the sin to just belong to the demon. I wanted to dig deeper.

What if *everyone* carries a sin in them? Not just the monsters. Not just the supernatural. But everyone—humans included. Because let's be honest: we're all a little prideful, a little greedy, a little wrathful. Some of us just hide it better.

The universe of The Devil's Bargain is built around that idea. Each bloodline, each sin, each soulmate bond is tied to something deeply flawed and deeply human. It's not about good vs. evil—it's about choice vs.instinct. Resisting the part of you that wants more. Or worse—giving in.

That's where the Devil's Bargain series came from. One sin per book. One soulmate bond that pushes everything to the edge.

Because I didn't want this to be about salvation. I wanted to write about what happens when the thing inside you—the worst part—is also the most powerful.

And what it means when that part isn't something you fight... It's something you *become*.

The soulmark concept came from this simple thought: if something is bound that deep in your soul, it should hurt. It should leave a mark. Not soft. Not glowing. Not romantic. But physical. Real. Unavoidable.

I didn't want a system built only on fate. Fate is part of it, but not the fairytale kind. This isn't "meant to be" in a warm and fuzzy way. It's "meant to be" in the sense that you can't escape it. You don't get to choose when the mark burns or who it's for. You just survive it.

And sometimes? You don't.

I've always found the idea of soulmates hard to explain. People talk about it like it's beautiful. Like you'll just know. But sometimes you don't. Sometimes it sneaks up on you, too late to stop it. And when that connection shows up before you're ready, before you're willing to admit what it means, it feels more like a loss than a gain.

So, I created a bond that reflects that. A bond that doesn't wait for your permission. That carves into your skin and forces you to confront something you're not prepared to face. It doesn't promise love. It doesn't protect you. It just exists—loud, painful, and permanent.

Once that bond was in place, the rest of the world started building itself around it. If soulmarks are real, people will fear them. Worship them. Exploit them. Entire bloodlines would be shaped by them. Power would be passed through them. Legacies would be tied to who you're marked for and what that mark can do.

Because in this world, the bond doesn't save you. It ruins you. And maybe, if you survive it, it remakes you too.

Acknowledgements

Well. We made it. Somehow. Emotionally unwell, sleep-deprived, probably dehydrated—but here we are. A whole-ass book.

To the characters who hijacked my brain and refused to shut up until I wrote their morally gray mess of a love story—thank you, I guess. Ophelia, you're the emotional equivalent of a locked door in a burning building. Julian, you're a red flag with cheekbones. I love you both. Please stop haunting my dreams.

To my mom, Jeanine, and my husband, Travis—thank you for keeping me grounded while I spiraled into a fictional mental breakdown. Mom, you cheered for me even when I looked like a hopeless and exhausted goblin muttering about demons in the kitchen. Also, sorry for the spice... kind of. Travis, you survived plot holes, mood swings, and my very specific version of writer's block. You deserve a trophy. Or at least a nap.

I love you both more than Julian loves a dramatic entrance. And that's saying something.

Brandy, you fixed everything I broke and somehow made it sound intentional. You're a miracle in editor form. Tawny, thank you for keeping me organized, on-brand, and emotionally supported through all the mayhem. Pia, you turned "dark, dramatic, maybe cursed?" into art. Dani, you hyped this book louder than I did and somehow made it look strategic. Chessa, you're the reason I have functional formatting and blurbs that make sense. Ashley, you walked in, handled everything like a pro, and made me wonder how I ever did this without you.

This book wouldn't exist without you. Or if it did, it'd be held together with duct tape and a desperate Google Doc.

Thank you for being part of the madness. Truly.

Up Next

Up Next in The Devil's Bargain Series...

Gilded Lies *(Book Two – Greed)*

He doesn't want a soulmate.

She already belongs to someone else.

But Greed doesn't care what's forbidden.

It only wants what it was never meant to touch.

Coming August 21, 2025

About the Author

Deliciously Dark, Beautifully Twisted

Sara McClaflin writes dark romance with feelings, flaws, and just the right amount of emotional damage. Her stories are character-driven, morally gray, and often ask one very important question: what if love was a little dangerous—and we liked it that way? After years of reading and reviewing books with too much angst, she finally started writing her own.

She lives on the West Coast with her husband, their chaotic dog, and more book boyfriends than she's willing to admit. Her TBR pile is a cry for help, her playlists are 80% heartbreak, and she's always chasing the next character who'll ruin her in the best way.

Newsletter Sign Up: https://subscribepage.io/saras-newsletter

amazon.com/stores/Sara-McClaflin/author/B0CR8VHBHJ?ref=ap
_rdr&isDramIntegrated=true&shoppingPortalEnabled=true&ccs_i
d=1fcaa1c2-62ac-4142-ab01-dce9c490e471

bookbub.com/profile/sara-mcclaflin

goodreads.com/author/show/47632250.Sara_McClaflin

instagram.com/authorsaramcclaflin/

facebook.com/profile.php?id=61551822185090&notif_id=174422
8205391402&notif_t=page_user_activity&ref=notif#

tiktok.com/@sara.mcclaflin

Also by

The Huntington Brothers Series

Destined for Love

Tangled Hearts

Promises to Keep

Standalone Novels

The Keeper's Secret

Love on the Edge

Anthologies

Head in the Clouds: A Romantic Comedy Anthology

Desperate: A Deadly Thriller Anthology

If Ophelia's emotional damage and Julian's obsession made you scream, swoon, or seriously question your standards—go leave a review. You're already in too deep, might as well make it official.